Reginald Hill

Reginald Hill is a native of Cumbria and a former resident of Yorkshire, the setting for his outstanding crime novels featuring Dalziel and Pascoe, 'the best detective duo on the scene bar none' (*Daily Telegraph*). His writing career began with the publication of *A Clubbable Woman* (1970), which introduced Chief Superintendent Andy Dalziel and DS Peter Pascoe. Their subsequent appearances, together with the adventures of Luton lathe operator turned PI Joe Sixsmith, have confirmed Hill's position as 'the best living male crime writer in the English speaking world' (*Independent*) and won numerous awards, including the Crime Writers' Association Cartier Diamond Dagger for his lifetime contribution to the genre.

The Dalziel and Pascoe novels have now been adapted into a successful BBC television series starring Warren Clarke and Colin Buchanan.

By the same author

Dalziel and Pascoe novels

A CLUBBABLE WOMAN
AN ADVANCEMENT OF LEARNING
RULING PASSION
AN APRIL SHROUD
A PINCH OF SNUFF
A KILLING KINDNESS
DEADHEADS
CHILD'S PLAY
UNDER WORLD
BONES AND SILENCE
ONE SMALL STEP
RECALLED TO LIFE
PICTURES OF PERFECTION
ASKING FOR THE MOON
THE WOOD BEYOND
ON BEULAH HEIGHT
ARMS AND THE WOMEN
DIALOGUES OF THE DEAD
DEATH'S JEST-BOOK

Joe Sixsmith novels

BLOOD SYMPATHY
BORN GUILTY
KILLING THE LAWYERS
SINGING THE SADNESS

FELL OF DARK
THE LONG KILL
DEATH OF A DORMOUSE
DREAM OF DARKNESS
THE ONLY GAME

REGINALD HILL

EXIT LINES

A Dalziel and Pascoe novel

See how the world its veterans rewards!
Pope: *Moral Essays, Epistle 2*

HarperCollins*Publishers*

HarperCollins*Publishers*
77–85 Fulham Palace Road,
Hammersmith, London W6 8JB

This paperback re-issue 2003

1 3 5 7 9 8 6 4 2

Previously published in paperback by
Grafton in 1987 and reprinted seven times

First published in Great Britain by
HarperCollins*Publishers* 1984

www.harpercollins.co.uk/crime

ISBN 0 586 07253 5

Typeset in Meridien by Palimpsest Book Production Limited,
Polmont, Stirlingshire

Printed and bound in Great Britain by
Clays Ltd, St Ives plc

Acknowledgments

My thanks to the following: Joseph Addison (Chapter 2), Julius Caesar (12), Charles II (14), Thomas Coryat (11), William Cowper (7), Elizabeth I (20), George V (15), Johann Wolfgang von Goethe (16), William Hazlitt (8), O. Henry (13), Thomas Hobbes (26), James V of Scotland (27), Jehoram King of Judah (23), Somerset Maugham (9), Thomas More (24), Captain Oates (1), Lord Palmerston (3), William Pitt the Younger (6 and 10), François Rabelais (19 and 29), Sir Walter Rayleigh (24), Philip Sidney (18), Sydney Smith (5), Lytton Strachey (22), Jonathan Swift (25), Lord Tennyson (21), James Thurber (17), the Emperor Vespasian (28), and Oscar Wilde (4).

Requiescant in pace.

Chapter 1

'I am just going outside and I may be some time.'

On a cold and storm-racked November night, while Peter and Ellie Pascoe were still celebrating with wine and wassail the first birthday which their daughter Rose had greeted with huge indifference, three old men, who felt far from indifferent, died.

Thomas Arthur Parrinder, 71, was aroused for the last time by a warm wetness amid the freezing rain which had been lashing his face for almost four hours. He opened one eye and saw above him, silhouetted vaguely against the dark sky, a long animal head with pricking ears, and he glimpsed also the gleam of tooth and inquisitive eye as the beast stooped down to lick at him once more. His mouth gaped and a rattle that may have been a laugh spilled out with it a single word. 'Polly!' No other word passed his lips, and precious little breath either, before an overworked hospital doctor pronounced him (not without some guilty relief) dead on arrival.

At just about the same time, Robert Deeks, 73, was being hooked back from a long slide to oblivion by the ringing of a distant bell. A little earlier another bell had rung for some considerable time, but that had eventually ceased. At last this new one stopped too. Then a door opened. A voice called out. Other doors. Opening and shutting. Footsteps below, hurrying, scurrying; a voice growing in volume and alarm; footsteps and voice together on the stairs, ascending. He took another lurch back to reality. He was in a bathroom, his own bathroom. To register this was quite a triumph and, thus encouraged, his mind took a further step. He was in the bath! He looked down at the russet-coloured water lapping his chest, grey and flimsy as a sodden newspaper blown against a picket fence. His mind suddenly broke through fact into feeling. It would be a shaming thing to be found in the bath, especially when he had made it so dirty. It was a special old people's bath with a non-slip bottom and padded grips to help him ease himself in and out. He reached for the grips now, but his nerveless and swollen-knuckled fingers could find no purchase, and even if they had, he knew there was no strength left in his arms to pull himself upright. He let his arms fall. Fact and feeling were beginning to retreat at an even pace. He felt himself slipping away with them. A cry of horror from the open door inhibited the process for one last moment. Slowly he turned his head and saw his daughter in the doorway, paralysed at the shock of seeing him bathed in his own diluted blood. He opened his toothless mouth and said, 'Charley.' The next bell to ring was the ambulance bell but he was moving beyond recall towards a more urgent summons by then.

Philip Cater Westerman (70) felt the rain bouncing off his plastic mac and the wind trying to get under it as he mounted his bicycle and rode out of the car park of The Duke of York. At least the wind was behind him as he turned left towards The Towers. That this narrow, country thoroughfare was called Paradise Road did not strike him yet as ironical. Then he saw lights coming towards him, making nothing of the wind, ripping through the curtain of rain with arrogant ease. The car must have covered a hundred yards in the time he took to cover ten, even with the wind at his back. And in the same instant as the thought, the lights were twisting and brakes screaming in an attempt at evasion both desperate and vain. He was facing the car when he and it almost simultaneously came to a halt. He saw the two front doors burst open and two figures come running towards him, one broad and bulky, the other as tall but thinner. The image remained in his mind, surprisingly powerful, indeed almost analgesic in its strength, as he was hurried to hospital. There, the same harassed houseman who had registered the first two septuagenarians d.o.a. saw that another mile in the ambulance would almost certainly have given him three in a row. As it was, this poor devil was hardly worth preparing for surgery, but the doctor was not yet so advanced in his profession as to be quite certain he was God's agent, and he set the wheels in motion. As if to confirm this decision, Philip Cater Westerman opened his eyes and said, 'Hello.'

'Hello, old chap,' said the doctor. 'Take it easy. Have you right in no time.'

But no time was precisely what Philip Cater Westerman knew he had.

'Paradise,' he said reflectively. Then he added with great indignation, 'Paradise! Driver . . . fat bastard . . . pissed!'

And died.

In the Pascoe household, the telephone rang.

Pascoe groaned, Ellie made a face and went to answer it. Pascoe listened at the open door for a moment but when he heard Ellie greet her father, his face relaxed and he returned to his celebratory Marks and Spencer Burgundy. He grinned at his wife on her return, inviting her to share his relief that it hadn't been the duty sergeant with the once flattering but now fearful message that yet again Mid-Yorkshire CID could not function without its favourite Detective-Inspector.

Ellie did not return his smile, so he returned her worried frown.

'Trouble?' he said.

4

'I'm not sure. It was Dad, ringing up to wish Rose a happy birthday.'

'So?'

'It's the second time. He came on the line when Mum rang this morning.'

'He's so proud of his granddaughter, he wants to do it twice,' said Pascoe. 'What's the problem?'

'I said it was nice of him to do it twice and he seemed puzzled. Then Mum came on.'

'And did she wish Rose happy birthday again too?'

'No,' said Ellie in exasperation. 'She just said to take no notice of Dad, he'd be forgetting his own head next!'

'Sensible woman, your mother,' said Pascoe.

''Tis distance lends approval to the view,' said Ellie ironically. 'But she sounded worried. Dad hasn't really been right since that bad turn he had two years ago. Mum didn't say anything, but I can tell. Peter, I think I ought to pop down there and check things out.'

Down there was Orburn, a small market town south of Lincoln, about eighty miles away.

'Why not?' said Pascoe expansively. 'When?'

'Tomorrow would suit me,' said Ellie. 'If that's all right? They haven't seen Rose for a bit. It's been awkward for them since Dad gave up the car. I'd stay the night. It's too far there and back in a day with the baby. Would you mind?'

Pascoe sipped his wine reflectively and said, 'You know, if you really let yourself go and give it all you've got, you could easily shatter your own record for getting close to asking my permission! Now, that would be nice. But I'd need the request in writing, else who's going to believe it?'

'Bastard,' said Ellie. 'I'm merely consulting your convenience.'

'Let's keep Andy Dalziel out of this,' grinned Pascoe. 'Hadn't you better consult your mum's too?'

'Yes. I'll ring her back now,' said Ellie, retreating through the door.

'And this time, leave the phone off the hook,' called Pascoe after her. 'If I'm going to be deprived of my marital rights tomorrow, I claim double ration tonight.'

But before Ellie could reach the phone, it rang.

He heard Ellie give the number, there was a pause, then she said, 'All right, Sergeant Wield. I'll get him.'

'Oh shit,' said Pascoe. 'Shit, shit, shit!'

Chapter 2

'See in what peace a Christian can die.'

'Back door,' said Wield. 'Glass panel broken. Key in lock. Hand through. Open. Easy.'

Sergeant Wield was in fine telegraphic style. He also seemed to have been practising not moving his lips, so that the words came out of his slant and ugly face like a ritual chant through a primitive devil-mask.

Pascoe put the unkind thought aside as best he could, which was not very well. His resentment at being called out had not as yet been assuaged by explanation. Wield had been even more economic of words on the phone and when Pascoe had hinted a complaint shortly after his arrival at 25, Welfare Lane, in the middle of a Victorian terrace which even Betjeman might have hesitated to save, the Sergeant by the flicker of an eye inside the devil-mask had underlined the inhibiting presence of Constable Tony Hector.

PC Hector had been the first officer on the scene and was therefore a potential source of illuminating insights. Unfortunately he was to Pascoe the last person he would have wished first. His principal qualification for the police force seemed to be his height. He was fully six feet six inches upright, though at some stage in his growth he had reached a level of embarrassment which provoked him to shave off the six inches by curving his spine forward like a bent bow and sinking his head so far between his shoulders that he gave the impression that he was wearing a coat-hanger beneath his tunic. He was one of a trio of young constables whom Detective-Superintendent Dalziel had unkindly nicknamed on their arrival two months earlier Maggie's Morons, suggesting that their recruitment into the force was more the result of Mrs Thatcher's economic policies than a natural vocation. Twice already Pascoe had had occasion to see Hector in action and Dalziel's judgment had still to be refuted. But Pascoe was a kindly, sympathetic man and had not altogether given up on the youth.

'Tell me about it,' he now invited the constable.

'Sir?' – with a puzzled note.

'About what happened. Tell me what you found when you got here,' said Pascoe slowly and distinctly to make sure he was heard above the inappropriately loud din of a television set coming from the house next door.

'Oh, yes, sir,' said Hector, producing his notebook

and coughing discreetly behind his hand. 'I came on duty at six P.M. on Friday, November . . .'

'No, no,' said Pascoe. It was, of course, Hector's fondness for the orotund constabulary style which had driven Wield so far towards telegraphese. 'From when you got here. And in your own words, please.'

'These are my own words, sir,' said Hector, brandishing his notebook with the beginnings of indignation.

'Yes, I know. But you're not in the witness-box. I mean, just *talk* to me as you'd talk to your . . . to your . . .' Pascoe tailed away helplessly. Friends? Father? However he ended his sentence it was going to sound ridiculous.

'Self,' interposed Sergeant Wield. His eyes met Pascoe's and the Inspector had to resist an urge to giggle, an urge he quelled by recollecting that a particularly unpleasant murder had occurred a few feet above his head not very long before.

The thought also made him feel guilty about his sense of grievance at being called out.

Am I getting callous, or what? he wondered.

'Go on, son,' he said to Hector.

'Well, sir, when I got here, I found Mrs Frostick and a lot of other people . . .'

'Hold on. Who's Mrs Frostick?'

'Mrs Frostick is Mr Deeks's daughter, sir. Mr Deeks is the deceased, of this abode.'

Pascoe looked sharply at Hector, hoping to see the gleam of intelligent life in his eyes which would mean he was sending him up. But all was earnest blankness.

'And these other people? Who were they?'

'Neighbours mainly, I think, sir.'

'Think? You've got their names and addresses, haven't you?'

Hector's head sank a little further between his shoulders. Perhaps it was fully retractable, like a tortoise's.

'Some of them, sir,' he said. 'It was all a bit confused. A lot of people had come rushing in when Mrs Frostick called for help . . .'

'Called? You mean, literally, called?'

Again the blank yearning after understanding.

Wield said, 'There is a telephone, as you saw, sir. But Mrs Frostick seems to have been a bit hysterical and after she found her father she ran out into the street, yelling and banging at neighbours' doors.'

'Neighbours' doors? Several doors? So there would have been several neighbours? And also anyone casually strolling by who might have been attracted by the commotion?'

'It's a nasty night, sir,' said Wield. 'Not many pedestrians, I shouldn't think.'

'No. Well, all these people, some of whose names you have, what were they doing?'

'Some of them were upstairs with the deceased . . .'

'Was he, by then?'

'Sir?'

'Deceased.'

Another inch of retraction.

'He didn't look good, sir.'

'The murdered man did not look good,' murmured Pascoe, tasting the phrase with a kind of sad pleasure. 'So, some were upstairs. Some I presume were downstairs . . .'

'Yes, sir. Comforting Mrs Frostick, making her cups of tea, and that sort of thing, sir.'

'In the living-room, was that?'

'Mrs Frostick was in the living-room,' said Hector, screwing up his face in search of preciseness. 'The tea was being made in the kitchen. That's where the oven is, so they'd have to make it there. Mr Deeks was on his bed, in his bedroom. There's only one bedroom, at the front. The other bedroom's the bathroom. Converted.'

Keen to spot glimmers of hope, Pascoe said with the same approval as if he'd been talking about Castle Howard, 'You've got the geography of the house sorted, then.'

The head emerged a little and Hector said, 'Yes, sir. Well, it's just like my Auntie Sheila's in Parish Road round the corner, except that she had a bathroom extension built out over the wash-house in the yard.'

'An extension? Excellent!' approved Pascoe. 'To return to Welfare Lane, what did you do when you got here?'

'Well, I had a look around, sir, then I went outside to call for assistance.'

'I see. You had a look around. And what did you see? I presume you saw something?'

The blank was shot through with agony now, the agony of not asking, 'Like what?' Pascoe looked at him wriggling, wished he could unhook him and throw him back, sighed and said, 'You say you went *outside* to call assistance.'

'Yes, sir. I thought reception would be better and it were a bit crowded in the house with all them people,' complained Hector.

Pascoe gave up. It was clear that like the useless lamp-post he resembled, the young constable was not going to cast any useful light.

'Thanks, Hector,' he said. 'That'll do for now. Stop on the front door, will you, and help keep the sightseers away. Oh, and I'll want a list of everyone you found in the house when you arrived. Heads of families will do where you didn't have time to make a comprehensive census.'

Looking puzzled, relieved, and also slightly disappointed, Hector departed.

Wield and Pascoe exchanged glances.

'Well, at least he was pretty quickly on the scene,' defended Pascoe, compensating for his final sarcasm.

'Yes, sir,' said Wield stolidly. 'He was just in the next street when the call went out. Having a cup of tea at his auntie's, I suspect.'

'You'd better tell me everything, Sergeant.'

And with the look of one who had been expecting to do no less ever since he found PC Hector on the scene, Wield began.

Dorothy Frostick, now being treated for shock

in the hospital to which she had accompanied her father's body, had become alarmed when her attempts to telephone the old man had been unanswered earlier in the evening. On arrival at the house, she had discovered him in his bath, bruised and bleeding. Unable to lift him out singlehanded, she had run outside, half hysterical, and roused the neighbours to help.

Principal among these, Wield had ascertained on arrival, was Mrs Tracey Spillings of No. 27, next door, where she was presently attending the Inspector's pleasure, and pursuing her own in the shape of *Dallas* from the sound of it.

'She says the old boy was alive, just, when they got him out of the bath, but reckons he was beyond recall by the time the ambulance got here. The hospital say he was dead on arrival. Mr Longbottom's been alerted to do the PM in the morning. I didn't think we need bother Dr Rackfell; the duty man at the City General should be able to give us all the preliminary details. Oh, and someone either rang the *Post* or Sam Ruddlesdin was listening in. He turned up shortly after I did. Asked a few questions, then set off for the hospital, I think.'

Longbottom was the Chief Pathologist at the City General, Rackfell was the police surgeon on call that night, and Ruddlesdin was the *Evening Post*'s chief reporter.

'You've got everything sewn up so nicely, Sergeant, I don't see why you needed to bother me either,' said Pascoe rather grumpily. 'Now there's no one at home at No. 23, you say? Why didn't whoever it was try there, I wonder? Well, let's go and see your Mrs Spillings at 27 and let this lot have a bit of space to move in.'

This lot were the forensic team and the photographer who were beginning to move methodically through the tiny house.

'Incidentally, why *did* you bother me?' wondered Pascoe as he led the way out of the front door, ignoring PC Hector's vain attempt to stand straight at attention. 'Mr Headingley busy, is he? And Mr Dalziel out of reach?'

George Headingley was the CID Inspector on duty that night. And Superintendent Andy Dalziel would certainly have expected to be informed instantly of any murder on his patch.

'I'm not sure what's going on, sir,' said Wield in a low voice as they walked towards No. 27. 'Something seems to have come up at the hospital.'

'Something to do with this case, you mean?'

'I don't think so, sir,' said Wield. 'What happened was, Hector buzzed in about this lot, said that the ambulance was just arriving to take Mr Deeks away. It sounded at the time as if the old fellow was still alive, so Mr Headingley said he'd go down to the hospital to see what was what and asked me to get things started down here.'

They'd covered the few yards to 27, but Wield did not offer to knock and the two men sheltered from the driving rain as best they could in the lee of a puce-glossed doorway.

'He contacted me about half an hour later, maybe more. Told me Deeks was dead and Mrs Frostick was under sedation. Then he said something had come up and it'd be best if I could get hold of you as he was going to be occupied with this other thing. I asked if he wanted me to try to get hold of Mr Dalziel too, but he said no, there was no need for that, no need at all. He was being very cagey, said he'd explain things to you later. Anyway, that's how I came to be disturbing your evening.'

'You could have told me this on the phone!' protested Pascoe. 'It might have made me a fraction less bad-tempered.'

'Thought you'd prefer to start off with a clear mind,' said Wield.

He was right, of course. Anything that could make a good, solid, down-to-earth copper like George Headingley slide out from under a murder inquiry must be serious. Already Pascoe's mind was spiralling off into the inane of speculation. He only hoped he could drag it back to earth and hold it there till he got this investigation properly under way.

He needn't have worried. Ballast was at hand.

The fluorescent door was flung open, revealing a brightly lit living-room where the full volume of a television set competed vainly with a clamorous wallpaper whose main motif was the display ritual of birds of paradise in a tropical jungle. Lowering his eyes, Pascoe met the glower of a short but enormously broad woman in a nylon overall which seemed to have been glossed from the same pot as the doorway.

'Are you buggers too shy to knock, or what?' she demanded. 'I didn't rudd that step just so's a pair of petrified coppers could stamp their hobnails on it. Are you coming in? I haven't got all bloody night, even if you have!'

The mysterious behaviour of George Headingley was quite forgotten. Meekly Pascoe followed Sergeant Wield into the house.

Chapter 3

'Die, my dear doctor – that's the
last thing I shall do.'

The mysterious behaviour of George Headingley
had its roots in what had happened out on the
Paradise Road earlier that evening; or perhaps even
in what had happened during Dr John Sowden's
medical training a few years before, for Dr Sowden's
ethical attitudes had matured much more rapidly
than his clinical knowledge.

As a second year student, he was already
proclaiming a doctor's first duty was to his patient,
not to some semi-religious philosophical abstrac-
tion. He found no difficulty with abortion; the
mother was his patient, not the foetus. And at
the other end of existence, the only difficulty
he found with euthanasia was its illegality, but
he would certainly not strive officiously to keep
alive patients who ought to be switched off.

These were the pragmatic points of view which

deserved to be maintained by a modern young doctor. Somewhere within their clinically rigid framework, there should have been a space perfectly tailored to contain the death of Philip Cater Westerman, to whom surgery could at best have given only a couple of years of probably bedridden life. Yet in some peculiarly illogical way, even though he had done everything possible for the man, which in all truth was precious little, it was to Dr Sowden as if the *thought* that Westerman would be better off dead had somehow transplanted itself into action. Incredibly, he felt guilty! Another few minutes and he would have been dead on arrival like the other two. But because he had technically entered into his care for those last few minutes of life, he, Dr Sowden, prospective snapper-off of life-support systems and generous dispenser of terminal tranquillizers, felt guilty. Or responsible. Or resentful. Or something.

Puzzled and irritated by this feeling, he went to the waiting-room where a nurse had told him that some visitors were eager for news of Mr Westerman.

There were three men there; one fat, flushed and middle-aged, staring gloomily into space, the only sign of life being the movement of his right hand down his right sock as he attempted to scratch the sole of his foot inside his shoe; the second slightly younger and much better preserved, with a reflective self-contained expression on his sallow face and in his hand an expensive-smelling cigar whose smoke tendrils twined themselves around the no-smoking sign above his head; the third, sitting as far away from the other two as possible and looking distinctly the most nervous of the trio, was a uniformed police constable.

Not relatives, decided the doctor; they must be from the car involved in the accident.

Addressing a neutral point of the room, he said, 'I'm sorry to say Mr Westerman is dead.'

The fat man stopped scratching momentarily; his companion raised his cigar to his lips; the constable stood up.

'The death will have to be reported to the coroner, of course,' said Dr Sowden to the constable, thinking that he was keeping the coroner busy tonight. 'If you'd like to come with me . . .'

He opened the door and waited. The constable glanced across at the two men as if in search of something but nothing was said.

He followed the doctor into the corridor.

'How'd it happen?' Sowden asked as they walked along together.

'Don't rightly know,' said the officer vaguely. 'He was riding a bike.'

'That,' said Sowden judiciously, 'is surely a circumstance rather than a cause. How was the breathalyser test?'

It was none of his business, of course, and had the policeman merely indicated this, he would probably have felt it was no more than his own bit of pomposity deserved and let the matter drop. But when the constable said evasively, 'I'm not sure,' Sowden said sharply, 'You did breathalyse them? Or rather him? The driver? That was him there, in the waiting-room, I take it?'

The constable's silence acquiesced.

'And you don't know if he's been breathalysed? Good lord, if even a dying man could smell the whisky, surely you didn't miss it? I could still smell the stuff in the waiting-room! And what's he doing there anyway? Shouldn't he be down at the station, helping with inquiries?'

'Not up to me, sir,' said the constable, stung to reply.

Sowden was prevented from any further probing by the intervention of the ward clerk who drew him aside and murmured. 'There's a police inspector to see you, Doctor. It's about Mr Deeks.'

Waiting in his office was a middle-aged man with bushy eyebrows and a kind of weary affability, like a country parson at the end of a long church fête.

'Headingley,' he said, offering his hand. 'Detective-Inspector. It's about Deeks. Dead, I gather?'

'Yes. Died in the ambulance.'

'Ah. His daughter's here too, is that right?'

'Yes, but you can't see her. She's in shock. I've admitted her for the night. She'll have been sedated by now.'

'Oh. I see,' said Headingley, looking towards the

frosted panel in the door against which the police constable's hat could be seen silhouetted. 'Is that one of our lads out there?'

'Oh yes,' said Sowden. 'But nothing to do with Deeks. A road accident. A cyclist was killed. In fact, if you've got a moment, you might have a word with your constable. He seems a bit vague about whether the driver was breathalysed or not. And the fellow's actually here, in the waiting-room, stinking of Scotch!'

'I'll look into it,' said Headingley without enthusiasm. 'About Deeks, cause of death?'

'Well, I haven't done a detailed examination of course, it's a bit hectic tonight. But I'd be surprised if it wasn't simple heart failure brought on by stress. He'd been beaten about the head, and there were several cuts around the throat and shoulders, nothing likely in itself to cause death, but the strain of undergoing such treatment must have been tremendous.'

'Some nasty people about,' said Headingley gloomily. 'We'll need a full scale PM, of course. Mr Longbottom's not about, I suppose?'

'I'll check,' said Sowden, picking up the phone.

'And I'll have a quick word with our lad out there,' said Headingley.

It took Sowden a couple of minutes to ascertain that the pathologist was not in the hospital. He got the exchange to dial Longbottom's home number and as it rang, he called, 'Inspector!'

Headingley returned from his conversation with the uniformed policeman looking very pensive.

'They're ringing Mr Longbottom at home,' said Sowden. 'You take over. It's not part of my remit to disturb consultants at this time of night.'

He smiled as he spoke, but Headingley did not respond.

The pathologist himself answered the phone and condescended to be available at 10.30 the following morning. Rather to Sowden's admiration, Headingley responded to brusqueness with brusqueness. After he had replaced the phone he said, 'The constable said you said something about even a dying man smelling whisky, sir.'

'That's right. Last words that poor devil uttered were, let me get it right, *driver, fat bastard, pissed*. That's a pretty straightforward death-bed declaration, wouldn't you say?'

'It would seem so,' said Headingley. 'Look, would you mind if I used your phone again?'

'Be my guest.'

'Er, privately, if I may.'

'Why not?' said Sowden. 'They'll be reporting me for malingering if I stay here much longer anyway.'

He left. As he walked down the corridor which led past the waiting-room, its door opened and the two men emerged. Suddenly Sowden's absurd buried guilt feeling about Westerman's death came surging to the surface.

'Hold on a second,' he called.

The men stopped and turned.

'Yes?' said the cigar smoker.

Sowden looked around. At the end of the corridor he saw the uniformed constable. Waving an imperious summons, he said, 'I think the police might like a word before you go.'

The men exchanged glances.

'Oh aye?' said the fat one.

The constable approached.

'Officer,' said Sowden, 'I just wanted to be quite sure for my own peace of mind that you had in fact administered a breathalyser test.'

The constable was nonplussed.

The fat man belched and said, 'Who to, friend?'

'I should have thought that was obvious,' said Sowden.

He heard footsteps hurrying behind him and turned to see, not without relief, Inspector Headingley approaching fast.

'I was just inquiring about the breathalyser test, Inspector,' he said.

'Yes. All right. Sorry, sir,' said Headingley.

It may have been that the man was out of breath but there seemed to be in that *sorry, sir* addressed to the fat man something more than mere constabulary courtesy.

'Excuse me, but just who are you?' said Sowden. 'Don't I know your face?'

The fat man looked at him speculatively.

'Mebbe you do and mebbe you don't,' he said. 'Dalziel's the name, Detective-Superintendent

Dalziel if you want the whole bloody issue. And you're Doctor Livingstone, I presume.'

Light dawned.

'My God! I get it now!' said Sowden triumphantly.

'Get what, Doctor?'

'Why all the fuss and keep it quiet! It's a nice little cover-up.'

'Cover-up?' echoed Dalziel softly. 'Of what? By who?'

'Of drunken driving causing death,' said Sowden challengingly. 'And by the police of the police.'

It was a dramatic little confrontation beginning to attract some distant notice from nurses and other personnel.

The cigar-smoking man intervened.

'No one's asked me who I am.'

'All right. Let's have your name and rank too,' said Sowden.

'No rank. Plain Mr Charlesworth. Arnold Charlesworth,' said the man. 'I'm not a policeman. I'm a bookmaker. And I'm more than happy to be breathalysed. Again.'

Sowden ignored the last word and said, 'Why should anyone want to breathalyse you, Mr Charlesworth?'

'It's the law, Doctor,' said Charlesworth in a friendly tone. 'You see, it was me that was driving the car that killed that poor sod back there. The Superintendent here was just my passenger. And my breath test was negative.'

He puffed a wreath of cigar smoke about Sowden's head.

'So stuff that in your stethoscope and diagnose it,' he said.

Chapter 4

'Either this wallpaper goes or I do.'

Mrs Tracey Spillings was in her forties, all the way down. She had a boldly handsome, no-nonsense kind of face, but her brusque manner did not mean she was entirely bereft of empathy, for, seeing the anguish on Pascoe's face (Pascoe's because it took more than mere noise to limn any detectable emotion on Wield's features), she gestured towards what looked like an empty armchair and said, or rather shouted, 'She means no disrespect, it's her only pleasure, switch it off and God knows what she'd be up to, ain't that right, Mam?'

A step nearer the chair revealed that curled up in its huge chintzy arms was a wizened old lady who reminded Sergeant Wield of a picture in his illustrated H. Rider Haggard showing what happened to Ayesha after her second immersion in the Flame of Life. That this frailness should at one time have contained this vastness was a concept requiring a greater effort of lateral thinking than he was inclined to make.

Pascoe showed why he was an Inspector by shouting, 'How do you do?' to the old lady whose eyes never left *Dallas*. Nor, from the size of the stack of tapes standing next to the VCR, did it look as if they would ever need to.

Mrs Spillings jerked her head towards the inner door which led to the kitchen. Here the noise level was reduced to that of a medium-sized steel foundry, but this was compensated for by a wall-paper design of huge tropical fruit whose violence was intensified by the confined space, the 1000-watt strip lighting, and highly polished kitchen units in the puce which was clearly Mrs Spillings's favourite colour.

Pascoe introduced himself and started to explain what he wanted, but quickly found that his explanation was neither needed or heeded. Mrs Spillings launched straight into narrative.

'This is what happened,' she said. 'You'd best make notes as it's the second time of telling and there'll not be a third. It were an hour back, no, I tell a lie, likely more. I'd just finished the ironing when Dolly Frostick came banging on my door, screaming blue murder. I went straight out, there was others at their doors and windows, but all hanging back, not doing owt. You'll know how backward folk can be about coming forward in your job, until they think they're getting something for nothing and then there's no hanging back. I said *Dolly, calm yourself, lass, and tell us what's up*. And she said *It's me dad, it's me dad!* and set off shrieking again. I saw I could be here till next Sunday waiting to get any sense out of her, so I went to have a look for myself. I saw right off the house were in a mess and I said to myself, *Hey up! burglars!* and I picked up the poker from the grate before I went upstairs.

'He were lying in the bathtub. The water were all bloody, so I pulled out the plug. I said, *Bob, Bob, what the hell have you been up to?* but he said nowt, just flickered his eyelids for a second. So I lifted him out of the bath – he were no weight at all, skin and bones, they all go like that, mine's just the same – and I wrapped him in a towel and I took him into the bedroom and put him on the bed and covered him over.

'There were a lot of others there by then. Where one goes, they're quick enough to follow. Not that any on 'em were good for owt but getting under my feet. I told Minnie Cope from 21 to put kettle on and make a pot of tea – that's about her limit – and I went downstairs myself and rang for the ambulance and for you lot. Dolly Frostick were back in the house by then. She'd quieted down a bit, so I gave her a cup of tea with a lot of sugar. Next thing someone said the police is here, but it was only that Sheila Jolley's nephew from Parish Road. He were always a gormless child and he's not improved much with ageing. I told him it were a serious matter and he'd best make himself useful by getting some proper bobbies down here, so he went off out with his little wireless. Then the ambulance came and they got poor old Bob away, just.

'I put Dolly in the ambulance with her dad and I sent Minnie Cope along for company. I'd have gone myself only I can't be sitting around all night in a hospital waiting on some black bugger's convenience. And I thought when you lot finally got someone with a bit of sense here, he'd likely want to know what'd been going off. So I stayed in the house till this one came. He's no oil-painting, but at least he's not simple like that Tony Hector. But *he* says I've got to wait and tell it all again to *you*, whoever you are. Well, I've waited, and I've told it and if you write it down, I'll sign it. Right?'

She spoke dismissively and it took all of Pascoe's courage for him to say, 'There *are* just a couple of questions, Mrs Spillings.'

'Like what?'

'Well, like, did you hear anything odd next door earlier this evening?'

Mrs Spillings looked at him in disbelief, then opened the door into the living-room, admitting a Force 10 gale of noise.

It was reply sufficient.

Mrs Spillings said, 'I'll let you two out the back way. That'll be the way he got in, you'll have worked that much out, I dare say. Me, I've got proper locks fitted and all, but Bob Deeks never bothered though I kept on telling him. Come on! Don't hang about.'

She opened the back door and with considerable relief the two policemen exited from the vibrant house. They found themselves in a tiny back yard with a brick wash-house, a bird-table and some kind of evergreen in a tub. Mrs Spillings unlocked a door in the high wall at the bottom of the yard and they went out after her into a narrow lane which ran between the backs of the Welfare Lane houses on one side and those of the Parish Road houses on the other. The lane acted as a wind tunnel, sucking icy darts of rain into it horizontally at vast speed. Mrs Spillings seemed indifferent to the weather. She walked a couple of paces to the next door and gave it a push. It was a ramshackle affair and lurched creakingly on one hinge.

'That's how the bugger'll have got in,' she re-affirmed. 'Listen. Bob Deeks were a miserable old sod, but I never found any harm in him. You lot want to get this sorted proper.'

'We'll get him all right,' assured Pascoe.

'Oh aye, you'll likely get him,' said the woman. 'It's what *he* gets that bothers me. Suspended sentence! I'd suspend the buggers!'

'It's a tenable position,' said Pascoe, trying to re-grasp the initiative. 'I may need to talk to you again.'

'Any time you like, sunshine,' came the voice drifting back along the lines of sleet. 'Any time, as long as I'm not busy.'

Pascoe and Wield went through into the yard of No. 25 and let themselves into the house. The fingerprint man was hard at work in the kitchen.

'Anything?' asked Pascoe.

'Millions,' came the cheerful answer. 'I reckon there's more dabs here than there is in the North Sea.'

'Ha ha,' said Pascoe. 'And thanks a lot. Sergeant, we'll need everyone who was in the house for elimination. Get a start on it, will you? Combine it with door-to-door along the street. Anyone see or hear anything? Any strangers wandering around? Why am I telling you this? You know the drill at least as well as I do. Use Hector and anyone else you can lay your hands on. I'll get some extra hands drafted in as soon as I can.'

'Where will you be, sir?' inquired Wield.

'At the hospital,' said Pascoe. 'Talking to Mrs Frostick, if possible, and checking on what killed Deeks.'

He paused at the door, turning his already dripping raincoat collar up as the wind outside shrieked its joy at the prospect of having another go at him.

'And if I find George Headingley in intensive care,' he added bitterly, 'it might just about justify getting me mixed up in this lot.'

Chapter 5

'Bring me all the blotting-paper there
is in the house!'

In the event, it took George Headingley only five
minutes to convince Pascoe that there were worse
things to be mixed up with than murder inquiries.
'You've got yourself a real mess there, George,' he
said feelingly. 'A real mess!'

'You can say that again,' said Headingley. 'I'm
sorry I got you called out, but I got this feeling I was going to be needed mopping up after
Fat Andy, and as things are turning out, I was
right.'

The two men were talking in the comfortably
appointed foyer of the main modern wing of the
City General Hospital. Headingley had contacted
Wield a couple of minutes after Pascoe's departure
from Welfare Lane, and learning of his destination
had hastened to intercept him.

'Arnie Charlesworth! What the hell was he

doing driving round with Arnie Charlesworth?' demanded Pascoe.

'Be careful what you say,' objected Headingley. 'He's regarded as a respected member of the community.'

'We've all got things we regard as respected members,' said Pascoe, 'but we're in trouble if we start flashing them round in public.'

'You know,' said Headingley, 'you've always been Andy's golden boy, but there's no need to start sounding like him! All right, so Charlesworth's a bookie and a bit of a hard case, and not the kind of man we should be seen taking favours from. But he's completely legit, and he's a big charity man. The mayor's parlour, the Rotary, the Masons, anywhere they make decisions and influence people, he's welcome.'

'All right. So it's only suspicious sods like you and me who'll be worried about Dalziel hobnobbing with this respectable citizen.'

'I hope so,' said Headingley. 'But I've got a nose for trouble, Peter. It's not the Charlesworth connection that bothers me. It's this other thing. And it's Sam Ruddlesdin who's got a pretty sensitive nose himself. He rang me a little while back, asked about the Deeks killing. I told him you were on the case and would, I was sure, be only too pleased to cooperate fully with the Press. Then he said, dead casual like, *Oh, by the way, this accident out on the Paradise Road, Mr Dalziel was a passenger in the car, is that right?* I said I believed he was. He asked if he was OK and I said I understood so, and he said that he believed Arnie Charlesworth was driving and I said yes, and then he said, *But it was in fact Mr Dalziel's car?* That shook me rigid. I'd no idea if it was or not. I'd just assumed it had been Charlesworth's car. Well, I waffled round it, but it got me worried. And then something else began to worry me too. Listen.'

Pascoe listened. At the head of the foyer were six lifts, seemingly in constant use even at this hour. They announced their arrival with a melodic *ping!* The *pings* were pitched at slightly different levels and as Pascoe listened their interval and sequence suggested the communications code from *Close Encounters*. At last! he thought. An explanation of why hospitals always give the impression of being run by aliens disguised as human beings.

'See the pay-phone over there?' said Headingley. 'All the time Ruddlesdin was talking I could hear those bloody pings! The bastard was here!'

'So what?' said Pascoe. 'He came round here to check on Deeks. Sergeant Wield told me.'

'Mebbe. But he must have got here not long after I'd got Mr Dalziel out of the place. Christ knows what that daft doctor said to him.'

'But what could Sowden tell him?' asked Pascoe. 'That he thought the old fellow said something about the driver being pissed before he died? What's that mean? Anyway, why should Sowden get himself involved in something so vague?'

'Christ knows,' said Headingley. 'He seemed to

have managed to work up a fair head of steam for some reason. Even when Charlesworth said he was the driver, this didn't calm him down. Not that I didn't have some sympathy with him. Bloody Charlesworth just stood there, puffing out cigar smoke, a bit of a sneer on his face like he was saying, *That's my story. Prove different.*'

'George,' said Pascoe quietly. 'You don't think there could be anything different to prove, do you?'

Headingley shook his head.

'No. No. Not Andy, it's not his style. Mind you, Peter, he was as drunk as I've seen him, no doubt about that. I always thought he was unsinkable, but by Christ he'd hit an iceberg tonight. I've as good as locked him in his office and I told the lads on the exchange that no calls were to be put through to him.'

'You're taking a risk, aren't you?' said Pascoe admiringly.

Headingley shook his head.

'Not me. Soon as Ruddlesdin rang off, I got on to the DCC and put him in the picture in case the *Post* started after him. I'm covered, Peter. The DCC approved my action, even unto the passing of this Deeks inquiry to you. Not that I wouldn't rather have it back and leave some other poor sod to deal with old chubby cheeks!'

'Well, thanks for putting me in the picture,' said Pascoe. 'I'll tread carefully with the dastardly doctor.'

'You do that,' said Headingley. 'Just you be nice and noncommittal if he starts pushing. By the way, I told him I was just holding the fort, so to speak, till our murder expert could be brought off another case. Didn't want him thinking I was more worried about my Chief than about an investigation. So better wear your deerstalker!'

The two men separated, Pascoe continuing into the depths of the hospital where he finished up kicking his heels for twenty minutes in a tiny office. The desk top was covered in papers, mostly handwritten in a scrawl which convinced him that doctors did not after all develop a specially illegible hand just for prescriptions. Sowden arrived suddenly and quietly enough to discover him trying to interpret one of the sheets.

'Ah,' said the doctor. 'The ace detective, I presume. Trying to keep your hand in?'

Somewhat abashed, Pascoe dropped the paper back on to the desk and said, 'Sorry, but it's a bit like an archaeologist stumbling on the Rosetta stone. I'm Pascoe. Detective-Inspector Peter. How do you do?'

He held out his hand. After a second, Sowden shook it.

'John Sowden,' he said. 'Sorry you've had to hang around, but things happen in convoys out there. With luck I may have two minutes before the next lot heave into view. So what can I do for you? I think I told the other chap all I could.'

Pascoe looked at him sympathetically. In his

twenties with the kind of dark continental good looks that must have the nurses falling over backwards for him, he looked at the moment too tired to take advantage of such gymnastics.

'Yes, I've looked at what you told Mr Headingley,' he said. 'There are a couple of things I'd like to ask you, though. And I'd like a look at the body for myself.'

'Just in case I've missed anything?' said Sowden.

'Not really,' said Pascoe. 'But I bet if a cop tells you that your rear offside light isn't working, you always walk round the car to have a look.'

Something vaguely related to a smile touched Sowden's face.

'All right,' he said. 'Come on, I'll take you along and you can ask your questions as we go.'

They set off together down the corridor, the doctor's pace a little faster than Pascoe found comfortable.

'It's really a matter of what might have caused these wounds on Deeks's head and neck,' he said.

'At a guess I'd say that most of the contusions could have been the result of simple blows from a fist,' said Sowden.

'Hard enough to damage the knuckles?' asked Pascoe.

'What? Oh, I see what you mean,' said Sowden. 'Possibly. I don't really know. This isn't really my field, you know. You're the murder expert, so I was told. Or was the other chap exaggerating?'

'Very likely,' said Pascoe. 'And the cuts? What

kind of instrument should I be telling my chaps to look out for?'

'I don't know. A knife.'

'Blunt knife, sharp knife?' prompted Pascoe. 'Broad blade or narrow? A knife for stabbing or a knife for cutting?'

'Something with a sharp point,' said Sowden. 'Yes, certainly that.'

'And sharp on both sides of the point? Like a stiletto? Or a round-bladed point, like a long nail, or a spike?'

'More like a stiletto except broader,' said Sowden, becoming interested. 'Yes, there was certainly evidence of the sharp point digging in, with the skin and flesh being severed cleanly on both sides. Here we are. See for yourself.'

The chill air of the hospital morgue touched the skin with none of the violence of the wild cold November wind outside, but Pascoe did not have to pause to consider his preference. There were three bodies as yet unparcelled for the night. Sowden glanced at the labels on their toes, his face troubled.

'Not a good night for the old,' he said. 'This is your man. Robert Deeks.'

He pulled back the cover. Robert Deeks, his face a player's mask of grief with its deep hollow cheeks and gaping toothless mouth, stared accusingly up at them. Quickly and efficiently, Sowden pointed to the location of the wounds and bruises and offered his interpretation of them.

'Thanks,' said Pascoe, making notes. 'That'll do fine till Mr Longbottom takes a look.'

He meant no slight, but tired men are easily piqued, and Sowden, covering Deeks's face with an abrupt movement, pointed to the body on the next slab and said, 'At least you won't need Longbottom to tell you how this one died.'

'No? Why's that, Doctor?' asked Pascoe courteously, though he had no doubt of the answer.

'Philip Cater Westerman,' said Sowden, drawing down the sheet. 'Road accident. Hadn't you heard?'

Philip Cater Westerman had contrived to pass away with an expression of amused bafflement on his face which was not altogether inappropriate.

'Hard to keep track of all the road deaths, more's the pity,' evaded Pascoe. 'And the third? What about him?'

He thought his efforts to divert the trend of the conversation were going to fail for a moment, but Sowden contented himself with a sardonic stare, then covered Westerman's face.

'This one? Straightforward. Poor devil died of exposure on a playing field, would you believe? You couldn't go three hundred yards in any direction, so they tell me, without hitting houses.'

He drew back the cover and Pascoe saw Thomas Arthur Parrinder's thin aquiline face, which might have been carved in marble except for a stain of discolouration round a patch of broken skin on the left temple. Pascoe sniffed. A non-medical smell had caught his nose. It was rum.

'What happened?' he asked. 'Drunk, was he?'

'No, I don't think so,' said Sowden. 'The smell's from a half bottle of rum he had in his pocket. It smashed when he fell but as far as I could see, the seal on the cap was unbroken.'

'You're doing our work now,' said Pascoe drily. 'So, what did happen?'

'Slipped in the mud as he was taking a short cut across the recreation ground. Broke his hip, poor sod. He must have lain there for hours. It was such a nasty night, no one was out. He wasn't very warmly clothed. Hypothermia kills hundreds of old folk indoors every winter. Expose them outdoors . . .'

'Yes,' said Pascoe. 'Terrible. That bruise on his head . . .'

'He must have gone down a real wallop,' said Sowden. 'Cracked his head on a stone; it probably stunned him so that by the time he was conscious enough to cry for help, he'd already have been weakened so much by the cold that his voice would be too feeble to carry far.'

'Yes,' said Pascoe. 'Probably. Which hip did he break?'

'Hip. Let me think. The right one. Why?'

'He'd break it by falling on it?'

'Sorry?'

'I mean it'd be a fracture by impact rather than by stress. I'm sorry to sound so untechnical.'

'No, I take your meaning,' said Sowden. 'By impact, yes. I see. What you're saying is –'

'What I'm asking,' interrupted Pascoe, 'is whether you wouldn't expect any damage to the head incurred in the same fall that broke his hip to be on the right side also?'

'It would be more likely,' agreed Sowden. 'But the body is capable of almost infinite contortions, especially an old, poorly coordinated body out of control in a fall. As for a mugging, which I take it you're hinting at, I looked in his pockets to get his name. I got it from his pension book which had several bank notes folded inside it. And there was also a purse, I recall, with a lot of silver. No, I think you and your colleagues, Inspector, could usefully take a course in suspicious circumstances, what to follow up, what to ignore.'

Again that note of challenge. Pascoe made a note of Parrinder's name and said, 'Thank you for your help, Doctor. Now I know how busy they keep you here, so I won't hold you up any more.'

Pascoe was congratulating himself on having evaded any head-on conflict. He guessed that after Sowden had enjoyed a few hours' sleep, he would relegate the road accident to that deep-delved and well-locked chamber where doctors and police-men alike try, usually successfully, to store yester-day's horrors as they relax and prepare themselves for today's.

But this one was not yet ready for inhumation. With no great pleasure he recognized a lanky figure chatting intimately to a nurse outside the doctor's office. It was Sam Ruddlesdin, the *Post* reporter.

Inclination told him to keep walking by with a cheerful wave of the hand. Instinct, however, told him that Ruddlesdin would only have returned to the hospital if he had some mischief in hand, and it might be well to get a scent of it. So when Ruddlesdin greeted him with a cheerful, 'Hello, Mr Pascoe. How are you?' he stopped and said, 'As well as can be expected, in this place, at this time. What brings you here?'

'Same as you, I dare say,' said Ruddlesdin with a saturnine grin. He had a good line in saturnine grins to go with a nice line in scurrility, which made him an entertaining companion for about two and a half pints, and generally speaking his relationship with the police was finely balanced on a fulcrum of mutual need.

Pascoe said, 'You mean the Welfare Lane killing? Mr Deeks?'

'That too,' said Ruddlesdin. 'I was down there earlier, before you in fact. Talked to Sergeant Wield. He seemed to think Mr Headingley would be on the case. But when I was here earlier, I gathered from Dr Sowden that he'd just left with Superintendent Dalziel and that you were taking over. The murder specialist. Is that an official designation in Mid-Yorkshire now, Inspector?'

'It doesn't carry any extra money if it is,' said Pascoe, looking at Sowden, who returned his gaze defiantly with just a hint of guilt. 'Anyway, you've caught up with me now. Shall we talk on our way out to the car park?'

Ruddlesdin said, 'I'd certainly be glad of the chance to talk with you, Mr Pascoe, but I'd really like a quick word with Dr Sowden first.'

He looked at Sowden, who made no move to invite him into the office; then at Pascoe, who made no move to take his leave. Ruddlesdin let another saturnine grin slip down from beneath the brim of his slouch hat.

'It was really just to check again on what you thought Mr Westerman said before he died, Doctor,' he said.

'Look,' said Sowden, suddenly uneasy. 'I'm not sure I should really be talking about this with you. A patient's dying words, I mean, in a sense they're, I don't know, confidential, I suppose.'

'Like in confession?' said Ruddlesdin, swapping the grin for a parody of piety. 'Yes, I can see that. And I'm not going to quote you, Doctor. Well, probably not. But something else came up. You see, after I talked to you earlier, I did a little bit of research on the ground. Paradise Road runs past The Duke of York where Mr Westerman had been drinking, past The Towers, the old folks' holiday home, which was where he was heading, and then past nowhere at all for another three miles till you arrive at Paradise Hall Hotel. I can't afford their restaurant prices very often myself, but I *have* been there. Very nice. Excellent menu, top class

43

clientele. Just the place for a pair of distinguished citizens to eat, I thought. And I was right! Mr Charlesworth and Mr Dalziel ate there tonight.

'Mr Abbiss, the owner, was very discreet, but I got just a hint that Mr Dalziel had been a trifle the worse for wear when he left. Not that that signifies, as he was the passenger, of course. Only . . .'

Pascoe refused to be the one who said, 'Only what?' but Sowden was less resilient.

'Only what?' he said.

'Only when I called in at The Towers just to get some background on the poor old chap who'd died, I got talking to a Mrs Warsop who is by way of being their bursar. Quite by chance it seems that she too was dining at Paradise Hall tonight. Now, she doesn't know Mr Dalziel from Adam, but she *is* acquainted with Mr Charlesworth by sight. And as she was leaving the Hall, she saw them in the car park together, getting into a car. And the strange thing is, she's quite adamant about it, that it wasn't Mr Charlesworth, but the (I quote) fat drunk one who got into the driver's seat and drove away!'

Chapter 6

'I think I could eat one of Bellamy's veal pies.'

Andrew Dalziel awoke to sunlight and birdsong, both of which filtered softly through grey net curtains. It was almost a month since, following his usual habit on bad mornings of hauling himself upright with the help of the hideous folk-weave drapes which were a sort of memorial to his long-fled wife, he had pulled the curtain rail right off the wall. Time had not yet effected any great healing, and now only the flimsy net and an erratic window-cleaner maintained the decencies. There was no way, however, that the net could maintain his weight, so now, belching and breaking wind, he pursued his alternative levée strategy of rolling sideways till he hit the floor, then using the bed for vertical leverage.

Upright, he had the misfortune to glimpse himself in a long wall mirror. Clad in a string vest and purple and green checked socks, it was an image to engage the unwary eye like a basilisk. He approached closer and addressed himself.

'Some talk of Alexander,' he said softly, 'and some of Hercules.'

Slowly he peeled off the vest. The string had printed a pattern of pink diamonds over his torso, from broad shoulders down to broader belly. He scratched the pattern gently as a musician might run his fingers over harp strings. His head felt heavy, his tongue felt furry, his legs . . . it occurred to him that he couldn't feel his legs at all.

He nodded his huge head, like a bear who sees the dogs circling and, though chained to a post, yet believes that the sport may still be his. His strength he did not doubt. Nothing was wrong with him physically that a scalding shower and an even scaldinger pot of tea had not a thousand times already set to rights. But his mind was troubled by something like the sound of a bicycle wheel whistling round in the rain.

The shower and the tea had to be negotiated with care, but they allayed the basic physical symptoms sufficiently for him to risk a small Scotch to calm the mind. And now, he told himself with the assurance of one who believed in a practical, positive and usually physical response to most of life's problems, all he needed to complete this repair of normality was a platterful of egg, sausage, bacon, tomatoes and fried bread. Bitter experience had taught him in the years since his wife's departure to eschew home catering. It wasn't that a basic cuisine was beyond his grasp; it was the cleaning up afterwards that defeated him. And while a man could live with a broken curtain rail, only a beast would tolerate fat-congealed frying-pans. Fortunately the police canteen did an excellent breakfast. Gourmet cooking they might not provide, but what did that matter to a man who – for Pascoe's benefit anyway – affected to believe that *cordon bleu* was a French road-block? And a slight blackening round the edge of a fry-up was to a resurrected copper what the crust on old port was to a wine connoisseur – a sign of readiness.

His ponderous jowls shaved to danger point, his few sad last grey hairs brushed to a high gloss, his heavy frame clad in an angel-white shirt and an undertaker-black suit, with knife-edge creases breaking on mirror-bright shoes, he set off at a stately though deceptively rapid pace towards the city centre.

He was, of course, carless. His reason for being carless he continued to keep carefully out of his mind. Nor did he in any way appear to register the momentary lull in noise as he entered the canteen. To Edna, the weary siren behind the counter, he said, 'Full house, love.'

Under his approving gaze, she filled his personal willow-patterned plate till the pattern disappeared. Seizing a bottle of tomato sauce from the counter, he made for an empty table, sat down and began to eat.

It was here that George Headingley found him.

He sat down on the opposite side of the table, himself a large man, but dwarfed by Dalziel, an effect intensified by something in his demeanour of the schoolboy waiting to be noticed before the headmaster's desk.

'Sir,' he said.

''Morning, George,' said Dalziel. 'This murder in Welfare Lane – Deeks, is it? – how're we doing?'

'Well, Pascoe's handling that, sir,' said Headingley, slightly taken aback. Of course, Dalziel had been in the station for an hour or so last night, but he hadn't given the impression he was taking anything in.

'So you said. What made you dig him out? Weren't it his lassie's birthday yesterday?'

Headingley decided that straightforward was the best route.

'The DCC's just come in, sir. He'd like a word if you don't mind.'

'Is that what he said? If I don't mind?' said Dalziel disbelievingly.

'Well, not exactly,' admitted Headingley.

'Oh aye. Well, you go and tell him, George; you tell him . . .'

Dalziel paused, attempted to spear a rasher of bacon, was defeated by its adamantine crispness and had to scoop it up and crunch it whole: 'You tell him I'll be along right away.'

Three minutes later, his plate clean and his mouth scoured with another cup of red-hot tea, he made his way upstairs.

The Deputy Chief Constable was not a man he liked. It was Dalziel's not inaudibly expressed view that he couldn't solve a kiddies' crossword puzzle and had only been promoted out of Traffic because he couldn't master the difference between left and right. More heinously, he rarely dispensed drink and when he did it tended to be dry sherry in glasses so narrow that it was like reading a thermometer looking for the bloody stuff, which in any case Dalziel regarded as Spanish goat-piss.

'Andy!' said the DCC heartily. 'Come you in. Sit you down. Look, I'm sorry, thing is this, we have got ourselves a bit of a problem.'

This recently developed speech style, modelled on that of a Tory cabinet minister being interviewed on telly, was taken by many as confirmation of rumours of the DCC's political ambition. A desirable stepping-stone to becoming first a personality, then a candidate, was the acquisition of the office of Chief Constable when the present incumbent, Tommy Winter, retired in nine months' time. Winter, who had never shown a great deal of enthusiasm for his right-hand man, had none the less given him a late opportunity to shine by suddenly deciding to take a large accumulation of back-leave visiting his daughter in the Bahamas. The DCC had decided the old boy was at last getting demob-happy, but now, regarding the menacing bulk of his head of CID, he began to wonder uneasily if Winter could have had some presentiment of this potentially scandalous development.

'You've got a problem, you say?' said Dalziel, leaning forward. 'How can CID help? Something personal, is it? Someone putting the black on, eh? Photos, mebbe? You can rely on me, sir.'

The man was bloody impossible, thought the DCC wearily. Impossible. It was a small consolation that no television interviewer in the world could even approach his awfulness!

Like Headingley before him, he decided to ignore dangerous side-roads and press straight on.

'You were involved in a car accident last night,' he said.

'I was in a car that was involved in an accident, that's right,' said Dalziel.

'It was your car,' said the DCC flatly. 'So you were involved whether you were driving or not.'

'Whether?' said Dalziel wonderingly. 'There's no whether about it! I wasn't, and that's that!'

'I've had the editor of the *Post* on to me,' pursued the DCC. 'One of his reporters has unearthed a witness who says she saw you getting into the driver's seat of your car outside the Paradise Hall Restaurant and driving away.'

'She?'

'She. A lady of unimpeachable character and, as far as I know, excellent eyesight.'

'She saw me driving away from Paradise Hall?'

'So she alleges.'

Dalziel scratched his armpit thoughtfully.

'Had she been drinking, mebbe?' he said finally.

'Not so that anyone noticed,' said the DCC acidly. 'Though you apparently had.'

'That's likely true,' said Dalziel seriously. 'That'll be why I didn't drive. Arnie Charlesworth drove. Likely you'll know him, being a gambling man? Arnie's not a drinker himself. Was once, now he doesn't touch the stuff. It'll all be in his statement. You've got his statement, have you, sir?'

'Yes, Andy. I've got his statement.'

'Grand!' said Dalziel. 'Now let's get on to this problem of yours, shall we?'

The DCC sighed deeply and turned half-profile to Dalziel's camera-rigid gaze.

'Andy, what you must understand is our need to appear absolutely impartial in this. Fortunately the editor of the *Post* is as aware as I am of the need to foster good and mutually beneficial police, public and press relationships.'

'You mean he doesn't want us stopping his paper vans parking on double yellow lines,' growled Dalziel.

'He has behaved very responsibly by putting the information in my hands . . .'

'Information? What information? I've told you what happened. Is someone trying to make a liar out of me?'

Ignoring the belligerent stiffening of Dalziel's body which had the effect, noted with terror by many a criminal, of turning what seemed mere flab into solid muscle, the DCC said, 'There's also the matter of Dr Sowden at the City General

51

who claims that Mr Westerman, the deceased, said something before dying which appeared to imply that he thought you were the driver of the vehicle that hit him. The testimony of Mrs Warsop, that's the witness in the car park, and of Dr Sowden could certainly be presented in a very damaging way if the *Post* decided to use it. Worse, of course, it might be that one of the less scrupulous national papers would take it up.'

Dalziel stood up.

'I've had enough of this,' he said angrily. 'Bloody journalists – I've shit 'em! Who runs the police in this country? Us or the bloody newspapers?'

Suddenly the DCC had had enough too. His tellypersona vanished like a whore's smile at an empty wallet. He became total policeman.

'Sit down!' he bellowed. 'And shut up! Now, Mr Dalziel, let me tell you something else. All that's bothering the Press at the moment is whether a drunken police officer is trying to wriggle out of a manslaughter charge. That bothers me too, but what bothers me almost as much is what the hell you were doing consorting with Arnold Charlesworth?'

'Why? What's wrong with Arnie?' asked Dalziel, slowly subsiding.

'Has it somehow escaped your notice, you who usually manage to know what's in my in-tray before I get near it,' said the DCC with heavy sarcasm, 'that Arnold Charlesworth is currently being investigated by Customs and Excise for evasion of betting tax? Just imagine what the Press will make of *that* when it comes out? Senior police officer entertained by crooked bookie! What the hell are you playing at, Superintendent?'

Dalziel said defiantly, 'There's nowt been proved against Arnie. He's an old mate of mine. Any road, I notice you don't ask who else was eating with us.'

'Not the Archbishop of Canterbury?' said the DCC, essaying wit.

'No. Barney Kassell, Major Barney Kassell.'

'And who the devil's he? Something big in the Sally Army?'

'No,' said Dalziel. 'He's Sir William Pledger's estate manager. You'll have heard of Sir William Pledger, I expect, sir? Big mate of Mr Winter's I gather. Major Kassell knows Mr Winter pretty well too, from arranging shooting parties and the like.'

The DCC was taken aback. William Pledger, a Harold Wilson knight who'd survived the elevation, was a powerful figure in the financial world. He'd made his reputation in the Far East in the 'sixties and early 'seventies, and was currently Chairman of Van Bellen International Holdings which was to date the nearest thing to efficient supranationalism to emerge out of the EEC. Pledger's shooting parties on his Yorkshire estate were usually high-powered affairs, with guests flown in from Europe, though the local connection was not neglected, as evidenced by the Chief Constable's frequent presence. Pledger's estate manager would certainly be a different kettle of fish from a local bookie, no matter how rich.

Dalziel pressed home his advantage.

'Arnie Charlesworth's been out to Haycroft Grange, shooting, too. That's how he knows the Major. Thought I might try it myself. Sir.'

The DCC who'd never even had a sniff of such an invitation said, 'I'm not much in favour of blood sports myself, Andy. Anyway, this is all beside the point. A policeman's got to be more careful than anyone else, you know that. What's all right for the public at large may not be all right for him.'

He frowned and went on, 'Look, you know how some people like to make mountains out of molehills. What would seem a good idea to me would be for you to keep your head down for a couple of days. You must be a bit shaken up. Have a couple of days off. You've got plenty of back-leave, you've been pushing yourself a bit hard lately, Andy.'

'Oh. You want me to take some of my holidays then, not sick leave?' said Dalziel mildly.

'Holiday, sick leave, whatever you like!' snapped the DCC. 'Go to Acapulco, Tibet, *anywhere*, so long as you don't talk to Ruddlesdin or any reporter, or *anyone!* Understand?'

Dalziel nodded and rose.

The DCC as if encouraged by this silence said boldly, 'Andy, you're *quite* sure you weren't driving?'

The fat man didn't even pause but left the room without closing the door behind him.

It was not a very positive gesture, but the best he could manage. Usually he regarded any confrontation with the DCC as a mismatch, but today had been different. The trouble was of course that the long streak of owl-shit had a secret advantage today in the shape of an old man looking up into the headlamp-bright tracers of rain with unblinking blue eyes. Dalziel could see him now if he wished, suspected he might start seeing him even if he didn't wish. It was a ghost that was going to take some exorcising.

'Hello, Mr Dalziel. What's your pleasure this time?'

It was Edna, the canteen girl. For some reason his feet had brought him back to the basement while his mind wandered aimlessly in the past.

'Full house,' he said automatically.

'*Again?*'

Of course, he'd had it once. On the other hand, it was a silly copper who quarrelled with his feet. Exorcism probably required as full a stomach as most human activities.

'Yes, please,' he said firmly. 'And this time, love, see if you can't get them rashers *really* crisp.'

Chapter 7

'What does it signify?'

Peter Pascoe allowed himself to be rehearsed in the whereabouts of fridge, oven, and his clean underwear for some minutes before interrupting with, 'And that's a chair, and that's a table, and there's a door! Darling, I haven't lived with a liberated woman these past seventy years, or whatever it is, without becoming moderately self-sufficient.'

'Bollocks,' said Ellie. 'And any more of that crap and I'll leave Rosie in your tender care while I drive off to Orburn.'

'I wouldn't mind,' said Pascoe. 'Even her muckiest nappy's a pleasanter prospect than anything I've got to look forward to. Still, I suppose it's good timing. It could've spoilt a weekend when you were staying at home.'

He kissed the pair of them fondly.

'See you tomorrow night, then,' he said. 'Love to the old folk.'

It was nearly ten o'clock, a lateness explained though possibly not justified by the hour at which he'd finally got to bed. Pascoe assured himself that the lie-in had been necessary in the interests of his personal efficiency, but he wondered whether he'd have chanced it if he hadn't suspected Dalziel was going to have other things on his mind that morning than checking on his staff.

His first stop was the hospital where he found that Longbottom, the pathologist, presumably eager to take advantage on the golf-course of the bright November day which had succeeded the stormy night, had already started on Robert Deeks.

A native of Yorkshire whom education had deprived of his accent but not of the directness which usually accompanied it, Longbottom summed up his findings in simple non-technical language.

'You can try murder, but it'll probably end as manslaughter,' he said. 'Injuries to the head and face caused by slapping and punching. Possibly by someone wearing a leather glove. Injuries to neck, shoulders and scalp caused by narrow-bladed double-edged knife with a sharp point. None of these injuries severe enough to be fatal of itself. But he was old and frail. I'm surprised he was still living by himself, really. Cause of death, in lay terms, shock. Oh, and there was a bit of bathwater in his lungs. He must have gone under a couple of times.'

'Been forced under, you mean.'

'Could be,' said Longbottom. 'Why not? I presume whoever knocked him about was trying to force something out of him. Certainly wasn't self-defence. But that's your problem, Inspector. Now, let's see. What else do we have?'

He checked a list.

'Road accident and a broken hip with death from exposure? No urgency there, I presume. I'll leave them over for a rainy day.'

'I think,' said Pascoe hesitantly, 'though it's nothing to do with me directly, that an early report on the road accident would be appreciated.'

'Oh?' said Longbottom. 'All right. If I must, I must.'

'And as a matter of interest,' pushed Pascoe, 'the other one, I happened to see him last night. His right hip was broken, I believe, as a result of a fall. And he's got a nasty bruise on the left side of his head which Dr Sowden seemed to think could have been caused in the same fall. I'd be interested in your opinion.'

'Trying to get me to drop a colleague in it, Inspector?' said Longbottom, smiling thinly. 'Dr Sowden? Young man, rather pretty?'

'That's the one.'

'I know him. Good face for a doctor. Fatigue just makes it a bit more romantically haggard. Let's have a look.'

Thinking that Longbottom's rather frighteningly sallow and bony features perhaps explained his decision to concentrate on the dead rather than the living, Pascoe followed him to where an attendant,

sensitive to his master's wishes, had already produced Thomas Arthur Parrinder's cadaver.

Longbottom ran his fingers along the fractured
hip and studied the contusion through a magnifying-
glass.

'Thinking of assault, are you?' he said.

'It's a conditioned reflex,' said Pascoe.

'Any special reason?'

'No,' admitted Pascoe. 'As far as I know there's
no evidence of robbery or of any other person
being involved.'

'As far as you know?' repeated Longbottom
sarcastically. 'So this is another one that's really
nothing to do with you? You must find time
hanging heavy on your hands, Inspector. Or do
you just want to prove Dr Sowden is fallible?'

Pascoe considered this. He didn't think it was
true, but when it came down to it, he wouldn't be
too troubled if he undermined that young man's
confidence, and it might even persuade him to
greater discretion in the Westerman business.

'If you could just tell me your opinion,' he
said.

'No opinion without proper examination,' said
Longbottom. 'That's one of the few perks of working with corpses. But you might care to examine
the ground where he fell and see if you can find
a stone or some other solid protuberance at least
two inches in diameter. Or is that someone else's
business?'

*　　*　　*

At the hospital inquiry desk, Pascoe discovered that Mrs Dolly Frostick had discharged herself an hour earlier. This was a nuisance as it meant he would have to make another diversion to see her at home.

Home, he discovered from the hospital records, was 352, Nethertown Road, a ribbon development of nineteen-thirties semis running alongside the main easterly exit route from the city. In front of the house, like a matchseller's tray, a tiny square of green-tinged concrete was set with boxes of roses and other ornamental shrubs. This geometric artificiality contrasted strangely with the front of 352's Siamese twin, 354, where an untended lawn and flower-beds had been allowed to run riot, and summer's profusion lay wrecked but not drowned by the storms of winter.

A small man with a thin moustache and a discontented face answered his ring.

'Yes?' he said aggressively.

Pascoe introduced himself with the aplomb of one used to being greeted as something between a brush-salesman and a Jehovah's Witness.

The man was Alan Frostick and while part of his aggression sprang from a natural instinct to defend his wife, a great deal of it seemed to be chronic and indiscriminate.

'You'll not have caught anyone yet?' he said as he closed the door behind Pascoe with a last glower at his concrete garden. 'More stick, that's what's needed. More stick.'

Whether the extra stick was to be applied to the criminals or to the police was not clear. A door whose woodwork had been painted over with brown varnish, into which a wood grain pattern had then been combed, opened into a main sitting-room where two women sat. Mr Frostick had at least not made the little man's common matrimonial error of biting off more than he could chew. His wife was a good inch shorter than he was, a not unhandsome woman in her forties, perhaps even a pocket Venus in her day, but now haggard with grief and fatigue. Her friend, introduced as Mrs Gregory from next door, looked to be in much the same state, though whether this was sympathetic or merely coincidental did not at first emerge.

Mrs Gregory offered to make a cup of tea. Alan Frostick sat on the sofa next to his wife and put a comforting arm around her shoulder.

'Make it quick, will you?' he said. 'She's been upset enough.'

'Yes,' said Pascoe. 'Of course. Mrs Frostick, could you tell me what happened last night? I believe you tried to ring your father earlier in the evening?'

'That's right,' said the woman in a reassuringly firm and controlled voice. 'About half past six. Alan had just had his tea. I always like to ring him if I haven't been able to get round in the day.'

'Do you go round most days?' inquired Pascoe.

'When I can. It's two bus rides away, you see, so

it's not always convenient. It used to be all right a couple of times a week maybe, but for the last year or so, since he had his turn . . .'

'His turn?'

'Yes. He was ill, had to go into hospital. When he came out, he stayed with us for a bit till he was fit again. But he was never the same.'

'But he became fit enough to go back to his own home?'

'He wanted to,' interrupted Frostick. 'That's what he was always saying. Only place for a man is his own home. He wanted to go back.'

Mrs Frostick nodded agreement.

'That's when we put the phone in . . .'

'And the bath,' interrupted her husband. 'Don't forget that bath.'

'Yes, dear. But it was the phone that was most important. It meant I could keep in touch easily. And Mrs Spillings next door was very good at keeping an eye on him. Anyway, when he didn't answer at first, I wasn't bothered. He might easily have gone down the road for a paper. And even when I tried again later on and still got no reply, I wasn't too worried. He usually has a bath on a Friday evening and he can never hear the phone in the bathroom. But by the time it got to eight o'clock, I was getting worried.'

'You didn't think of phoning one of the neighbours?'

'Well, Tracey, that's Mrs Spillings, doesn't have the phone. In fact there's no one in the Lane with it that I know well enough to bother. So I thought I'd best get myself round there. It was a terrible night but I was lucky with the first bus. Well, it stops just opposite and you can almost see it coming from our front window.'

'I see. You went by bus,' said Pascoe. There was a wooden garage beside the house and he felt sure he'd glimpsed a car through the partially opened door.

'It's Alan's club night,' explained Mrs Frostick quickly. 'He was out with the car. I had a long wait for the next bus, though, and it was well after nine by the time I got there. I rang the bell, he always likes you to ring the bell, he's that independent. But when he didn't come, I let myself in with my key. I shouted out to him and had a look downstairs. When I saw what a mess things were in, I began to think something terrible must have happened, I was almost too frightened to go upstairs but I went anyway. I was still shouting though I think that now I was really shouting to warn off anyone who might be up there, if you know what I mean. I went up and up, it's just a short stair but it seemed to go on for ever somehow, and even though I thought I was ready for the worst, when I went into the bathroom and saw him lying there, I . . .'

The transition from control to collapse was sudden and complete. One moment the voice was firm, the narrative clear and remarkably frank in its analysis of her feelings: the next she was weeping and sobbing convulsively. Frostick patted her shoulders helplessly and glared at Pascoe as if he were to blame. Mrs Gregory returned with a tray set with teacups, which she carefully deposited on an old-fashioned sideboard before sitting next to the weeping woman on the arm of the sofa and taking her in an embrace which completely excluded Frostick.

After a while the sobs declined to an occasional soft-bursting bubble and the narrative resumed.

'I'm sorry, Inspector. When I saw him, I just stood and shrieked. I tried to lift him out, but even though he weighed next to nothing, he was too much for me. He seemed all slippery and sort of waterlogged and I thought I was likely just to hurt him more by dragging him over the edge of the bath. Or perhaps that's what I thought I thought later. What I remember vaguely is running down the stairs and into the street and banging on people's doors and shrieking and shouting. I couldn't stop. It's funny. I had this feeling that when I stopped, that's when it was really going to hurt, so I just went on and on. And then there was the ambulance, and getting to the hospital, and that doctor telling me he was dead, there was nothing they could do. Nothing. Just like that. Nothing. It was all over. All that living, all that worrying. I just couldn't make any sense of it. No sense at all. It's not how it should be, is it? It's not how it should be!'

It was a poignant moment, suddenly and brutally interrupted by a tremendous hammering noise from the other side of the party wall and a high-pitched male alto voice calling what sounded like *Teeny! Teeny! Where's my tea?*

'Oh Dolly, I'm sorry, he must know I'm in here, I don't know how,' said Mrs Gregory.

Frostick leapt to his feet and banged his fist against the wall, bellowing, 'Shut up! Shut up!' And now another voice was heard next door, a hoarse bass, rumbling powerfully but incomprehensibly beneath the alto whose cries of *Teeny!* only increased in pitch and volume. Then the bass exploded; there was a sharp crack; and silence . . . till like dimples on a smooth flowing stream there came a little run of soft sobs like a child's comfortless crying.

'I'd better go,' said Mrs Gregory. 'I'll be back later, Dolly. I'm sorry, Alan. Goodbye, Inspector.'

She rose and left swiftly. Frostick, looking spent after his outburst, said, 'She never mashed the tea,' and went out, presumably to the kitchen.

Pascoe looked inquiringly at the woman on the sofa and after a while she said, 'It's Mabel's father. He's nearly eighty. He gets very confused. They've had to put his bed downstairs now, he's so awkward on his pins. I don't think he knows where he is half the time, but he always knows where Mabel is.'

'What was he calling?' asked Pascoe, thinking a brief diversion to her friend's problems might have some therapeutic value. 'It sounded like *Teeny*.'

'That's right. It's what he called Mabel's mother. That's who he thinks Mabel is most of the time, when he recognizes her at all.'

'It must be pretty awful,' said Pascoe.

'Oh yes.' To his horror he saw that tears were forming again in her eyes. 'It's been like that for three years and more now. I don't know how she stands it. It's just about driven her Jeff mad and Andrea, that's her daughter, up and left home earlier this year. That's why we didn't want Dad to stay with us, partly anyway. It was bad enough when he was convalescing after his turn. Him and Alan got on each other's nerves and, I've got to be honest, it got on mine too a bit. But he seemed all right by himself after that, till just recently. He'd been getting more awkward and forgetful and we'd been talking about having him back here to live with us. I'd say it'd just be for a while till he got right again, but Alan'd say no, it'll be for ever, or at least for as long as he lives, and look at him next door, we shouldn't kid ourselves, it might be a long, long time. So we've talked and talked and sometimes I've thought there's no way round it but he's got to come, and then I've seen Mabel, or heard the noise from next door, and I haven't been able to face it, and that's the truth, Inspector.

'And now I know that maybe if I had been able to face it, he'd be here now and alive instead of . . . instead of . . .'

She stared unblinkingly at Pascoe through eyes big and bright with tears.

'It's not so much him being dead,' she said. 'That's all there was for him, I reckon. But not like that! Not like that!'

Frostick came in with the teapot and Pascoe waited for a new outburst from him for upsetting his wife. But all the man said was, 'You take milk?'

'Thank you. No sugar. Mrs Frostick, I'm sorry to bother you when I can see how upset you are, but I have to ask these questions. Did your father keep any money or other valuables around the house?'

'I don't know,' said the woman. 'No valuables certainly. He never had anything that was worth very much.'

'But money perhaps?'

'He used to keep money,' said Frostick, handing Pascoe his tea. 'He liked to settle for things in cash. Never had a bank account or a cheque-book. He wasn't badly off, either. He had a tidy pension from his work as well as the State. About seven or eight months back, Dolly came across a pile of notes he'd stuffed in an old kettle. More than a hundred pounds, wasn't there?'

'Yes, but I really got cross with him,' said Mrs Frostick. 'I made him go into town with me and I stood over him while he paid most of it into his building society account. I didn't often lose my rag with him, but when I did, he knew better than to try and outface me.'

'Do you think you cured him of the habit?' asked Pascoe.

'I doubt it,' said Frostick. 'He was a wilful old devil. He'd just hide the next lot somewhere that Dolly wouldn't find it, that's what I reckon.'

'Well, perhaps we can check to some degree by looking at his building society pay-in book and seeing if he's drawn much out recently,' said Pascoe. 'I'm afraid we'd very much like it if you could come down to the house as soon as you feel able, Mrs Frostick, and check over everything to see what, if anything, is missing.'

'Do I have to?' she said in a low voice.

'There's no one else can do it, is there?' said Pascoe.

'You'll have to go some time, Dolly,' said her husband. 'Tomorrow morning, Inspector. That suit you?'

Pascoe would have preferred today, but looking at the woman and understanding now something of the burden of self-reproach she was carrying, he didn't have the heart to press her.

'One last thing,' he said. 'Your father was still alive when you found him. Did he say anything at all that you remember?'

'No,' she said. 'Nothing. Only *Charley*.'

'Charley?'

'That's our son,' she said. 'He and his grandad were very close. He must have wanted to see him, or get me to tell him something.'

Her voice broke again.

Pascoe looked on her grief with genuine sympathy, but he was a policeman as well as a fellow human and the best he could do was to try and keep his policeman's thoughts out of his voice as he said casually, 'How old's your son, Mrs Frostick?'

'Eighteen,' she said.

'Is he at home at the moment?'

The note of casual, friendly inquiry might have lulled a doting mother but Frostick was both sensitive and aggressive.

'No, he's bloody well not!' he snapped. 'He's in Germany, that's where he is!'

His wife, bewildered by his aggression, said, 'Charley's in the Army, Inspector. He couldn't get a job, you see, so he joined up this summer. It was all right at first, he was out at Eltervale Camp doing his training with the Mid-Yorkies, so we saw plenty of him. Then he got sent off to Germany three weeks ago. It's not right really, he's just a boy, and he'd just got himself engaged to Andrea, that's Mrs Gregory's girl next door, you'd think they'd have kept him a bit nearer home . . .'

'Best reason on earth for going abroad!' interrupted Frostick. 'Lad of his age engaged! Stupid. And to that scheming trollop! He's a good lad, our Charley, Inspector. He wasn't content to sit around on his arse collecting the dole like some. He did something about it, and he'll make a real go of things, if he's let!'

Frostick's voice was triumphant. Clearly the

wider the gap between Charley and the toils of Andrea Gregory, the better he would be pleased.

But on the sofa Mrs Frostick was weeping quietly and steadily, not only, Pascoe guessed, for a dead father, but also for a lost son.

Chapter 8

'Well, I have had a happy life.'

Detective-Constable Dennis Seymour and Police-Constable Tony Hector had little in common except size and a sense of grievance. Seymour was five inches shorter than Hector, but compensated with breadth of shoulder and depth of chest. Not too privately, he reckoned Hector was something of a twit and part of his grievance at being diverted from the Welfare Lane inquiry lay in having to suffer such a companion. But Sergeant Wield had been adamant. Mr Pascoe wanted this done and Seymour had better make a job of it.

Hector's sense of grievance went deeper, partly because he felt he had a personal stake in the Welfare Lane murder, and partly because he could not altogether grasp what they were meant to be doing on the Alderman Woodhouse Recreation Ground.

'We're looking for a stone or a bit of hard

wood, something that, if you fell and hit your head on it, would break the skin and leave a dent,' said Seymour patiently. He had bright red hair and an underlying Celtic volatility of temper which he knew might prove a hindrance to advancement if he did not keep it firmly underlaid.

'Couldn't this old fellow just've banged his head on the ground when he fell?' objected Hector.

'The ground was soft, it had been raining,' said Seymour, stamping his foot into the muddy grass which the November sun's puny heat had not begun to dry.

'It's going to be a hell of a job finding something like that, just the two of us,' grumbled Hector, looking glumly out across the broad open space which included three football pitches and a children's play area.

'*Not* finding it's the important thing,' said Seymour smartly. And this is where he lost Hector, to whom the easiest way of *not* finding something seemed to be not to look for it very hard.

Convinced at last that looking was essential, he said, 'Wouldn't it be better if we had some idea of where to look before we started?'

He was right, of course, for Seymour had made the error of driving directly to the Recreation Ground instead of diverting first to talk with the man who'd discovered Mr Parrinder. He regarded Hector with new eyes, and made the discovery that being not quite so stupid as he looked increased rather than diluted the fellow's unlikability. At least before he had been reliable.

'You start looking,' he said. 'If you find anything, bag it and mark the spot. I'll go and talk to the fellow who found him.'

The witness was called Donald Cox. He turned out to be a small, voluble, middle-aged man with worried eyes and a rather insinuating manner who lived with his wife, four children and a Great Dane in a basic semi about half a mile from the Alderman Woodhouse Recreation Ground. Or perhaps, thought Seymour, it would be more accurate to say that the Great Dane occupied the house and the Cox family fitted round it as best they could.

'He needs his exercise, don't you, Hammy?' said Cox proudly. 'Only reason I was out. He'd missed his afternoon walk, I usually take him morning, afternoon and evening, three times a day, well, I've got the time now, haven't I, since they closed the works and put us all on the dole. I wish I could claim for Hammy here, you'd think they'd make an allowance, wouldn't you, he's like one of the family, and it was very nasty all afternoon so I thought, I'll just wait till later, it might fair up, but it just got worse and worse. Not a night to put a dog out in, they say, but this dog's got to go whatever the weather, if a day goes by without he's put at least five miles on the clock, there's no peace. He'll run up and down the stairs till three in the morning if that's the only way he can get his exercise, won't you, Hammy? Round and round the recreation ground he goes, round and round, by Christ I wish I had his energy. Don't worry, lad! He's got a lovely nature!'

It was Hammy's lovely nature, in fact, which was bothering Seymour as the dog attempted to demonstrate its affection by scrambling on his lap.

'If you could just show me where you found Mr Parrinder,' he said, trying in vain to rise.

'Pleasure. Hammy'd love a run out, wouldn't you, boy? You've brought your car, have you? Well, he likes a ride too, though you'll have to have your windows open, can't bear to be shut in a confined space.'

It was a chilly and chilling return journey to the recreation ground. The dog occupied the whole of the back seat with its head protruding from one window and its tail wagging out of the other. An amiable fog-horn bark into the ear of an overtaking motorcyclist nearly caused an accident.

'It's the white helmet,' said Cox complacently. 'He thinks it's a bone.'

Between the barking and the apologetic waves at the other road-users, Seymour managed a few questions. No, there'd definitely been no one else in sight on the recreation ground. Only idiots and Great Dane owners were out on such a night. Mind you, it had been very dark. In fact, Cox would likely not have seen the prostrate man if it hadn't been for Hammy finding him. No, the man hadn't been calling out, looked too far gone for that, poor sod. But yes, he had said something, just as Cox arrived to see what it was Hammy was looking at.

'And what did he say?' inquired Seymour.

'I'm not sure. It sounded like, mebbe, *Polly*,' said Cox. 'That's the nearest I can get to it. *Polly*. And seemed to sort of laugh, though what there was for him to be laughing at, I don't know. Delirious, I should think. But he certainly seemed to be dying happy, so you can't knock it, can you?'

'Did you touch him at all?'

'I tried to lift him up, but I could see he was unconscious and his leg was sprawled out underneath him at a funny sort of angle, and I guessed he'd broken something. So I thought it best to go for help. What's all this about, but? I thought the poor old devil had just had a fall and hurt himself. It was treacherous, the surface, what with the sleet and everything. I nearly went over a couple of times myself and Hammy's legs were going all ways!'

'Oh, it's just routine,' said Seymour.

The entrance to the recreation ground was just a wide gap in the wire-netting fence flanked with a small forest of bye-laws ranging from *Official Vehicles Only* to *All Dogs Must Be Kept On Leash*. Parking by the latter sign, and noting that either Cox couldn't read or didn't count Hammy as a dog, Seymour went in and looked for Hector. A schoolboy football match had started on one of the pitches and Seymour saw with mingled amusement and exasperation that Hector's search pattern, which consisted of walking in a straight line across the whole breadth of the recreation ground, was at the moment taking him along the touch line, much to the annoyance of the proudly spectating dads. From time to time Hector bent down to pick up a stone or other substantial piece of debris which he put in a plastic sack. He then marked the spot by digging a hole with his heel. Presumably this next traverse would take him on to the pitch itself. It was a confrontation almost worth waiting for, but when Cox pointed confidently towards one of the other pitches not in use, Seymour, for the sake of the reputation of the Force rather than on humanitarian grounds, waved his arm and shouted till he caught the lanky constable's attention and beckoned him to join them.

'You're certain this is where he was lying?' he asked Cox, who was now indicating a specific square yard of ground indistinguishable from any other.

'The very spot,' said Cox with complete conviction. 'Look, I walked round from the entrance and I got as far as that goalpost there, and I leaned up against it and tried to light a fag, but it wasn't any use in that wind. Then I saw Hammy galloping towards me and suddenly he stopped and started getting interested in this sort of bundle on the ground, so I went to have a look.'

Examination of the goalpost revealed half a dozen confirmatory matchsticks at its base.

'All right,' said Seymour. 'Let's take a look.'

He turned to address his invitation to Hector and was delighted to see that Hammy, having at last found a human he could really look up to, was standing with his forelegs on Hector's shoulders so that he could lick his new friend's terrified face. Hector retreated, Hammy advanced, the pair spun round together in a parody of a waltz, till finally the constable's legs slid away from under him and he crashed heavily to the ground.

'That's one way of looking for this stone,' agreed Seymour. 'But what I think Mr Pascoe had in mind was using our eyes.'

He began systematically to search the area round the spot indicated by Cox, spiralling further and further out. From time to time he spotted a stone, but none that looked of a possible size or to have any signs of recent contact with broken skin. Still, it had been raining hard overnight and the microscope might see something he couldn't, so he popped each stone into a plastic bag and charted its position conscientiously. Finally he decided he'd gone far enough and returned to where Cox was standing by the goalpost smoking a cigarette, watching his dog make playful assaults on Hector's legs.

'Thanks for your cooperation, sir,' he said to Cox. 'Would you mind if I left you to find your own way home? I'm going across the ground, see, to where Mr Parrinder lives, out the other way. That's why he'd be walking this way, it must have been a regular short cut for him.'

'Braver man than me,' grunted Cox. 'I wouldn't come this way in the dark, not without Hammy. No, you get on, Officer. Hammy needs all the exercise he can get. We'll walk back in a moment, though he'll be sorry to part company with your mate here!'

It didn't look as if the parting would be equally sorrowful on both sides. But Seymour, not without malice, said, 'No need for that just yet, sir. Constable Hector, would you cast around a bit longer, see if there's anything else you can find. I'll pick you up on my way back. Goodbye, Mr Cox. 'Bye, Hammy.'

He strode away jauntily. Perhaps after all there might be more in this for him than wandering up and down Welfare Lane doing house-to-house inquiries. The word was old Dalziel was having a spot of bother. Tough on the old sod, but it had only been a matter of time before his behaviour caught up with him. With Dalziel edged out, there could be a nice bit of upgrading all round, and who was better equipped to be a sergeant than Detective-Constable Dennis Seymour?

He flung his arms wide in a spontaneous gesture of self-congratulation, and Hammy, who had come running after him reluctant to lose even one of his new friends, mistook the gesture for invitation and drove himself upwards, bringing his huge forepaws down against Seymour's shoulders and sending the amazed detective-constable crashing full length on the muddy ground.

Chapter 9

'Dying is a very dull, dreary affair. And my
advice to you is to have nothing whatever
to do with it.'

Welfare Lane when Pascoe arrived at noon was
remarkably free of sightseers even for what was
basically a pretty unfashionable murder. Indeed,
apart from a couple of shopping-laden women
trudging along the pavement, the only person in
sight was the constable outside No. 25.

The reason soon became clear. As he parked
his car behind the police caravan outside Deeks's
house, the puce portal of No. 27 burst open and
Mrs Tracey Spillings swept out on a wave of *Dallas*.

'All right, sunshine!' she bellowed. 'On your
way! Oh, it's only you.'

'I'm afraid so,' said Pascoe. 'I'm sorry, did you
want this parking spot . . . ?'

'What'd I do with a parking spot?' she demanded,
adding with a significant glance up and down the

street and an increase in voice projection which Pavarotti would have envied, 'Not that there's not plenty round here as drives in limousines to draw their dole.'

'Is that so?' said Pascoe, thinking that anything short of a chariot of fire would scarcely be a fit vehicle for Mrs Spillings. 'Then why did you . . .'

'I'm not having folk hanging round here gawking,' she said fiercely. 'Sick, some people are, and with nothing better to do. He's worse than useless –' indicating the uniformed constable who studied the rooftops opposite, perhaps in the hope of snipers – 'but I've sent 'em packing, no bother.'

No, thought Pascoe. He didn't imagine there had been any bother!

'I'd like to have a word if I may,' he said. 'Perhaps we could . . .'

He hesitated, glancing at the almost visible din emanating from the Spillings household.

'We'll go in your caravan,' said Mrs Spillings. 'You'll not be able to hear yourself think in here. She's been bad this morning. Worse she gets, louder she likes it. She reckons when she can't hear no more, she'll be dead. *Mam, I'll just be five minutes!*'

The last sentence ripped like a torpedo through the oncoming waves of sound. Pulling the puce door to, Mrs Spillings set out towards the caravan which dipped alarmingly as she placed a surprisingly small and rather delicately shaped foot on the step.

Inside, Sergeant Wield was working his way through a sheaf of statements and reports. His rugged face expressed no surprise at the sight of the woman.

'Door to door,' he said to Pascoe. 'Nothing. You had any luck, sir?'

'I don't think so,' said Pascoe. 'Mrs Spillings, you knew Mr Deeks well, did you?'

'Pretty well. We moved into 27 when I got wed twenty-five years ago. Dolly Deeks got married from that house two years later. Her mam died four or five years back and the old man had been on his own since then. So you could say I knew him pretty well.'

'Did you ever know him to keep a lot of money in his house?'

She thought for a moment then said, 'Aye. Once. I recall Dolly getting right upset because she found a lot lying around. She's a quiet soul, Dolly, but she really gave him what for that day!'

'Yes, she told me about it,' said Pascoe.

'She's all right, is she? Out of that hospital? That's no place for a well woman. Not much use for a sick 'un either, from all accounts.'

'Yes. She's at home. She'll be coming here tomorrow. To get back to the money, did he still keep any in the house? More important perhaps, did he have any reputation locally for keeping large sums about the place?'

She saw what he meant at once.

'No, he weren't thought of as the local miser or

owt like that. Though there's no accounting for the daft ideas some buggers get into their heads! As for still keeping money in the house, I don't know. I recollect him telling me he'd loaned young Charley – that's his grandson – the money to buy that lass of his an engagement ring, but whether it were cash he had or whether he had to draw it out special, I don't know.'

'But he discussed his finances with you?' said Pascoe.

Tracey Spillings laughed and said, 'Not old Bob. He were very close! But this were different. Charley's the apple of his eye, but he would never sub him after he left school. If you can't live on your dole money, he'd say, get a job. He paid no heed to all this unemployment. There's always jobs for them as wants them, he said. They're always after likely lads in the Forces, or even the police.'

Pascoe ignored the implied order of merit and said, 'It doesn't sound as if he'd have been very happy to dish out money so Charley could get engaged, then?'

'Normally, he wouldn't. Specially as he didn't much like the lass. But Charley timed it nicely, I gather. Told his grandad he'd signed on with the Mid-Yorkies, and then touched him straight after. That's how I got to know about the money. Old Bob mentioned the loan when he was telling me about Charley joining up. He were that pleased, even though he knew how much he'd miss the lad.'

'And the lad himself. He was fond of his grandad too?' said Pascoe. 'He'll be upset to hear what's happened.'

'Oh aye. He liked the old boy and I've no doubt he'll be upset,' said Mrs Spillings. 'But you know how it is with young 'uns. You never get back what you give.'

'Your mother seems to be getting a pretty good bargain,' smiled Pascoe.

'You reckon? There's times I could gladly kill her. That's not a right way to feel about your own mam, is it?'

Slightly taken aback by this frank admission, Pascoe found he had no reply. But Wield, without looking up from his records, said, 'I dare say when you were a squawking baby in the middle of the night, there were times she could gladly have killed you, Mrs Spillings.'

The woman considered this, then a wide grin opened up her face, letting out a lively, pretty, perhaps even slim young girl for a moment.

'Mebbe you're right there, sunshine,' she said. 'Mebbe it does even out in the end! I'd best get back and see to her. If ever you feel like a cup of tea, don't knock, I'll not hear you. Just come on in.'

She left.

Pascoe said, 'Interesting woman.'

'Interesting, aye,' said Wield. 'What was all that about Charley?'

Pascoe explained, adding thoughtfully, 'But I'll

maybe just give them a ring at Eltervale Camp just to make sure he's gone.'

'You're getting cynical, sir,' observed Wield. 'By the way, Mr Headingley rang. Said he'd be having a bit of lunch at The Duke of York if you're interested.'

'What's he think I'm on, my holidays?' snorted Pascoe. 'I haven't time to drive all that way out just to socialize.'

'Didn't get that impression, sir,' said Wield neutrally. 'Thought he might be after having a chat about Mr Dalziel's spot of bother. Not that he said owt, you understand.'

There were no secrets in a police station, thought Pascoe. He also thought that he really ought to stay as far away as he could get from this Dalziel business, but did not much like the feeling accompanying the thought.

'Did you want to speak to the Army now?' said Wield, reaching for the phone. Before he could touch it, it rang. The Sergeant picked it up and listened.

'No, sir,' he said. 'Not yet. Half an hour unless he's held up. Right.'

He replaced the receiver and said, 'That was Ruddlesdin. He was hanging around earlier. Mrs Spillings spotted him. He tried to interview her.'

He smiled at the memory.

'How the hell does he come to be ringing us here?' wondered Pascoe. 'Oh, and is that me you're expecting in half an hour?'

'That's right,' said Wield. 'He's keen to talk to you. He's on his way and he'll see you here at twelve-thirty. Unless you're held up.'

'Yes,' said Pascoe slowly. 'You know Sergeant, perhaps I should call in at Eltervale Camp rather than ring them. The Army tends to be a bit protective about its own.'

'Yes, sir,' agreed Wield. 'Face to face is best. And you'd have to go quite near The Duke of York, wouldn't you? To reach the camp, I mean.'

'So I would. Good. You'll know where to get me, then.'

'Unless Sammy Ruddlesdin asks, I will,' grinned Wield.

'Sergeant, you're a darling man. By the way, did you send Seymour and Hector off to the recreation ground?'

'Aye,' said Wield. 'And I've heard nothing since. Hector's likely got lost, and Seymour will have found himself a bird to chat up. What's it all about, sir?'

He sounded disapproving and Pascoe said airily, 'Could be something or nothing, Sergeant. See you later!'

As he left, Wield shook his head sadly. Something or nothing! He much admired Pascoe, but there was no getting away from it, sometimes the young inspector did get his head full of daft notions.

Though in this case, Wield, who was a man of considerable sensitivity beneath his harsh and rugged exterior, wondered how much Pascoe's present 'hunch' wasn't just a mental space-filler, delaying him from admitting just how upset he really was by Dalziel's spot of bother.

The Sergeant's stomach rumbled. No *Duke of York* for him, but he had been relying on Seymour's return so that he could slip away for a quick snack. Where was the man? Chatting up a bird, he'd suggested to Pascoe. Wield's inner sensitivity did not extend to forgiving DC's who kept him from his food while they chatted up birds.

He chewed on the end of his pen and planned reprisal.

The Sergeant's suspicions about Seymour were to some extent justified, but not in every particular. Women delayed him, but only in the way of duty.

Castleton Court where the late Thomas Arthur Parrinder had lived was a block of local authority retirement flats, in no way an old people's home, though there was on the site a widower in his early sixties who had undertaken the job of warden, which meant for the most part channelling complaints to the Housing Office and responding to the flashing lights and sounding bells which meant a tenant was in trouble.

The warden was called Tempest, a thick-set ex-miner who took his new duties as seriously as he'd taken his old. His cheerful face was shadowed as he let Seymour into Parrinder's flat.

'He were a good lad, Tap. That was what every-one called him, from his initials I suppose, though some says it was because when he was down on his luck with the hosses, he'd be tapping anyone he could for a bob or two. Well, I never knew it; a good lad, spry and lively and right independent. Mebbe a bit too much. Makes a change from them as is never off your back, but there's a happy medium.'

'What do you mean?' asked Seymour.

'Well, look at this,' said the Warden. 'See these alarm switches on the wall in every room? They set off the light and the bell outside the door. See how they've got cords reaching down to the floor? Idea is, if anyone has a fall, he can still pull the switch, right? Well, look at this.'

He opened the bathroom door.

'See. There's the switch, but where's the cord? They take 'em off! Afraid they might pull it by accident instead of the light cord, see, and I might come rushing in and find them in the bath or on the pot. It's daft, really, but that's folk for you.'

Old Deeks could've done with one of those, thought Seymour. But likely he'd have been the same and put it out of action.

'One old lady,' continued Mr Tempest, leading him back into the small but comfortably appointed living-room, 'set her alarm off once by accident, she were so embarrassed, next thing I knew, she'd taken the fuses out so the bloody thing wouldn't go off at all! Can you beat that, eh?'

Seymour who was still young enough to feel immortal shook his head in general bewilderment at the vagaries of age and studied the room. Television, two armchairs, low table with transistor radio, glass-fronted cabinet with the remnants of a good tea-set, not much of a reader but a pile of old *Dalesman* magazines and not so old racing papers by the fireplace.

'He was a racing man, you say?' he said with the approval of one who shared the interest.

'Oh yes. Waste of time and money if you ask me,' said Tempest, insensitive to Seymour's enthusiasm. 'Not that he went over the top, I'm not saying that. He always kept it within bounds as far as I could see. I suppose it's a hobby like any other.'

'Any family?'

'Daughter in Canada, I think. No one closer, not as comes to see him anyway. His wife died fifteen years ago. He was the only man by himself in this block, the rest is all widows. Gentler sex, they say. I don't know about gentler but they're certainly tougher! I used to have a laugh with him about it. He said it was like most chances in life – came too bloody late!'

'I know the feeling,' said Seymour with the insincerity of the young. 'Any particular friends?'

'I don't know about his own mates – certainly he didn't get many visitors. Among the old girls? Oh, there's two or three he's quite thick with. They play cards for pennies and they like a flutter on the gees. Tap'd put it on for them. There's Mrs

Campbell in 24, nice woman, full of life, takes care of herself – you know, hair-do's, make-up. Could pass for fifty. I often wondered if Tap had chanced his arm there! Then there's Mrs Escott at 28. She was probably the closest, only, last six months or so, she's started going.'

'Going?' said Seymour. 'Where?'

'Upstairs,' said the warden significantly. 'SD. Senile dementia. It's just on and off at the moment, but once they start that game, there's no road back. I've seen it too often. They get muddled and start wandering, mentally and physically. In the end they can get to be a menace to themselves. And everyone else. Turn the gas on, go out without lighting it, that kind of thing. It's early days yet for Mrs Escott, but she's going, poor dear. I've had a word with her son. He says he's noticed nowt, but he's noticed all right. Trouble is, with the telly and everything, people are getting wise these days.'

'Wise to what?' inquired Seymour, to whom all this was literally as well as figuratively territory antipodean, his two surviving grandparents living close to their eldest son, Seymour's uncle Andy, in New Zealand.

'The old folk problem,' said the warden. 'People live a long time these days. Trouble is they don't stay young longer, they stay old longer. It's when they start needing looked after, either because they can't get about any more, or because they're into SD, that the bother starts. I see it coming on, I just pass the word to the social workers.

They start working at the relatives to take the old people to live with them. They say it's best for them. Well, maybe. It's certainly best for the local authority. Once you get an elderly relative being looked after in your house, you've got a hell of a job to get shut of him! There's not the hospital beds, you see. The authority just doesn't want to know. But now folk are getting wise, they've seen it on the telly, old folk don't come home to die any more, they come home to live and be a worry and a bother and a burden for years maybe.'

'So what happens?'

'If no one takes 'em in, the authority's got no choice. But you've got to be really hard not to take your old mam or dad in just for a couple of weeks, haven't you? Hello, Mrs Campbell. Here's a nice young bobby for you to dazzle. Always said you were a bobby-dazzler, didn't I?'

Mrs Campbell who had appeared with a shopping basket was a great relief to Seymour. All this talk about senile dementia had filled him with foreboding, and it was a pleasant surprise to see this bright-eyed, handsome woman in an elegant fur coat and a truly remarkable hat which seemed to be composed entirely of orange feathers. She gave him a cup of tea and in the round, confident tones of the middle class expressed her great distress at the sad news about Tap Parrinder.

'Such a nice man. So independent, and good with his hands too. It's so nice to have a man about the place, Mr Seymour, someone you can turn to if you need something lifted or fixed. Mr Tempest, the warden, is very obliging, of course, but he's not the same as a real neighbour, if you know what I mean. I do hope we get a replacement as nice, and preferably another man. We do seem to be rather top-heavy with females, I'm afraid. Not that I'm complaining, Mr Seymour. I never anticipated finishing my days in council accommodation, but to tell you the truth, I've been quite delighted with the class of person I've met in the flats, quite delighted!'

After another cup of tea, Seymour finally got down to extracting firm answers to his questions.

She had last spoken to Parrinder on Friday morning.

'He'd been a little under the weather for the past few days, just a cold, but he hadn't gone out. I called to ask him if he wanted anything from the shops when I went out later as I usually do on Friday. He said no, he was still all right.'

'Still?'

'Yes. I'd looked in from time to time earlier in the week. I offered to collect his pension but he said he might as well let it stand as he had plenty of stuff in his fridge to keep him going.'

'Did he say anything about going out later?' asked Seymour.

'Oh no. I'd have certainly told him what I thought if he'd even hinted it. It was so nasty, even I put off my shopping till Saturday, after all. He was standing looking out of his window as we talked and I remember saying to him I might change my mind and not go till Saturday if it didn't get any better and he said something about yes, but it makes the ground nice and heavy, doesn't it? As if that was a good thing! And then he goes out in it without telling anyone. But he was such an independent man. Independence! It's your greatest fault and your greatest virtue, you men. You have to do things your own way, Mr Seymour. Your own way. There's no denying you!'

She smiled coyly at him and Seymour finished his tea and took his leave, promising to call in again if ever he were passing.

He almost gave the demented Mrs Escott a miss, but he had a fairly strongly developed sense of duty and also knew that those omissions which the sharp eye of Sergeant Wield didn't spot, the milder but no less perceptive gaze of Inspector Pascoe would surely pick up.

Mrs Escott was even more of a relief than Mrs Campbell. Instead of some wild woman of the woods, with mad eyes and unkempt hair, he found himself in the presence of a very ordinary-looking, rather dumpy lady with neat grey hair whose only sign of disturbance was that her soft brown eyes filled with tears when she discovered his mission.

She bustled around making a pot of tea which Seymour didn't really want but guessed was a therapeutic response. He placed himself so that he could see into the tiny kitchen and check that she actually lit the gas. Everything was carried out swiftly and efficiently and the tea tasted fine, no salt instead of sugar, or any other mad substitution. His expression of gratitude must have been slightly overdone for he caught her looking at him as if she suspected *he* was slightly odd, a disconcerting reversal.

She was able to fill in a little more of Parrinder's Friday timetable. She had called in to see him at about two o'clock that afternoon. He was watching some racing on the television and she had made a cup of tea and they had sat together and talked for about an hour. He had made no mention of any plans for going out later, but that didn't surprise her. Not that he was a secretive man, but he was certainly one who made his own decisions independent of anyone else.

'Did he drink a lot?' wondered Seymour.

'Oh no,' she said. 'He liked a drop of rum when he could afford it, but he wasn't what you would call a drinker.'

Seymour made notes. It was beginning to seem possible that Parrinder had met his 'accident' as he was heading across the recreation ground on his way into town later that evening rather than on his return, though the latter was by no means ruled out. It had been ten o'clock when Mr Cox found him. Presumably he had been lying there for some time for the wet and the cold to strike home with such deadly effect. It would have been dark by five o'clock on such a dreary day and very few pedestrians would have been out and about in such a place in such conditions.

'Mr Seymour,' said Mrs Escott in her rather gentle voice which had a great deal of the West Country beneath its patina of Yorkshire vowels and usages. 'All these questions – was Mr Parrinder attacked by someone? When I heard about it this morning, they just said he'd fallen and broken something.'

For a woman whose mind was failing, she was sharp enough to be the first to ask the question direct, thought Seymour.

'We don't know,' he said, adding reassuringly, 'But don't you worry about it. Maybe it was just an accident. That's what I'm trying to find out.'

'That recreation ground,' she said, her eyes filling again. 'It's a dreadful place when it's dark. All those muggings you read about. I won't go near the place, I don't even like it much in daylight either. Poor Tap, poor Tap.'

The double dose of tea had got to Seymour and he asked permission to use the bathroom.

'Yes, of course,' said the woman, directing him, and drying her tears at the same time.

Seymour went in. It was a ground-floor flat and Mrs Escott, not trusting to frosted glass to protect her privacy, also had heavy curtains drawn so that the room was in deep gloom. Seymour reached out, grasped the light cord and pulled.

No light came on, at least not in here, and distantly he heard a double-noted bell begin to clamour an urgent summons.

'Oh shit,' he said.

Chapter 10

'Oh my country! How I love my country!'

George Headingley had had a mixed morning.

He just missed Arnie Charlesworth, learning at
his main betting shop that the bookie was on his
way to a race meeting at Newcastle.

The DCC had passed Major Kassell's name on
to him and he had rung Sir William Pledger's
mansion, Haycroft Grange, which was about ten
miles out of town, to learn that he'd just missed
Kassell too. The good news was that he was coming
into town, to the local airport to be precise, to meet
a plane.

The plane in question turned out to be a Cessna
Utililiner, the property of Van Bellen International,
which was bringing some of Sir William's weekend
shooting guests from the Continent. The plane had
already landed and there seemed to be quite a lot
of activity around it as Headingley drove towards
the clubhouse of the local gliding club which was

the only building on the site with any possible pretensions to being a passenger terminal.

To his surprise, there was a familiar figure standing at the side of the clubhouse, beating his arms against his sides to keep the blood circulating in the cold November air. It was Inspector Ernie Cruikshank, dowager of the uniformed branch, who usually had to be bribed to expose himself to the open air before May was out.

'Ernie, what the hell are you doing here?' asked Headingley.

'Same as you, likely,' said Cruikshank gloomily.

'I hope not,' said Headingley. 'What's going off, then?'

'Don't you know? It's your boss who set it up! Special request from Customs and Excise. For some reason best known to themselves, they're giving yon plane a right going-over and they asked if we could provide a presence in case we were needed. I ask you, bloody Saturday morning too, with them Rovers hooligans piling into town off every train for the match this afternoon, not to mention your precious poof Pascoe helping himself to my lads for his bloody murder inquiry!'

Headingley smiled, guessing that Cruikshank had opted for the outside duty which he felt entailed minimum exposure. The reference to Pascoe was best ignored. Cruikshank made little effort to conceal his opinion that the young DI was a jumped-up, supercilious, intellectual twit.

He pressed for further information and learned that Pledger had got a special dispensation for his company plane to land here during the shooting season.

'Cost him a bit to get it made OK, they reckon,' said Cruikshank. 'Normally it's nowt but gliders here and the odd light plane.'

'Well, that's hardly a *heavy* plane,' said Headingley judiciously, looking at the Cessna.

'Bit bigger than they normally have here,' said Cruikshank with the defensiveness of one whose expertise had just been garnered via a ten-minute chat with an Excise officer.

'And what's all this about a Customs check?'

'Well, seems normally they have a token chap here when Pledger's plane arrives, just to make sure the formalities are observed. It's top people, usually, and you know how them buggers get kid-gloved in this bloody country,' said Cruikshank with a class-bitterness, Marxian in intensity, but which didn't stop him voting Tory. 'This time, but, Customs have had a tip, someone's bringing in a load of naughties. They're all very tight-lipped but it must be something big to make it worth upsetting Pledger and his mates.'

'And you got this detail via Mr Dalziel, you say?' said Headingley.

'Aye. It'll likely come to nowt. He doesn't give away easy collars, that bugger! But uniformed'll do when it's a case of standing round in the bloody cold, wasting time!'

This analysis of Dalziel's priorities was too close to the mark to bear discussion, so Headingley went into the clubhouse in search of Major Kassell.

He spotted him instantly, not because of anything particularly military in his appearance, but because he was clearly mine host on this occasion, making sure that guests were minimally inconvenienced by this unfortunate delay, dispensing coffee and/or alcohol among the half-dozen new arrivals, four men, two women, lounging at their ease in the club room.

Kassell was about forty, a strong face with a prominent nose and deepset eyes which seemed always on the move and watchful, even as the mobile mouth twisted in a social smile. He had prematurely grey hair, silky and elegantly coiffured, which far from ageing him seemed to set off the liveliness of his features. He registered Headingley's arrival at once, and also that his presence had nothing to do with the current situation.

The Inspector stood quietly by the door, knowing that Kassell would be with him shortly.

When he finally broke free from his hostly duties, Kassell did not speak at once but gestured to Headingley to step outside into the narrow passageway.

Headingley introduced himself and stated his business.

Kassell nodded and said, 'Yes. I'd heard. Dreadful accident. Poor Charlesworth. Must have shaken him up.'

'I dare say, sir. Though it's business as usual this morning.'

Kassell looked at him, bushy grey eyebrows raised in surprise.

'He's hardly going to close down for a week's mourning, is he? How can I help, Inspector?'

'Just routine, sir. Get the facts straight. Did you come out of the restaurant with Mr Charlesworth and Mr Dalziel?'

'No. I was a little behind them, I recall.'

'Oh. Why was that, sir?'

'I can't see that it matters, but I had a brief word with one of the waitresses.'

About what? wondered Headingley. Didn't they say something about men with big noses being extra lecherous?

He let none of this show, but went on. 'So you didn't actually see the other two getting into their car?'

'No, I didn't.'

'So you couldn't say who was driving?' said Headingley.

'Now why should I need to say that?' said Kassell quizzically. 'Though as a matter of fact, I could.'

'Really, sir? How?'

'My car was round the side of the Hall. As I walked to it, their car passed me on its way out of the car park. I gave them a wave.'

'So you did see who was driving?'

Suddenly Kassell was pure military, stirring up long-forgotten, deep-hidden memories in George

Headingley who had served with some discomfort and little distinction as a National Serviceman in Korea.

'Of course I did. Do you think I'm blind, man?' snapped the Major.

'And?' pursued Headingley doggedly.

'It was Charlesworth, of course. Who else?'

Peter Pascoe had had no personal experience of military service so Eltervale Camp, the Mid-Yorkshire Infantry's training depot, aroused no strong emotions in him.

The adjutant, summoned from his pre-lunch drink in the officers' mess, looked Pascoe up and down, decided he could pass for a gentleman and invited him to return with him for a peg.

Pascoe declined, apologized for his untimely call, and explained the purpose of his visit.

The adjutant, a pock-faced captain called Trott, said, 'Frostick, you say? Can't say I recall the name. Sergeant Ludlam's your man. He knows everything.'

Ludlam turned out to be the sergeant in charge of the Orderly Room, a round son of Leeds, who looked Pascoe up and down, decided he could pass for an NCO, and returned Trott's compliment after that gentleman had retreated by opining that *he* knew fuck all.

'Frostick, Charles,' he said. 'He's the lad whose grandad's been killed?'

'That's right,' said Pascoe, surprised.

'His father was on to us this morning asking if we could get his CO in Germany to pass the news on,' explained Ludlam. 'I dealt with it. Captain Trott, he don't take much in at weekends. Sad case. He'll likely get compassionate. Now, what do you want to know?'

Feeling rather foolish that he had already learned all he wanted to know, i.e. that Charley Frostick was definitely in Germany, Pascoe said vaguely, 'Oh, just a bit of background. What kind of lad he is, that kind of thing. Routine.'

The Sergeant regarded him shrewdly.

'Routine, eh?' he said. 'There's no such beast for you buggers. Let's see what the files say, shall we?'

The files said that Charley Frostick was a fair soldier, a good shot, reliable and conscientious, possibly NCO material.

'The only black he put up was getting back late a couple of mornings,' he said.

'Mornings?' said Pascoe. 'I thought you soldier boys were all tucked up safe and sound by nine P.M.?'

'You've got the wrong decade, mister,' said Ludlam. 'During the basic training period, it's very strict and regimental. Once they've passed out, however, they're like the rest of us – as long as you're spick and span on first parade, which in his case'd be seven-thirty A.M., you're OK.'

'You mean he could have been sleeping at home during that time – how long was it?'

'Just a couple of weeks before he went on draft. Could've been sleeping where he wanted,' grinned the Sergeant. 'Tell you who'll know more than me. Sergeant Myers of our regimental police.'

'Well, really, I don't know if I need to bother him,' said Pascoe, glancing at his watch.

'No bother. He'll be down at the guard house. You've got to go past it on your way out. I'll stroll along with you.'

Sergeant Myers and a couple of his minions, all distinguished by their white webbing, were sitting round a heat-pulsating stove, drinking pint mugs of tea. Conversation halted at the sight of Pascoe but Ludlam quickly reassured them he was harmless.

'It's all right, Micky,' he said, grinning. 'It's not the brass. I just thought you might like to meet a real cop.'

Neither Myers nor his colleagues seemed very impressed.

Myers, an ill-tempered-looking man with wire-rimmed spectacles, said, 'One of our lot in trouble, is it?'

'Not the way you think,' said Ludlam. 'Do you remember Charley Frostick, last draft? His grandad was done in last night, you'll be reading about it in the papers likely. The Inspector here's seeing about getting him back on compassionate.'

It didn't sound a likely story, but it was well-intentioned, Pascoe assumed, and he nodded his agreement.

'What happened?' asked Myers.

'He was attacked in his bath,' said Pascoe. 'Presumably in the course of a robbery.'

'Poor old sod. How'd they kill him?'

'Well, he was beaten and stabbed and half drowned,' said Pascoe. 'But in the end I suppose his heart just gave out.'

Myers shook his head.

'Layabouts,' he said savagely. 'Give 'em to us for a few weeks, we'd soon straighten them out.'

Ludlam said, 'You had to straighten young Frostick out, didn't you? Wasn't he getting back at all hours?'

'That's right. He was screwing the arse off some bint worked in a hotel, isn't that right, Corporal Gillott?'

The man addressed, a lance-corporal with a ramrod straight back so that even sitting down he seemed to be at attention, pulled at his ragged brown moustache and said, 'That's what I heard, Sarge.'

'Didn't you never meet her, Norm?' asked the third r.p., a burly full corporal with heavy jowls. 'I thought you was a bit of a mate of Frostick's, letting him sneak in late, and that.'

'What's this? What's this?' demanded Myers sharply. 'I'll have no favourites round here, so you'd best be sure what you're saying, Corporal Price!'

'Only joking, Sarge,' said Price, grinning maliciously at Gillott. 'I saw her once at a camp dance.

Painted like a fairground sideshow she was, but I wouldn't have minded rolling my penny down her chute!'

'Less of that, less of that,' ordered Myers. 'Show some respect. Anything else we can do, Inspector?'

Pascoe, always interested in crime and punishment, said, 'What do you get for being late?'

'First offence, couple of days' jankers,' said Myers. 'Which reminds me. Corporal Gillott, isn't it time you was out there, checking on our customers?'

Gillott stood up. Could a man really be as straight as that without some artificial aid? wondered Pascoe.

'What'll I have them doing this afternoon, Sarge?' he asked, each syllable glottally stopped so the words came out like the sound of a typewriter.

'Leaves,' said the sergeant. 'There's leaves all over the fucking place. Come nightfall, I don't want to see a fucking leaf anywhere around this camp.'

'Come nightfall, you can't see anything anywhere,' said Ludlam, laughing.

He and Pascoe followed the lance-corporal out and watched him marching smartly away.

'Well, there's our police for you,' said Ludlam. 'Remind you of your mob, do they? No, don't answer that!'

Pascoe made for his car. He was beginning to feel strangely shut in, the same kind of feeling he had when his work took him into a prison. That was probably unfair. No doubt a monastery would have much the same effect.

He said as he unlocked his door, 'How long have you been in the Army, Sergeant?'

'Me? We'll have been together now for twenty years come next spring,' said Ludlam. 'I haven't made up my mind yet whether to make a career of it!'

Pascoe laughed with the man. It did occur to him to wonder if advancement to sergeant was the best a lively intelligent man could hope for over twenty years in the Army, but it would have been crass to put the question. However, a more general philosophical query did seem in order.

'Twenty years,' he said. 'Before the big unemployment. Tell me, Sergeant, what motivated men to sign on in your day?'

The sergeant leaned down to the open window and with wide-eyed surprise at being asked such an obvious question said, 'Why, patriotism, Inspector. Pure and simple patriotism!'

Chapter 11

'Sack, Sack! . . . Pray you give me some sack!'

As Pascoe switched off his engine in The Duke of York car park, the passenger door opened and George Headingley slid in.

'Thought it was you,' he said. 'I'd just about given you up. Look, I'm on my way to The Towers to see this Warsop woman. Then I thought I'd go on to Paradise Hall. Why don't you come along? In fact, why don't you drive me, seeing as you're sitting there with your engine warm.'

'I've got work of my own, remember?' protested Pascoe. 'And what about my lunch?'

'Oh, I'm sure they'll let you at the left-overs at Paradise Hall,' said Headingley. 'And you wouldn't like it in the Duke anyway. They've taken against cops there since last night. I don't know who's been putting ideas in their heads – Ruddlesdin, likely – but they're muttering about drunken policemen already. Come on, let's go!'

With an exaggerated sigh, Pascoe let in the clutch and drove out of the car park, turning left along the narrow winding country road known locally as the Paradise Road.

It took its name from the Hall, five miles away, and the Hall, rather disappointingly, took *its* name not from the naughty antics which local tradition insisted used to go on there, but from the Paradise family who built it in the mid-eighteenth century.

The Towers two miles closer was a half-hearted gesture in the direction of Victorian Gothic. Rumour had it that its last private owner, an old lady who died in the mid-'thirties, had been so incensed by a quarrel she'd had with the owners of Paradise Hall that she had willed her own property to the local authority with the intention that it should be used as a lunatic asylum. What she seemed to have in mind was some sort of Yorkshire Bedlam from which shaven-headed madmen would escape from time to time to swarm all over her neighbour's grounds. Happily, provision for the mentally handicapped in the district was already good, and with plans for future development well advanced, The Towers looked like being a white elephant till a legal ruling was obtained which permitted the authority to ignore the specific terms of the will so long as the building was dedicated to the ends of community care in a much more general sense.

And so it had become what was basically an old people's holiday home, providing short breaks in the countryside for inhabitants of city centre retirement homes and also for old people living with their families who needed somewhere to stay while the family had a break.

Philip Westerman had been one of the former. He had been coming to The Towers for four years now and was during his stays a popular visitor to The Duke of York.

Headingley filled Pascoe in on his morning's work, taking his interest for granted. Pascoe who had promised himself not to get involved felt to some extent trapped, but recognized that it was a trap of his own rather than Headingley's setting.

'So Kassell confirms that Charlesworth was driving,' he said hopefully. 'There you are. Nice, respectable witness. Cut and dried.'

'You'd think so,' said Headingley. 'Only he knew all about the accident without me telling him. Now, the *Post* doesn't appear till this afternoon, so who's been talking to whom?'

Pascoe shot him a glance.

'You're not suggesting collusion, are you?'

Headingley shrugged.

'What's in it for him?' he asked. 'Could've been Ruddlesdin again, though Kassell didn't mention being bothered by the Press.'

'Anyway, what's your line with this Mrs Warsop?' asked Pascoe.

'Just listen to her story. Hope she's a bit vague. And try to suggest politely that she really ought to keep her big mouth shut!'

In fact, it turned out that Mrs Warsop had a rather small mouth with a tendency to purse up as she considered any question closely before offering a well expressed and far from vague answer.

She was in her late thirties, a small erect woman with black hair bound severely back from a not unattractive face. She reminded Pascoe of the kind of Victorian governess who gets the master of the house in the last chapter.

She would also make an excellent witness in court, coroner's or Crown.

She repeated the story she had first told Ruddlesdin the night before. Standing in the entrance of the hotel, waiting for her friend, she had observed Dalziel get into the driving seat of his car and drive it away. She was adamant that it was in fact Dalziel she had seen.

'I had observed him earlier in the restaurant. He was with two other men whom I do not know personally but who have been pointed out to me on other occasions as Major Kassell from Haycroft Grange, and a bookmaker called Charlesworth whose betting shops seem to clutter up most shopping precincts in town.'

'And why did you *observe* Mr Dalziel, as you put it?' asked Headingley with a slight edge of sarcasm. He soon regretted it.

'Because of his vulgar and boisterous behaviour,' she replied with distaste. 'He was extremely loud and he kept on patting the waitress's *person*, though I must say she did not look the type to be

111

offended. I had no idea, of course, as I observed this behaviour, that this noisy boor was in fact a senior police officer.'

Headingley tried his best, suggesting that a view through a glass doorway into a dark car park could easily lead to error. To which the woman replied that the front of the hotel was very adequately lit and as she had actually stepped outside to take a breath of air in the shelter of the entrance porch, the obstacle of glass did not apply.

A big-boned, open-faced woman came into the room and said, 'I'm sorry to interrupt, Mrs Warsop, but Mr Toynbee's complaining about the soup again, and Cook's busy with the pudding. Could you spare a moment, do you think?'

This was Miss Day, the matron of The Towers, responsible for the health care and social well-being of the residents while Mrs Warsop, officially designated bursar, was in charge of the catering and general maintenance administration. Pascoe sensed the kind of antagonism between the two women which usually manifested itself in delicate and serpentine borderlines between areas of responsibility.

'You would think Mr Toynbee was accustomed to the Dorchester,' observed Mrs Warsop. 'Yes, I'll speak to him. I think these gentlemen are finished?'

'Just one more thing, Mrs Warsop,' said Pascoe. 'Did you see Major Kassell go out into the car park after the other two men?'

She considered. 'No,' she said. 'There were just the two of them. The other man must have remained in the dining-room, I suppose.'

'And how long was it before you finally got away yourself?'

'Five minutes, perhaps,' she said.

'Your friend kept you waiting,' observed Pascoe. 'You were in the same car?'

'Yes. I drove her home, but not along the road which goes past The Towers, if that's what you're wondering. It was more convenient to go in the other direction towards the south by-pass and get back into town that way. I had just returned to The Towers when that newspaperman turned up with his questions. It seemed to be my duty to answer them honestly.'

She stared at Pascoe as if expecting him to challenge this. Then, with a dismissive nod, she left.

'Very efficient lady, that, I should think,' said Headingley.

'Oh yes, she's certainly that,' said Miss Day without enthusiasm. 'Poor Mr Westerman! It's really knocked me back.'

'It must have put a damper on the others too,' said Pascoe.

'The residents? Yes, I suppose so. Though in a funny way, a death often rather bucks them up, as long as they aren't too close to whoever it is!'

She laughed as she spoke. Pascoe grinned back at her.

'How many do you have at a time?' he inquired.

'Oh, we can take up to eighty and we've squeezed a few more in from time to time, especially during the summer.'

'That'll be when the big demand from families comes, is it? Wanting to get away to the Costa Brava without gran?' said Headingley.

'Partly,' she replied. 'Though there's a constant demand for that kind of accommodation all the year round. It's not just people wanting to get away on their own summer holidays, you know. It's people who need a break in their own homes without having the old person on their backs twenty-four hours a day. You've no idea what it can do to people. And it can be very awkward for us at times.'

'How's that?'

'Oh, when it comes to going home time. Sometimes the family ring up and say it's not convenient, could the old person stay here another day or two? Or very occasionally they just don't turn up at all to collect them and when they're contacted, they say that's it, they've had enough, the State can look after them now! But worst of all is the old folk who don't want to go back themselves. That's really heartbreaking.'

She ushered them to the front door and waved them off with the same geniality Pascoe was sure she bestowed on her elderly residents.

As they drove off, Pascoe asked Headingley, 'How was the bike, by the way?'

'Sound as a bell, which it had,' answered Headingley. 'It was the old boy's own, he rode it round town regularly, always insisted on bringing it down here so's he could get to the pub. Good lights, back and front. Good tyres. Steady hand-brakes.'

They continued in silence till they saw the sign Paradise Hall Country House Hotel and Restaurant. A smaller notice attached to the ornately scrolled board announced that the hotel was closed until Easter, but the restaurant was open as usual.

The drive wound its way through fields filled with sheep and cattle rather than the lunatics hoped for by the owner of The Towers. Of the original extensive grounds only the neglected formal garden immediately surrounding the house had been retained. The Hall itself was an undistinguished but not unpleasant building, slightly in need of a lick of paint and a spot of pointing. Pascoe had never eaten in the restaurant but had heard mixed reports. Detractors and enthusiasts alike were agreed upon the impudence of its prices and when Pascoe glanced at the luncheon menu standing on the unattended bar, he said in amazement, 'Pissed or sober, there's no way Andy Dalziel'd pay *that* for a bowl of soup!'

'Doesn't seem likely he was paying, does it?' said Headingley, helping himself to a handful of peanuts.

'Charlesworth, you mean? Or Kassell? I can't see where this guy fits in, can you? Estate manager at Haycroft Grange. William Pledger's shooting parties. It doesn't sound like fat Andy's scene.'

'He's very respectable, that's the main thing,' said Headingley, who wasn't looking for aggro.

'Maybe. But his story doesn't gell with Warsop's, so who's making mistakes? What was he a major in, by the way?'

'The Mid-Yorkies,' said Headingley. 'I looked him up. Got out in 1975. He'd been out in Hong Kong, made some contact with Pledger out there, followed it up, and landed this job.'

'You've been working fast,' admired Pascoe.

'No sweat,' said Headingley complacently. 'There's this lass works on the Council switchboard. She knows *everything*.'

Pascoe laughed and then said seriously, 'George, what precisely is it you're doing? I mean, how do you see your function?'

'I wish I could be precise, Peter,' said Headingley. 'I'm going through the motions without going through the motions, so to speak. Which is to say, I'm doing a proper job, but mainly, I reckon, so the DCC can say, if he's asked, which he's still hoping he won't be, that yes, of course we've done a proper job of looking into this accident, and here's George Headingley to prove it!'

'Sam Ruddlesdin'll ask,' forecast Pascoe.

'Sam Ruddlesdin's got a boss who might take a wider view,' said Headingley. 'But it's nothing to do with me. I'm just poor bloody infantry. Good day. Would Mr Abbiss be in, please?'

A woman had come into the bar. She was very striking, with jet black hair tumbling over her shoulders and a pale, consumptive pre-Raphaelite face from which huge dark eyes stared like visitors from another world.

'I'm Stella Abbiss,' she said. 'Can I help you?'

Stella and Jeremy Abbiss wish you bon appétit it said at the foot of the menu. Husband and wife, Pascoe assumed. Partners anyway. He settled back to see if nice old-fashioned George Headingley would press for the man.

But Headingley had suffered enough from antagonistic mine hosts that day and he smiled sweetly and flashed his warrant card and said in his best, hushed we-don't-want-to-embarrass-the-customers voice, 'It's just a small matter of clearing up a couple of points regarding the accident last night. You've probably heard about it?'

'The old man near The Duke of York?' she said in a low voice which throbbed like a 'cello string.

She was *la belle dame sans merci*, Pascoe thought with delight. I shall become obsessed with her. But first I must bring Ellie here to approve. She deserves a good meal. He glanced again at the prices and changed his thought to: She deserves a nice drink. Could that delicious shadow round the eyes be real, or did she put it on with a feather?

'That's the one.'

'We had some reporter round this morning asking questions,' she said.

'I'm sorry to inconvenience you again,' said

Headingley. 'It's just a matter of getting the picture clear.'

'You want to know how drunk the fat man was, is that it?'

Such directness allied to such feyness! It was a dizzying concoction. Were their sauces like this? If so, well worth the money!

'Well, yes, for a start,' said Headingley manfully.

'Depends how drunk five large Scotches, a bottle and a half of Burgundy and three balloons of cognac would make him,' she said.

'And in your estimation, how drunk would that be?' asked Pascoe, just for the privilege of engaging in commerce with this creature.

Those strange compelling eyes joined his for a lovely moment. This was true Paradise, this was the primal idyll with everything possible and no sin, no shame. Then her gaze slipped his and moved to a point just above his right shoulder.

'Why don't you ask him yourself?' she said.

'Beer!' boomed a familiar voice. 'A pint of your best for me, lass, and pints of your second best for this pair of trainees who ought to be too bloody busy to drink it!'

Pascoe turned. The primal idyll was over. Approaching with the weary wayworn smile of a fallen archangel whose heavy pinions have at last deposited him safe on Eden was Andrew Dalziel.

Chapter 12

'Et tu, Brute?'

Dalziel's arrival produced at least one bonus. To the three pints of beer which she drew for them, Stella Abbiss, without any direct request being made, added three portions of cold game pie.

'Delicious,' approved Dalziel. 'I tried it last night. The fruits of your own gun, if I remember right, love?'

She nodded slightly. To Pascoe's mental video library was added the slow-motion sequence of this frail, pale beauty clad only in gumboots tracking a low-flying pheasant across a frost-laced stubble field with her hot, smoking barrel.

He was jerked rudely out of his reverie by Dalziel, who said, 'Now, Peter, what are you doing here? I knew old George had been set to sniff around after me, but I thought you had other things on your plate. Just along to see the fun, is that it? Heard

119

the fire engine and couldn't resist chasing along to see the fire?'

The sheer unjustness of the imputation made Pascoe speechless for a moment and Headingley said, 'He's along because of me, sir. We were meeting for a spot of lunch at The Duke of York and I asked him to give me a lift up here.'

'Oh aye? Carless, are you? Do a lot of drinking in The Duke of York, do you?'

Pascoe had recovered now and said coldly, 'More to the point maybe, what are *you* doing here, sir?'

'Me? I'm on holiday,' said Dalziel. He supped his beer and regarded Pascoe thoughtfully over the glass. When he put it down, it was empty. He said, 'Young cop, frequenting expensive places like this, doesn't look good, Peter.'

'It's even more expensive at night, they tell me.'

'And they tell you right. Difference is, I wasn't paying.'

'Me neither,' said Pascoe, glancing significantly at Headingley. 'But it does make a difference who's paying, doesn't it?'

'Like Arnie Charlesworth? Didn't give me a chance. I was still reaching for my wallet when he signed the bill. That's the way to be, my lads. So rich you don't bother about real money. Hey, lass, another three of the same.'

'Not for me,' said Pascoe, covering his glass in alarm. 'I'm not well into this one yet.'

'Nor me,' said Headingley, though with less conviction.

The woman approached with another pint which she put firmly in front of Dalziel. Pascoe smiled his thanks and something which might have been a responsive humour touched her pale narrow lips.

'Fancy a slice of that, do you?' said Dalziel. 'She's not your speed, lad. Burn you up with her exhaust while you're still looking for first gear. Any road, you should be ashamed of yourself, you with a fine wife to wash your linen and a bonny babbie to dandle on your knee.'

It was an interesting picture. Even Headingley grinned and said, 'It must be a comfort, all that clean linen, if you ever get knocked down by a getaway car.'

'Yes,' said Pascoe. 'Though Ellie does complain about skinning her elbows on the edge of the wash-tub. But to get back to what we were talking about, don't you think you should tell Inspector Headingley exactly what you *are* doing here?'

Headingley stopped grinning and hid his face in his beer glass. Even with the semi-official investigative authority he had received from the DCC, he wouldn't have dared essay so direct an approach to Dalziel. But it might be interesting to see how far the fat man would let his golden lad go before he came to a dusty answer.

'What do you think, Peter?' asked Dalziel through a mouthful of pie. 'Cover up my tracks? Cut out a few tongues? Any road, what's it to you? If it's jolly George here I should be pouring out my soul

to, how come you're asking the questions? I don't
see his hand up the back of your jacket!'

Pascoe said carefully, 'Just call it mere vulgar
curiosity, sir.'

'That's all right then,' said Dalziel, suddenly
relaxing. 'Mrs Abbiss!'

'Yes?' came the low, musical voice.

'You didn't find a spare hat when you tidied
up last night, did you? Trilby, I suppose you'd
call it. Grey wool, with a black band, size 7¾,
manufactured by Usher and Sons of Leeds?'

Silence, and then she materialized behind Pascoe,
reached over him and placed a grey trilby in
Dalziel's hands.

'Thanks, love,' he said. He placed it carefully on
his head.

'Fits, you see,' he said, eyeing Pascoe steadily.
'If it fits, wear it, that's what they say, isn't it?
This kind of weather, fifty per cent of heat loss is
through the top of your head, did you know that?
Like walking around with a fucking chimney!
Well, what've you got so far, Sherlock?'

The sudden switch away from Pascoe took
Headingley by surprise and he choked on his
beer. This occasioned a usefully cunctatory bout of
coughing, but the therapeutic blow Dalziel administered between his shoulder-blades extended this
to the nearer shores of death.

Pascoe answered.

'One of your fellow diners here saw *you* driving
away in your car.'

'Oh aye?' said Dalziel without interest. 'So the DCC said.'

'By chance she worked at The Towers where the man that got knocked over was staying at the moment.'

'Emotionally involved then? Not the best kind of witness,' pronounced Dalziel with Denning-like authority. 'Any road, she looks like a trouble-maker.'

He drained a good two-thirds of his second pint and smacked his heavy lips.

'You've seen her then?' asked Pascoe in alarm, thinking this could only mean Dalziel had paid a visit to The Towers.

'Only last night, lad,' said Dalziel, grinning as he read Pascoe's face. 'Leastways if she's the one I'm thinking of. She was hanging round the hallway waiting for her mate to finish tarting herself up when I came out. Late thirties, black hair, puckers her mouth up like a cat's arsehole when she's thinking? I noticed her earlier looking over at our table like she'd have been glad to chuck us out. Works at The Towers, does she? The way she ordered her grub and signed her bill, I'd have thought she were a princess of the blood at least.'

'Unfortunately your impressions are not evidence, sir,' said Pascoe. 'Either she's right or she's mistaken. Which?'

There's blunt for you, he thought. There's bold! There's bloody crazy!

But Dalziel seemed unoffended.

'Who knows?' he said. 'Mebbe she's right. Mebbe we stopped along the road a ways and changed over. Or mebbe she's mistaken. It was a nasty night, rain and sleet, lousy visibility. Easy to get things wrong.'

'Excuse me,' said Pascoe, rising. He was so angry that he didn't trust himself to say anything further at this point. He left the bar, went into the toilet and relieved himself. What the hell was Dalziel playing at? Keeping his options open till he'd checked with the other witnesses? It was time he got back to town.

When he came out of the toilet he almost bumped into Stella Abbiss coming out of the bar with a tray on which were two glasses of brandy.

'Hello,' he said. 'Could I have a word?'

'About last night? You'd better talk to my husband. He's in the kitchen.'

'I'd rather talk to you,' said Pascoe, smiling.

'I'm serving in the dining-room,' she said curtly.

'Surely one of your minions could manage that?'

'We have no minions,' she said wearily.

'*No one?*' said Pascoe, amazed, and also indignant at such labour being imposed on such frailty. 'You can't run a hotel single-handed.'

'The hotel closes down in October,' she explained. 'We don't get enough off-season custom to make it worthwhile. So there's just the restaurant. There's a girl comes in from the village, but only at nights. And we had another girl living in, but she's just walked out on us. Fortunately we're having a quiet lunch-time today. Neverthless, I'll have to go.'

She moved swiftly away through a door which led into the dining-room, a long and airy chamber looking out on to a falling garden whose shrubs and trees, ragged and depressed in the aftermath of last night's winter storm, must have presented a colourful prospect in spring and summer. The faded silk wall-hangings, wishy-washy water-colours, threadbare rugs and a heterogeneous collection of knick-knacks concentrated on the broad mantel above the large open fire, all contributed to the feel of the place as a room in a private house which must, Pascoe thought, be an economic ambience to opt for. There were tables for eighteen to twenty-four diners, depending on their groupings. At present there were only six people having lunch, a group of four middle-aged men and an elderly, almost mummified couple before whom Stella Abbiss set the brandy balloons. One of the men called to her 'See how it's coming along, love!' as she passed on her way to a door at the far end of the room which obviously led into the kitchen.

Pascoe walked swiftly after her and met her as she re-emerged bearing a coffee-pot. She did not look at him and he went on into the kitchen where he found a slender man of about thirty wearing stretch cords in lichen green, a lavender see-through silk shirt and an expression of great anger, standing over a stove beating something in a pan.

'*Yes?*' he said aggressively.

'Mr Abbiss?'

'*Yes!*'

'Detective-Inspector Pascoe. I wonder if . . .'

'In a minute!' said Abbiss. 'Can't you see I'm busy?'

The door opened and his wife came back in. She didn't speak but stood patiently by the entrance, watching her husband who Pascoe now saw was preparing *zabaglione*. He tried vainly to catch the woman's eye. Were she wearing a see-through shirt, he felt as if he might be able to see right through to the other side. She really did need care and attention, a loving man to pick her frail form up and carry it away to a cool, soft sick-bed and lay her down, and somehow at this juncture the administration of nourishing broths merged and melded into more primitive forms of healing involving the laying on of hands and of everything else the ingenious physician could possibly bring to bear on that thin white body with its . . .

He pulled himself up with a start. Abbiss had completed his own nourishing broth and was spooning it into four dishes which his wife had placed on a tray. Finished, she picked up the tray and left. They had not exchanged a word.

'Some pricks!' said Abbiss savagely. 'Some pricks!'

For a second Pascoe thought he was being attacked for letting his recent fantasy show too clearly, but Abbiss went on, 'He comes in here, only the third time he's been, the other twice with a grotesque creature with tits like turnips and taste to match (*darling, I drink Barsac with everything!*), and here he is, entertaining his business chums and acting as if he's bought the place! Lunch, you eat your puddings off the trolley. There's only the two of us, what do they expect? And have you seen our sweet trolley? *Trolley?* the gourmets cry. *No! it's a cornucopia on wheels!* But does the prick hesitate between the *Clafouti à la Liqueur* and the *Pêches Cardinal?* Does he draw his ghastly guests' attention to the *Riz à l'Impératrice?* No! The tiresome turd says, "*Hey, Jeremy* (twice before, and it's *Jeremy* already!) *what we really fancy is some of that Eyetie yellow stuff you do so well.*" "*Zabaglione?*" I say. "*Aye, and up yours too,*" says this Wilde of Wharfedale, this Coward of Cleckheaton. "*You can whip us up a bit of that, can't you, Jeremy?*" I demur. I am camp, but firm. This liver fluke in ill-cut shoddy tipsily rears himself out of his cow-plat and gets nasty. "*At these prices, you can surely do us that, Jeremy,*" he says. "*At these prices up here in Yorkshire, folk expect a hot meal. These aren't cold meal prices, Jeremy.*" I am torn. There is a *Mousseline au Chocolat* on top of the trolley which would mould itself perfectly to his mean little face. But what a waste! I think. What a waste! So I capitulate. I bow, I scrape. I come in here, and I create!'

'That is certainly what you're doing,' said Pascoe. 'Creating. In every sense.'

Suddenly Abbiss smiled and relaxed.

'Well, I have to get rid of it. Thanks for listening. Does me good.'

Yes, thought Pascoe. I think it does. He had observed with interest how the genuine naked indignation which had marked the beginning of the outburst had rapidly had its energies diverted to a shaping of the narrative itself. *A Wilde of Wharfedale, A Coward of Cleckheaton!* Not bad.

'Now, what can I do for you?'

Pascoe explained. Obviously his wife had already warned him of this constabulary invasion and its probable purpose, for the man expressed no surprise, but answered swiftly and with the appearance of frankness.

'Yes, your man Dalziel was a bit pissed. No wonder! He drinks like a man with a hollow leg, doesn't he? But he didn't get too obnoxious, at least not by the standards we've got to live down to round here. Even sober, most of our customers talk at ten decibels. Two kinds of noise we get here. Either it's the defiant bellow of self-made brass, like that little gang hopefully choking on the yellow Eyetie stuff, or the arrogant bray of inherited wealth. No, you've got to make a lot of noise before you get reprimanded at Paradise Hall.'

'Especially, I suppose, if you're a policeman and you're with Arnie Charlesworth,' said Pascoe slyly.

'Mr Charlesworth is a valued, and valuable customer,' admitted Abbiss. 'As is Major Kassell who made up the party. As I hope will be Superintendent Dalziel now he has discovered us. But, in answer to your unsubtle insinuation, I had no idea I was feeding the fuzz last night until that jerk-off journalist greased his way in here this morning.'

'What about your other customers? We might want to talk to some of them, especially any who left at the same time as Mr Charlesworth.'

'I can't say I noticed who left just then,' said Abbiss. 'We were, happily, very busy last night.'

'Not even Mrs Warsop?'

'Mrs Warsop?' he said in a puzzled voice.

'Mrs Doreen Warsop, bursar down at The Towers. She was dining here last night and left at the same time as Mr Charlesworth.'

'Really? Well, I can't be expected to remember everyone's name and all their comings and goings,' he said. 'As I say, we were very busy. Our girl who comes in was in a state of pre-menstrual tension or some such thing which borders on idiocy, and our girl who lived in until a couple of hours ago was clearly determined on farewell sabotage. So last night in particular I hardly had time to notice a face. The diners were just human wallpaper, Inspector. Just human wallpaper!'

'Bollocks,' said Pascoe kindly. 'You've got regulars. You've got people actually signing their bills! You're telling me you don't know where to send their accounts? And any casuals who ring up to book, you mean to say you don't ask for a telephone number *just so we can get in touch to let you know of any significant changes in our menu, sir.* Or do you go so far as asking new boys to send a deposit? Keeping a table for non-showers must be damned expensive when you're working to tight profit margins.'

'Don't let my shabby appearance fool you,' said Abbiss. 'We're doing all right. And yes, of course I could put you in touch with most of my customers. Only, quite frankly, I don't believe I want to. Can you think of anything more likely to frighten my regulars away than the thought that they're under surveillance? Good lord, I had a chap in here last week, was declared bankrupt in the afternoon and celebrated with two hundred quid's worth of booze and nosh for him and his loved ones the same night!'

'The sight of your name in the paper for impeding the police might have an even more powerful deterrent effect,' said Pascoe.

Abbiss smiled and shook his head. He was, Pascoe had concluded with rueful regret, far from being the archly gay restaurateur so beloved of straight diners. That was an act for the customers. Stella Abbiss, whatever else she needed, did not need rescuing from a mismatch.

'No,' said Abbiss. 'That would be splendid free advertising, giving the world my address and telling them how loyal I was to my patrons. In any case, Inspector, I'd need legal advice, but it does seem to me at a glance that you're on a rather sticky wicket. I mean, what reason can you give for wanting these names?'

'We want to interview witnesses,' said Pascoe.

'Witnesses of what? To what? Has a crime been committed? Certainly not here. Where then? Along the road? The accident? Mr Charlesworth, I believe, says *he* was driving. I can certainly vouch for Mr Charlesworth's sobriety, as can my wife. In any case, I believe he took a breathalyser test.'

'You're well informed.'

'You can thank the insinuating Mr Ruddlesdin for that,' said Abbiss. 'So what can the state of Mr Dalziel's health have to do with anything? Perhaps I should consult further with Mr Ruddlesdin.'

Oh dear, thought Pascoe. Threats, and not altogether idle. He glanced at his watch. Jesus! He ought to be back at Welfare Lane by now. And he should have rung in. As far as Wield knew, he was either at Eltervale Camp or in The Duke of York.

Abbiss suddenly smiled as if scenting a weakening resolve, and said, 'Look, Inspector, surely we're on the same side in this. We all want a good press, don't we?'

On the whole, Pascoe preferred the threats. But the decision how to play this wasn't really his.

He said, 'Well, I think my colleague, Mr Headingley, will probably want to take this matter further, Mr Abbiss, but it's up to him.'

He took the spoon out of the *zabaglione* pan and licked it.

'Good,' he approved. 'I must come round and try it some day. But only if it's on the menu!'

'For you, sweetie,' said Abbiss, falling back into

131

his camp role, 'on, off, it's always on. We can't have our prettier policemen going short, can we?'

Pascoe returned to the bar, waving at Stella Abbiss en route. Headingley had succumbed and was half way through a second pint while Dalziel was finishing his third. Pascoe also noticed that his portion of game pie had disappeared and had little doubt of its destination.

He said, 'I'll leave you to it, George. I've really got to get back.'

'Hey, but my car's back at The Duke of York,' said Headingley in alarm.

'That's your problem,' said Pascoe with some irritation.

Dalziel finished his pint and said, 'No problem. You finish your business here, George, while I have another pint. Then I'll drive you back to The Duke. No need to look worried – it's not the car in the smash-up. I've borrowed one from the pool while they're looking over mine.'

This information seemed to contain little for Headingley's comfort and he looked at Pascoe like a man betrayed.

Dalziel said, 'You take care now, Peter.'

His tone was light and friendly. But Pascoe somehow felt the words were even more accusatory than Headingley's gaze and he left more irritated than ever at finding added to his already large burden of problems a quite unjustified weight of guilt.

Chapter 13

> 'Turn up the lights. I don't want to go
> home in the dark.'

'Out at Paradise Hall! And what the hell were you doing at Paradise Hall?'

It was unfortunate. Sammy Ruddlesdin, thwarted in his attempt to get hold of Pascoe to question him about the Deeks case, had rung up the DCC to 'confirm some facts' about the Westerman accident. It had clearly just been a fishing expedition, but during the course of it the DCC had rather pompously suggested that he was surprised to find the Press so interested in a road accident when a particularly unpleasant murder was being investigated. If it was such an important case, Ruddlesdin had wondered, why didn't the DCC summon his head of CID back from his sudden and local holiday? Nevertheless, he continued without pausing for an answer, the Press would be extremely interested in talking to the albeit rather junior officer in charge of the Deeks case, if only someone among his minions could be found who actually knew where he was.

Wield had been inhibited in his attempts to forewarn Pascoe by the presence of the DCC three feet behind him in the caravan.

It was not Pascoe's purpose to reveal that Dalziel had been present at Paradise Hall also, but the DCC, with a nose for evasion that would have done credit to the fat man himself, asked the question direct and Pascoe was not so stupid as to offer the lie direct. He did however essay the response obscure.

'Well, in a manner of speaking, quite unofficially of course, and only coincidentally with Mr Headingley and myself, rather as I was there coincidentally and unofficially with Mr Headingley, during my official refreshment break that is, and quite legitimately and understandably in pursuit of, or rather in order to retrieve or recover, if he had left it there, his hat.'

'His hat!'

The monosyllable made it difficult for the DCC wholly to emulate the incredulous *glissando* of Dame Edith Evans's *a handbag!* but he won the palm for volume, and Sergeant Wield, banished to the pavement for the duration of the interview, stepped back a pace from the door at which he was eavesdropping right into the unwelcoming and unwelcome arms of Constable Hector. Behind him, smiling with the contentment of a man who has enjoyed his full entitlement of lunch-break, was the red-haired Seymour.

'Where the hell have you been?' snarled Wield, adding ferocity to features already stamped with all the lineaments of fear. Seymour stopped smiling and said rather sulkily, 'On that job you said Mr Pascoe wanted done.'

'That was years ago!' growled Wield. 'I want an explanation. Come on! Speak out.'

Behind him the caravan door-handle turned.

'For Christ's sake, keep your mouth shut!' urged the Sergeant.

Seymour raised his bushy red eyebrows in surprise at this conflict of instruction. Hector merely retained his usual expression of a man not certain between steps which way his knees bent.

The DCC emerged.

'And what's this?' he said. 'A street rally?'

He stepped down and found himself having to look up at Hector despite the constable's efforts at total testudinal retraction. The sight did not improve the DCC's temper.

'And what have you been doing?' he demanded. 'Enjoying a five course lunch at The White Rose, is that it?'

'No, sir,' protested Hector, bridling at the unjustness of the accusation. 'Looking for stones, sir.'

'*Stone's*, is it? Not *Ward's* or *Tetley's*? Not *John Smith's* or *Sam's*? Only *Stone's* will do you, is that it?'

Not being a man much given to either wit or

beer, Hector missed the point of the joke which was, in fairness, much disguised by the violence of its delivery.

'No, sir, it was for Mr Pascoe, sir,' stuttered Hector.

'Then it's not *Stone's* you should be after, son,' said the DCC. 'It's your *Moët et Chandon*, it's your *fine champagne*.'

And, much to Wield's relief, the DCC, recognizing a good exit line, strode away to his car under the suspicious glower of Tracey Spillings who stood, arms folded and noise-framed, in her puce doorway.

'Wait here!' ordered Wield.

He entered the caravan. Pascoe was sitting at the worktop staring fixedly at the telephone.

'All right, sir?' inquired Wield.

'Sergeant, you don't happen to know the Samaritans' number, do you?' said Pascoe. 'I think I need help.'

'Yes, sir,' said Wield. 'Sir, Seymour's outside. And Hector. Just back from that job you sent them on.'

'Oh Jesus!' said Pascoe, roused by alarm. 'They didn't say anything to DCC, did they?'

'No, sir,' reassured Wield. 'Nothing important. Shall I wheel 'em in?'

'No!' said Pascoe firmly. 'It's the Deeks, the whole Deeks and nothing but the Deeks from now on in. What's new?'

He listened with a growing sense of the injustice

of life to Wield's assurance that nothing whatever which required his attention, much less his attendance, had occurred in the two hours since they had last talked.

'You'd think I'd been playing hookey for weeks,' he protested. 'Weeks!'

'Yes, sir,' said Wield. 'What now, sir?'

'Now? Carry on with house to house, pulling in likely lads, chatting to furtive Freds in greasy mass to see if there's any whispers. But it looks like amateur night to me, Sergeant. I don't think information received's going to be much help to us on this one.'

'Not unless something's been nicked and sold,' said Wield.

'It doesn't seem likely but we won't know for certain till Mrs Frostick takes a look,' said Pascoe gloomily. This had been another point the DCC had taken him to task for. According to him, Mrs Frostick should have been brought round to the house today, in handcuffs if necessary, to check her father's belongings.

'That bastard Ruddlesdin,' he said savagely. 'I've got a mind to . . .'

'Yes, sir?' prompted Wield.

'Cancel my subscription to the *Evening Post*,' concluded Pascoe. 'All right, Sergeant. Let's go through everything we've got one more time just to make sure nothing's escaped our eagle eyes.'

'Yes, sir. And Seymour, sir?'

'Oh, all right. Wheel him in. But not Hector!

He'd have to unscrew in the middle like a billiard cue to fit in here!'

He listened to Seymour's report with growing relief that the DCC hadn't questioned the man further. No, there'd been no sign of a stone near the spot indicated by Mr Cox, but the recreation ground was full of kids who might easily have picked up and chucked away any lump of brick they spotted, or alternatively Mr Cox's sense of location might have been out by fifty yards, say, and PC Hector had managed to collect a bagful of stones from other areas. None of them showed any sign of skin or blood, but it had rained very hard that night. Did the Inspector want them all sent to Forensic for examination?

Pascoe postponed decision on that and listened to Seymour's expurgated adventures at Castleton Court.

'So Mrs Campbell saw him on Friday morning and Mrs Escott was with him for a good chunk of the afternoon? Now if I remember right, he had his pension book on him with about thirty quid in it. Was that right?'

'Sorry, sir, I don't know,' said Seymour guiltily. 'I did call in at the station after lunch, but they said his things were still at the hospital. Mr Cruikshank wanted to know what I wanted with them. I just waffled on, but I noticed he had a chat with Hector. Did you want me to go to the hospital?'

Pascoe thought. It was a question of demarcation. Accidental death; uniformed's affair, and the next of kin would collect clothes and personal possessions from the hospital. Any suspicion of crime and all the belongings would be with Forensic getting a good going-over. Trouble was, the suspicion of crime was his alone, and so unsupported by any evidence that he didn't feel able to throw what weight he had behind it, especially not after his recent encounter with the DCC.

He said, 'No, don't bother. I expect it's just what it seems. Parrinder feels a bit better late on Friday afternoon, decides to have a walk out, picks up his pension, treats himself to a half bottle of rum to help his cold, slips on the way home, breaks his hip and lies there till he's almost dead, poor devil.'

He still felt far from satisfied. It was the kind of dissatisfaction he would have liked to plonk down before Dalziel whose keen eye and sensitive nose could often focus straight on the source of any doubt.

'Is there anything more you'd want me to do about Parrinder then, sir?' asked Seymour.

'Not just now,' said Pascoe decisively. 'I've probably been wasting your time already. Sorry.'

Seymour had never before had a senior officer apologize to him for wasting his time, though in his own estimation occasion had not been lacking. Like a child reluctant to relinquish a golden moment, he moved away slowly and even found an excuse to pause, saying, 'Oh, by the way, sir. He said something before he died. He said, *Polly.*'

'Polly?'

'That's right, sir.'

'Polly. Any friends called Polly? Anyone at Castleton Court? Or a relative perhaps?'

'Not that I've discovered,' said Seymour. 'According to Cox, the fellow who found him, he seemed to be saying it to his dog.'

'Whose dog?'

'Cox's. It's a Great Dane built like a horse. It's called Hammy. It was the dog as found the old chap, evidently.'

'Hammy? A great Dane? Perhaps by the same token Polly is short for Polonius!'

The attempt at a joke seemed as far beyond Seymour as doubtless time, interests and circumstances had placed it beyond Parrinder. With a verbal pat on the shoulder for a job well done, Pascoe dismissed him and rededicated all his attention to the killer of Robert Deeks.

It was dedication singularly unrewarded and when he finally headed for home at nine P.M. all he had to show for a long hard day was a headache and a touch of nervous dyspepsia. From time to time during the day he had found himself looking forward to getting back to a warm, well-lit house with the prospect of supper and a stiff drink and Ellie's tension-dissolving acidity on the subject of police investigations and Rose's round apple-cheeked face, faintly puzzled in repose, as though she had fallen asleep pondering the purpose of existence. Then he would recall that Ellie and Rose were down at Orburn visiting her parents.

Even with the background central heating, the house felt chill and unwelcoming. He put a frozen casserole in the oven, poured himself a Scotch and went to the telephone.

'Hello, love. I hoped it would be you,' said Ellie.

'That's flattering.'

'Yes, I wanted cheering up,' she went on, unconsciously pre-empting his own need. 'I'm really worried about Dad, Peter. He's looking very frail and he's getting so vague, repeating conversations he had with you half an hour ago, that sort of thing. And sometimes he thinks Rose is me!'

'Well, he is knocking on a bit,' said Pascoe. 'And we can all repeat ourselves. I do it all the time! What's your mother say to all this?'

'Oh, you know Mum. She likes to kid herself everything's just as it's always been. She must know something's wrong, but she just hopes it'll go away.'

Pascoe smiled. The mild-mannered, sweet-natured Mrs Soper was as unlike her daughter as could be and their relationship was based on exasperated affection bred of mutual incomprehension.

'Has he been to the doctor?' asked Pascoe.

'Only incidentally, to renew his old prescription. Mum says she mentioned his vagueness to the doc, but all he could say was it was old age and not to worry!'

Ellie sounded very angry and to Pascoe's concern for her and for his parents-in-law was suddenly and irresistibly added a pang of purely selfish dismay as he foretasted what was coming next.

'Peter, I think I really ought to stay on till Monday and see the doctor myself. In fact I rang him up this afternoon when Mum was out of the way – you know what she's like about bothering doctors at weekends; the great gods will be angry if disturbed! – but all I got was some other idiot who was on call and not feeling very helpful. Well, I suppose you can't blame him . . .'

'But you did anyway!' said Pascoe, laughing.

'Only slightly,' said Ellie with a responsive lightening of tone which was good to hear. 'Anyway, I'm afraid it's another night in a cold empty bed for you. At least I hope it's cold and empty.'

'I don't know. I haven't looked yet,' said Pascoe. 'Ellie, what about college?'

Ellie lectured in what was now called an Institute of Higher Education. This incorporated the remnants of the college where Pascoe had re-met his former university friend during an investigation some years earlier. The college had started as a tiny teachers' training establishment in the 'fifties, blossomed in size and variety of course during the expansive 'sixties and early 'seventies, then been hit by the decline of both economy and birthrate during the later 'seventies and early 'eighties. Now the delightful rural site had been abandoned, the high-flying academic courses phased out, and the remnants of staff and students sucked into this resoundingly named but hollow centred institute based on the former technical college in the city centre. *Clogs to barefoot in one generation* was how the cynics described it. Ellie had returned there after maternity leave in September and was far from happy with conditions, courses and many of her colleagues. To be made redundant with a moderate settlement would have been easy and she was certainly tempted. But, as she had put it to Pascoe, 'The bastards are so obviously keen to be shot of me that I may just stay on for ever!'

Now she said dismissively, 'I've got nothing important till the afternoon and I'll have to cancel that. Peter, I think this has made up my mind about college for me. Suddenly it all seems so inconsequential. I'm neither valued nor valuable there. I think I'll tell them to stuff it. After all, a wife's place is in the home, isn't it?'

'Good lord!' exclaimed Pascoe. 'You've been seeing Andy Dalziel behind my back, haven't you!'

They talked a little longer. Ellie asked after Pascoe's day and he replied noncommittally, even though he suspected she would regard his decision not to off-load his own depression at this juncture as typical masculine egotistic role-playing.

Still, even without the relief and even with the addition of Ellie's depressive news about her father's condition and her delayed return, he derived much ease of spirit simply from talking to her.

It didn't last long. The phone rang again as he replaced it.

It was Sammy Ruddlesdin. Having avoided him by design at lunch-time, Pascoe had managed to avoid him more or less by accident for the rest of the day.

'Inspector Pascoe!' he said. 'You know, I never thought of trying to get you at home before this. Perhaps I should have started here!'

'I'm just back, and I'm just about worn out,' said Pascoe. 'So make it quick. I doubt if there's anything I can add about the Deeks case to what's appeared in your evening edition, except perhaps balance.'

This was sharper than he'd intended after the DCC's admonitions, but he did have strong feelings about being pestered in his own home, even though tonight it felt more unhomelike than he'd ever known.

'Thanks, but it's not Deeks; well, not primarily,' said Ruddlesdin. 'In fact, it's hardly a professional matter at all. More personal curiosity, that's all. I believe you and Inspector Headingley went along to The Towers and spoke with Mrs Warsop today?'

'Look,' said Pascoe. 'I really can't say anything about that. I just drove George Headingley there, that's all.'

'But you were present during the interview?'

'Sammy, if you care to come and see me in the morning, before or after church, as you will, I'll be glad to talk about the Deeks murder investigation. Shall we say ten o'clock?'

'Hold on just a moment, please,' pleaded Ruddlesdin. 'All I wanted to learn from you is the magic words.'

'Sorry?'

'The magic words that you or George Headingley used to change Mrs Warsop's mind. The *close sesame!* In other words, why is it that last night when I spoke to her she was adamant that she'd seen Mr Dalziel driving away from Paradise Hall, and yet by this evening when I spoke to her again, she was suddenly doubtful. The weather was foul, the visibility poor, the distance great, and perhaps after all it wasn't Dalziel who got into the driving seat. Now why should this be, Mr Pascoe? As a humble seeker after knowledge, I should really like to know why!'

Chapter 14

'Let not poor Nelly starve.'

Determined that any further hints of delay should be dealt with at source, Pascoe himself called on Dolly Frostick to take her to her father's house on Sunday morning.

'We've got a car. I'd have fetched her,' protested her husband as though his virility had been slighted.

'It's in the public service, why should you pay for the petrol?' said Pascoe expansively.

He would have preferred Mrs Frostick by herself but there was no way of barring her husband from getting in beside her.

At the house, he escorted the woman quickly through the living-room, kitchen and bedroom, to get her adjusted to the evidence of ransacking. Not that it was bad; there'd been no deliberate vandalization; but the police examination for traces of the intruder hadn't exactly improved matters and he knew from experience how distressing these moments could be. Dolly Frostick went pale and very quiet but seemed to be holding together well enough.

Downstairs again, he said, 'Good. Now what I'd like you to do, Mrs Frostick, is go round everywhere very carefully, telling us anything you think has gone missing, anything that's been disturbed or shifted.'

There was a banging on the front door which admitted straight from the street into the living-room.

Pascoe opened it. Tracey Spillings stood there, crowding out, without difficulty, the attendant constable.

'Hello, Dolly,' she said. 'There's a pot of tea next door when you're done here.'

'Thanks, love,' said Mrs Frostick. 'I shan't be long.'

In the event, she was optimistic. Pascoe tried to keep the atmosphere brisk and businesslike, but he knew he was up against forces stronger than anything his own personality could conjure up. Every drawer or cupboard she opened, she was looking into memories; with every relict of her father's day-by-day existence she came across, she was hearing reproaches. Frostick against all expectation proved a godsend, comforting, directing, diverting, and by the time they had finished, Pascoe had forgiven him everything.

The list of missing items was not long. A small

transistor radio, half a dozen campaign medals (Deeks's own from the Second World War and his father's from the First) and a pewter-cased pocket watch with a gold sovereign welded on its chain.

'He always said that was to be Charley's,' said Mrs Frostick in a low voice. 'That and the medals. He wanted him to have the medals.'

'He'll be able to win his own now, won't he?' said Frostick. 'Come on, love. Don't fret. Your dad always wanted Charley to join up, you know that. He knew it would mean Charley going away, but he knew it was best for the lad too. Just think, love, you'll be seeing him soon, and he'll tell you for himself.'

His effort to dilute his wife's grief by the reminder of her son's imminent return failed miserably. Mrs Frostick gave out a half-choked sob and Pascoe got in quickly, saying in his best official voice, 'Now, Mrs Frostick, think hard. Was there anything else you noticed down here, anything unusual?'

She looked around helplessly, then pointed through the open living-room door into the kitchen and the broken pane above the outside door.

'I can't think what he was doing leaving the key in that door. He never used to do that. Whenever he locked the door, he always used to put it on the kitchen table. That was one thing he was most particular about. But he was failing, I knew he was failing, mebbe if we'd paid more heed . . .'

She looked pleadingly at her husband but he

interpreted it as reproach and said defensively, 'He wanted to be on his own, Dolly, you know that. And he might have been particular about not leaving the key in the door, but he was daft enough to keep a spare hidden in the wash-house, so where's the difference?'

'In the wash-house?' said Pascoe. 'Can you show me?'

Leaving his wife in Wield's care, Frostick led him outside and opened the wash-house door, pointing to an old-fashioned boiler.

'In there,' he said.

Pascoe lifted the lid. Among a pile of rubbish he found an old tobacco tin. In it was the spare key.

'Not clever,' said Pascoe. 'How many people do you reckon knew he kept this key here?'

'What's the odds?' asked Frostick. 'It wasn't used.'

'Precisely,' said Pascoe, very Sherlock Holmesish. 'That's the interesting thing.'

Frostick, clearly not one of nature's Watsons, looked unconvinced and said, 'Family, of course. Some of his mates, I shouldn't wonder. Her next door, certainly. She knows everything, that one.'

'Mrs Spillings? Yes. Incidentally, she was saying that Mr Deeks told her a few months back that he loaned your Charley the money to buy an engagement ring.'

'Did she? She's got a big mouth. What's it to you anyway?'

'Nothing,' assured Pascoe. 'It's just this question

149

of money, whether there was any lying around. Did Charley get his loan in cash, I wonder, or did his grandfather have to go to the bank?'

'You mean her next door didn't know? Bloody wonders never cease! Well, I don't know either. I know nowt about it, except that it was money badly spent!'

He spoke with such vehemence that Pascoe probed further, saying, 'Charley's grandad must've liked his girl more than you did.'

'No. He thought she were rubbish.'

'Then why make the loan?'

He didn't intend to inflect *loan* significantly, but Frostick flared up, 'Don't you be making imputations, copper! My Charley's no sponger. Loan it was and every penny'd be to pay back, rest assured of that!'

'You haven't answered my question,' insisted Pascoe.

'Who knows how an old man's mind works?' said Frostick. 'I never spoke to him much myself, the miserable old bugger. But we were agreed on Miss bloody Andrea, I tell you. I reckon he coughed up because Charley had just told him he was joining the Army. He'd be so overjoyed at that that he mebbe had a rush of blood to the head, decided that a few months' soldiering overseas would soon put paid to his daft romance.'

He turned away and went back into the house. Pascoe slipped the key into his pocket and followed.

In the living-room he was glad to see Mrs Frostick looking a little more relaxed. Perhaps Wield had been amusing her by pulling funny faces. But there was one more test for the woman to undergo.

'Just one thing more,' said Pascoe. 'Before you go, Mrs Frostick, I'd like you to take a look in the bathroom. I'm sorry to ask you, but we've got to be thorough.'

Earlier upstairs, she had come out of her father's bedroom and walked past the bathroom door with eyes firmly averted. Now she took a deep breath and nodded her agreement. She led the way up the narrow stairs, Frostick behind with Pascoe bringing up the rear.

The bathroom struck a strange note in this old-fashioned little house. It was a good-sized room, fully tiled in pastel blue with a seaweed motif. The bath with its non-slip bottom and rubberized support grips was in a matching blue fibreglass, neatly boxed in with dark-blue glossed hardboard. The floor was laid with cushion vinyl and the windows curtained with heavy towelling round whose folds a pattern of tiny fishes swam.

Frostick was looking at it with pride.

'Did a lot of this myself,' he volunteered. 'Not the plumbing, of course. Cost a pretty penny. But it puts value on the house, doesn't it? People expect a bathroom these days. I don't know how you managed without one when you were a kid, Dolly.'

His wife didn't seem to be listening. Her eyes were bright with tears.

'Please, Mrs Frostick,' said Pascoe helplessly. 'Just a quick look, say if you see anything that's changed.'

'Anything that's changed?' she echoed. 'I can see that, Mr Pascoe. This used to be my room when I was a girl. My room.'

Of course, it must have been. Two up, two down; a wash-house and an outside privy; basic working-class accommodation which solidity of building and pride of possession had prevented from becoming a slum. Dolly Frostick was weeping for more than her dead father; she was mourning for her childhood.

'Come on, Dolly,' said Frostick. 'Let's get that cup of tea from her next door.'

'No, wait,' said the woman. 'On the side of the bath. Them scuffs in the paint. And on the floor. Them marks. They weren't there.'

The scuffs in the blue-gloss where the hardboard boxing met the vinyl floor were clear enough, but Pascoe had to get down on one knee to see the indentations in the intricately patterned flooring which her houseproud eye had spotted.

'Probably a copper's big flat feet,' suggested Frostick, and indeed when Pascoe rose he saw that the vinyl surface was soft enough to have received the impression of the toe of his kneeling leg.

'Maybe,' he replied. 'Thank you, Mrs Frostick. If

you like to have that cup of tea now, I'll take you home in shall we say ten minutes?'

After the Frosticks had gone through the puce portals next door (behind which the sound seemed to have been turned down perhaps as a token of respect for the bereaved) Pascoe returned to the bathroom with Wield and together they examined the indentations.

'What do you think?' asked Pascoe.

'This stuff takes a print if you exert a lot of pressure,' said Wield, demonstrating with his heel. 'Then gradually lets it out. Mostly it'll have gone in a few hours.'

'So it'd need a lot of pressure to leave a mark like this. Looks to me like a boot print, wouldn't you say?'

'Hard to tell really,' said Wield. 'It's just the toes here that are really clear. Like maybe someone was standing right close to the bath and rocking forward on their toes, scuffing the paintwork here.'

He demonstrated.

'See. It could be our man, pushing the old boy under,' he said.

'Or someone trying to lift him out,' added Pascoe. 'We'll need to check everyone who was in here on Friday night. You've got Hector's list?'

Wield scratched his nose which sat on his face like a shattered boulder on a blasted heath.

'I've got Mrs Spillings's list,' he said. 'We've spoken to 'em all, of course.'

'Great. Speak again, and check on footwear. Someone should have spotted this.'

'Mebbe, sir. But the floor must've been full of impressions by the time Forensic got here. It's just that these have lasted. The print boys themselves would be kneeling down and making marks while they were dusting the bath and its surrounds.'

'Good point. Check if we've got any kinky boots on the strength. None of our lads would be wearing anything like that, would they?'

'No. It's all pussyfooting around these days,' said Wield. 'I'd better check Mrs Spillings herself, though. It wouldn't surprise me if she were into Army surplus in a big way!'

'Army surplus,' said Pascoe thoughtfully. 'There's a thought. It's not a studded boot, though. But do they still wear studded boots in the Army?'

Wield shrugged.

'They'll tell you at Eltervale,' he suggested. 'But if you're thinking of the grandson, I thought you said he was definitely in Germany.'

'Mebbe he left a pair of boots at home,' said Pascoe.

'You're not thinking of Frostick, are you, sir?' said Wield, faintly incredulous.

'It's always nice to keep it in the family, as Mr Dalziel would say,' replied Pascoe. 'Check everything. That's the key to success, Sergeant. Check everything.'

* * *

On the way back to Nethertown Road, he learned that Charley Frostick had been given compassionate leave and would be flying back home as soon as possible. He also learned that the Club where Frostick had been on Friday night was the local Trades and Labour, and he made a note to get confirmation of his attendance there. Not that he really felt the man was a suspect, but presumably the little house in Welfare Lane plus whatever money there was from savings and insurance would pass to Deeks's daughter. To ask Frostick outright if he owned a pair of boots was further than he cared to go, but when they reached the house, he surprised himself and probably them by accepting the woman's almost reflex invitation to step inside and have a cup of coffee.

As they got out of the car, Mrs Gregory appeared at the front door of the adjoining semi and said, 'Oh Dolly, here's Andrea come home.'

Behind her appeared a young woman, though how young Pascoe found it hard to say without the power to penetrate what seemed like an almost ceramic mask of make-up. Her hair was done in the style Pascoe thought of as 'startled', with its probably artificial honey-blondeness modulating into a certainly artificial magenta at the extremities. She was wearing a flouncy black blouse and a very short, very creased straight pink skirt, candy-striped leg-warmers and shoes straight out of the Inquisitor's instrument box. Yet despite all these aesthetic disadvantages, there was somewhere in the girl a current of vitality which leapt out and touched Pascoe as their eyes met and was just as quickly switched off as she looked away.

This, he presumed, was the Gregorys' daughter, Charley Frostick's affianced bride. Frostick was regarding her with the kind of expression he probably reserved for dogs caught crapping on his green concrete.

'Hello, Andrea,' said Mrs Frostick. 'Has your mam told you? Charley's coming home for his grandad's funeral.'

'Yeah, she said,' replied the girl in a flat, lifeless tone perhaps caused less by lack of enthusiasm than fear of cracking the mask. 'How are you, Mrs Frostick? Sorry to hear about your old dad.'

'Thank you, dear,' said Mrs Frostick.

'Have you got a moment?' said Mrs Gregory. 'I'd like a word.'

'Teeny! Teeny! Where are you, woman! I want my dinner! Where's my dinner!'

The voice came streaming out of the door behind her.

She turned and called, 'It's not time yet, Dad! Jeff! Can't you see to Dad? Jeff!'

'He'll not hear,' said the girl. 'He'll be down the garden.'

'I'm just going to make the Inspector here a cup of coffee, Mabel,' said Mrs Frostick. 'I'll pop round later, shall I?'

'Oh, all right,' said Mrs Gregory. 'That'll do. That'll be best.'

She sounded relieved as though postponing some unpleasantness. But before she could withdraw, Andrea said impatiently, 'What's up with you, Mam? Honestly, you'd think you were going to say something dreadful. It's nowt to do with you or anyone else anyway, is it? All she wants to say, Mrs Frostick, is when Charley comes home, I'm going to tell him I don't want no more waiting, I want to get married straight off.'

'Straight off, Andrea?' said Dolly Frostick. 'What do you mean?'

'I mean now, this week, while he's home, straight off.'

'But . . . I don't know . . . I mean there's the church, you'd need a licence, and I'm not sure if he's allowed to get married just like that . . .'

'Register office,' said the girl. 'I'm not bothering with no church, and my dad wouldn't want to cough up anyway.'

'But the Army . . .'

'They haven't bought him, body and soul, have they? His life's still his own,' retorted the girl with at last a flash of animation to confirm the existence of that hidden electricity Pascoe had sensed but was beginning to suspect he had mistaken. 'They've got houses over there in Germany, you know; they don't live in trees. There's married quarters. Charley wrote about them in his letters.'

'You'd want to go back with him?' asked Mrs Frostick, amazed.

'Well, I wouldn't want to stay on here by myself,' said Andrea.

'Are you in trouble, girl? In the club?' interposed Frostick tersely.

'No, I'm bloody not!' exclaimed the girl. 'Grow up. No one gets in trouble nowadays.'

'So what's the hurry all of a sudden?' demanded Frostick. 'Charley's got his way to make. I thought you'd decided to wait till he got posted back here? At the earliest? And that'd be a sight too early to my way of thinking!'

This last comment looked set to provoke the girl into some extreme of passion, but her mother intervened.

'She's lost her job,' she said wretchedly.

'Lost her job? Now we're getting to it!' exclaimed Frostick. 'What've you been getting up to, girl?'

'Nothing! I just got fed up. Slave labour it is there. The hotel's shut down till Easter, so there's just the restaurant and they want me working in there day and night. It's just boring, that's what it is. And they're probably glad to be saving my wages, not that there's much to be saved. Stupid pair of twats. Think they're God's gift!'

This confusion of reasons did not impress Frostick, who got straight to the heart of the matter as he saw it.

'I've got it! No job, nowhere to live, so you'll have to come back here which you don't much like, do you? So you think you'll jump on our Charley's back, don't you?'

'Listen,' flared the girl. 'I can get plenty of jobs easy. I've got contacts, you get noticed in a job like mine. So mebbe I won't go with Charley. But mebbe I will too, if I want to. *He'll* want to. It's him that proposed to me. We're engaged, or don't you remember?'

With a courage which Pascoe could not but admire, she stood up to Frostick and waved her left hand in front of his face. Beneath that eggshell of make-up fluttered a fully formed she-hawk! On her third finger glittered what looked like a not inexpensive cluster of diamonds, reminding Pascoe of the problem of Bob Deeks's money. Frostick glared at the finger as if he'd have liked to bite it off and exclaimed, 'Yeah, engaged! It was the worst day's work he ever did. The very worst!'

Looking as if he was about to explode, Frostick turned away and marched into the house. Pascoe followed him.

'Excuse me, Mr Frostick,' he said. 'I won't stay for coffee, I'm a bit busy, but if I could just use your bathroom . . .'

'That bloody girl! She's a trollop, you could see it when she were still at junior school, a trollop! Did you see the state of her? I wouldn't have let any girl of mine go around like that! She'd have been out, I tell you. Out!'

'I gathered she was out,' said Pascoe undiplomatically. 'Not living at home, I mean.'

'No, not her, not with the old man in there to look after. Help her mam, that one? No way! She's

159

a decent woman, Mabel, and she gets no help from any side. When they had to move the old lad downstairs, Andrea said that was it, she was off as soon as she could find somewhere to go. I wasn't sorry to hear it – not that she told me, like, but her mam told my Dolly – I thought she might get herself right away, out of our Charley's road. But she only goes as far as that hotel, chambermaid come waitress, that's what she is; supposed to be a classy place and they take on the likes of her . . .'

'Hold on,' said Pascoe, for whom this was ringing a bell. 'Which hotel was it?'

'That Paradise Hall place. Living in, that was the attraction, getting away from home; she'd not do that kind of work at home, I can't see her doing it properly away! When Charley joined up I thought, grand, at least *he'll* be out of the way now. I was worried she'd pester him into getting married soon as he'd finished his training, but he'd got sense enough to see that wasn't on. I never thought I'd be glad to see our lad go abroad, but I tell you I wasn't sorry. I reckoned that even if he didn't find himself someone else, she wasn't the kind to hang around without getting hold of some other mug. But now she's got herself sacked, nowhere to live except at home, and if I know Andrea, she's not the one to put up with that. So it'll be our Charley who has to suffer. Our Charley!'

Frostick had worked himself up into a fine frenzy. Pushing past Pascoe, he rushed back out of the front door, eager to rejoin the fray.

It was too good a chance to miss. Three minutes later, breathing rather hard, Pascoe had checked the Frosticks' wardrobe, the second bedroom (obviously Charley's), the spare room and the cupboard under the stairs without finding any sign of a pair of boots.

He went into the kitchen, tried the cupboard beneath the sink just on the off-chance. No luck. Outside in the back garden, which consisted of five yards of patio in pink and beige flagstones and one yard of border planted with dwarf conifers, stood a neat shed in green plastic. What implements a man with a garden like this kept in his garden shed teased the imagination, and it was in a spirit of philosophical rather than constabulary inquiry that Pascoe let himself out of the kitchen and moved across the patio.

The answer was . . . nothing! The hut was as empty as on the day of its erection. Its function was simply symbolic. But was it a last rude gesture at the whole idea of the suburban garden which Frostick had so manifestly triumphed over? Or was it the last piece in a jigsaw of self-delusion? Did Frostick really believe he *had* a garden? Or that others would believe he had one? Mystery!

Pascoe at this moment became aware he wasn't alone.

Just beyond the wire fence in the hugely neglected next-door garden, seated on an upturned grass-box almost invisible amid the grass it could never hope to contain, was a man smoking a cigarette.

He was in his shirtsleeves, slightly unshaven, and with the haunted look of a fugitive. He regarded Pascoe with the still indifference of a reservation Indian. 'I was looking for the lavatory,' said Pascoe, retreating beneath that haggard gaze.

This had to be Jeff Gregory, hiding here from the family altercation which was distantly audible with the occasional scream of 'Teeny, I want my dinner!' rising above it like the melodic line above the choral patter in a Gilbert and Sullivan song.

'I'd better be on my way,' said Pascoe. 'Goodbye now.'

The man didn't speak.

Pascoe moved swiftly away.

Chapter 15

'Bugger Bognor!'

Detective-Inspector George Headingley was not a
man of impulse, nor one who took risks readily.

Let the Pascoes of this world erect airy hypotheses
from which to make intuitive leaps; let the Dalziels
kick harem doors down and march boldly in,
crying 'Stick 'em up!' to the eunuchs. George
Headingley would proceed by the book and what
wasn't written in the book had better be written
and signed by a competent superior. He'd already
stepped off this straight and narrow line a couple
of times in this current business, most disastrously
at the very start when he had spotted Dalziel at the
hospital and, instead of heading back to Welfare
Lane at the speed of light, allowed himself to
become embroiled.

*You abandoned a murder case in order to involve
yourself with a road accident?* he could hear an
incredulous voice asking at the Court of Inquiry.

The DCC's approval had been a pleasant thing, he had to admit that. And he had allowed its balmy breath to waft him still further off a strictly official course. But winds could quickly veer, breezes blow up into typhoons.

But what did you imagine you were doing, Inspector? asked the voice in his mind. *Investigating a crime? Or covering one up, perhaps?*

Following orders, sir, he replied faintly.

Whose orders? Did anyone order you to drink four pints of beer with Mr Dalziel at the Paradise Hall Restaurant on Saturday lunch-time? Did anyone order you to interrogate Mrs Doreen Warsop of The Towers in such a way as to make her change her story? Answer, please, Inspector. Answer!

When the DCC had contacted him on Saturday night to ask him what the hell he was playing at, Headingley knew the time had come to get the answer to all these questions firmly on record.

He requested the favour of an interview with the DCC on Sunday morning and this was what he was enjoying as Pascoe drove the Frosticks to Welfare Lane.

'So nothing you said could be taken as covering or inducing Mrs Warsop to alter her story?' said the DCC.

'No, sir.'

'Then why did she alter it?'

'I don't know, sir. I just got a message from her early yesterday evening asking me to contact her. I rang her up and she told me she was concerned that she may have misled me into thinking she was absolutely certain Mr Dalziel had driven out of the car park. Well, she wasn't. It had been very dark and very wet and she'd been a good distance away, et cetera.'

The DCC thought for a moment, then said, 'After this cosy lunch you had at Paradise Hall, Mr Dalziel dropped you back at The Duke of York, you say?'

'Yes, sir.'

'At what time?'

'Half past three, sir.'

'Half past three!' The DCC's tone was precisely that of Headingley's incredulous mental voices. 'And which direction did he drive off in?'

'Sir?'

The DCC said patiently, 'Did he head towards town or turn back along the Paradise Road?'

'I didn't notice, sir,' said Headingley truthfully, but he sensed the continuing doubt in the DCC's gaze.

'Look, sir,' he went on. 'What's the odds? There's two perfectly good witnesses that Mr Dalziel wasn't driving. And one of them's even willing to admit he *was* driving.'

'How did Charlesworth strike you?' asked the DCC.

'A bit disconnected really,' said Headingley. 'He just states things very flatly as if he's not much bothered if you believe him or not. Mind you, I spoke to him last night after he'd got back from the races. Perhaps he was worn out counting his money! One thing's certain, though. He wasn't drunk. Breathalyser didn't register at all and they confirmed this at Paradise Hall. Nothing but Perrier water all night. Evidently that's all he ever does drink.'

'A teetotal bookie,' mused the DCC. 'Perhaps he's too worried to drink!'

He made a note to contact Customs and Excise in the morning to check on their investigation of Charlesworth's alleged betting-tax evasion.

'And of course there's this Major Kassell too,' he said, brightening. 'He seems a reliable kind of chap by all accounts.'

So you've been checking round too, thought Headingley.

'Yes, sir,' he said, and described his encounter with the Major. He'd already given the gist. This time he added the circumstance.

'You say Mr Cruikshank was at the airport?' said the DCC.

'Yes, sir. In case assistance was needed.'

'And was it?'

'No, sir. I checked with Mr Cruikshank later. All clear.'

'No doubt Sir William Pledger would be relieved. And you say that this stand-by at the airport was arranged with Customs via Mr Dalziel?'

'So Mr Cruikshank told me.'

The DCC was silent. He's bothered, thought Headingley. He's not sure if he should have known about this. In fact, he'll be searching his files after

I've gone to check if the Chief Constable left him any word about it that he's overlooked! It would be interesting to see how the DCC proceeded. Dalziel's assessment of the man's brain was that it had been fossilized so long that if you opened it up, you'd find dinosaur droppings in it. Headingley did not rate it so low. The DCC was treading a delicate path. To over-react and place Dalziel on suspension while a senior officer from another force investigated would have been stupid. Public accountability was the catchphrase of the moment, but in terms of a policeman's career, internal accountability was what mattered, and no amount of protestation of virtuous intent could compensate for lack of bottle. No, he'd need a lot more evidence of improper conduct before the present gentle investigation of the facts of the matter was formalized.

But it's the poor sod doing the investigation who runs the risks! thought Headingley indignantly. He decided on one last attempt to get things out in the open.

'Look, sir,' he said. 'I'm a plain man, a simple copper, and I like to know what I'm at. What I'm saying, if I get asked, you know, *officially*, what it is I'm doing, what do I say?'

'For heaven's sake, Headingley,' said the DCC. 'You're doing your job, that's all. It's a simple accident. The driver, who does not deny being the driver, was stone-cold sober. The victim, who cannot give evidence no matter what a tired young doctor alleges he heard, was old, had been drinking, was riding a bicycle in a howling gale on a narrow country road at night. Open and shut. Your function is merely preventive. If the Press, or anyone, should start making waves at the inquest, I want there to be an immediate and informed response, that's all.'

Headingley must have looked so unimpressed by all this that the DCC dropped his irritated tone and added with a real effort at warmth, 'Oh, and George, I shouldn't like to miss this chance of saying how pleased I am that you were the officer on the spot when this unfortunate business blew up. It's not going unremarked, you know, the way you're handling things, rest assured of that.'

A promise? A bribe? Worthless old flannel most likely, thought Headingley gloomily. But at least it emboldened him to make one last request.

'Sir,' he said. 'One thing. I wonder if, well, what I mean is, while I'm doing this investigation . . .'

'Clarification,' corrected the DCC.

'Clarification,' said Headingley, 'it's not all that helpful, from the point of view of discretion I mean, if, well, if Mr Dalziel's around and I sort of bump into him, like yesterday.'

He finished at a rush.

The DCC smiled sadly, sympathetically, consolingly.

'Yes. I understand,' he said. 'I'll make sure that you won't be troubled by such coincidental meetings again.'

After Headingley had left, he picked up his phone and dialled. It rang for at least a minute with no response but he didn't hang up. Another thirty seconds passed, then a voice bellowed, 'Yes?'

'Andy, is that you?'

'Depends who that is.'

'It's me,' said the DCC.

He spoke at length and in friendly tones about the troubled times, the subversive movement's anti-police propaganda, the prurient and sensational press; he spoke eloquently and persuasively; after a while he became aware of a noise on the line, a sort of distant buzz such as might be made by an electric razor in the room next to the telephone.

He paused and said, 'Andy? Andy? Are you there? Hello? Hello? *Superintendent Dalziel!*'

'If you're going to shout like that, where's the point in using the phone?' said Dalziel's voice reproachfully. 'What can I do for you, sir?'

'Superintendent, when I told you to take some leave yesterday morning, I suggested perhaps a little frivolously that you might care to sample foreign parts. Now I'm suggesting, not at all frivolously, that a short break out of Yorkshire might do you the world of good. I believe they're enjoying some very pleasant weather on the South Coast at the moment. I think it might do you good. What do you say to Eastbourne, perhaps? Or maybe Bognor Regis?'

A few seconds later, the DCC replaced the phone

with the gentleness of a man to whom even the softest click could be the last sound that shattered his vibrating eardrums. But in his head he could hear a voice quite clearly.

George Headingley would have been amused, or perhaps not, to recognize in this voice that same note of polite incredulity which was the dominating tone of his own mental Board of Inquiry.

He said what? And you did what?

I went to play golf, sir.

The DCC rose from his desk and went to play golf.

Chapter 16

'Mehr Licht!'

Ellie rang again on Sunday night. She sounded rather more cheerful, though she admitted that it was probably on a false basis.

'Mum says the same. Much of the time, *most* of the time, he's just like he's always been. Then he'll do something odd. Often it's trivial. He'll go and have a bath twice in an hour, quite forgetting that he's been already. Or he'll not bother with having a bath at all and when she pushes him, he looks puzzled and says he's just had one that morning. He forgets whole days. When he remembers them later, as he sometimes does, it really upsets him, you know, to *know* he's forgotten. From that point of view, I suppose it'll get better as it gets worse.'

'But he's been OK today?'

'Oh yes. Fine, completely like his old self. When I see him like this, I can't help but feel that all he needs is a course of pills to stimulate the old mental juices, you know, some kind of "upper" like we used to take before exams.'

Not me, thought Pascoe. Not you either, if I remember right. It wasn't just old age which found memory a trouble. As the dull plateau of middle age hove over the horizon, the broken landscape of youth got rearranged into more interesting patterns. But he kept his reflections for a better time.

After Ellie had rung off, he was just settling down in front of the television with a bottle of beer and a slice of cold pie when the doorbell rang.

His first reaction was irritation. For some reason he was certain it was Sammy Ruddlesdin, despite the fact that he'd seen the journalist that morning and given him as full an account as he could of progress on the Deeks case.

But the shape he saw through the frosted glass of the front door was unmistakable.

'Hello, sir,' he said. 'Is it a raid?'

'Them merry quips'll be your downfall, Peter,' said Dalziel. 'A lesser man might take offence.'

'There's a lot of them about,' said Pascoe, pressing back against the wall to allow the fat man to pass. 'Are you coming in?'

This last was addressed to Dalziel's neck as he progressed into the living-room. By the time Pascoe had joined him, he'd switched the telly off and was sitting in Pascoe's armchair looking speculatively at the beer and pie.

'Care to join me, sir?' said Pascoe.

'Why not?' said Dalziel. 'It won't do any harm. I'm trying this fibre diet everyone's on about, did I tell you? It's grand, you can eat just about anything as long as it's got fibre.'

'Well, this is pretty fibrous, as you'll find,' called Pascoe from the kitchen. 'Chicken 'n' ham, from the supermarket, not the fruits of anyone's gun, I'm afraid.'

He returned with beer and pie.

Dalziel leered at him and said, 'Tickled your fancy that one, didn't she, Peter? Ellie away for long?'

Whether this was deduction or information wasn't clear. Its insinuation was. Pascoe said, 'She'll be back tomorrow. And strange though it may seem, even were her absence longer, I would not be shooting off my gun all over Yorkshire.'

'I'm doing a bit myself,' said Dalziel, sinking his teeth into the pie. For a moment Pascoe thought this was the beginning of some unsavoury amorous confession and the fat man's eyes registered the thought as he washed the chicken 'n' ham down with half a pint of beer.

'Shooting,' he said. 'Bang, bang.'

'You mean shooting . . . *things*?'

'Aye,' said Dalziel gravely. 'They tell me *things* are in season.'

'Birds? You're going to go shooting birds!' exclaimed Pascoe, incredulity struggling with indignation.

'I asked about sheep,' said Dalziel regretfully. 'I

173

wondered if they'd let me start with sheep, being only a trainee, so to speak. Something a bit bulky and sort of static. Sheep-shooting's never caught on, they tell me. Stags, yes. But not sheep. You can do all kinds of things with sheep, especially if you've been stuck out on the moors a long time, but you can't shoot them. It has to be birds. I asked about swans then . . .'

Pascoe interrupted this ponderous frivolity.

'But why? It's not your bag, is it? I mean, you're not the . . .'

'Type?' said Dalziel. 'What you mean, Peter, is I'm not one of your tweedy twits, all upper crust, and brains like these chicken leftovers beneath it. Well, you're right. I'm not. I'm glad you've noticed. But it's not like that any more. It's a popular sport. Pricey but popular. Businessmen, professional people, foreigners, they're all at it. So why not me?'

'Do you want the general objections, or the specific?' asked Pascoe stiffly.

'Well, I doubt if anyone with the stomach for this battery-raised pap can make much of a case against killing birds in the wild,' said Dalziel, swallowing the last of his pie. 'So let's hear the specific. Don't be shy, lad. Speak free.'

'I don't know,' said Pascoe. 'It just doesn't seem the kind of thing you'd want to do, somehow.'

'Why not? The Chief Constable's a dab hand, so they tell me. Mebbe I'm a late developer. Mebbe I've got secret ambitions.'

'And secret funds too, from the sound of it,' said Pascoe.

'Oh, aye? And what's that mean?' said Dalziel softly.

'You said yourself it's pricey,' said Pascoe.

'It is that. Couple of thousand a day, basic, if you're hiring the shooting. That'll be for, say, eight guns, ten at the most. And then you've got the rest on top of it. Accommodation, entertainment, transport, guns, shells. It's a rich man's pleasure, no doubt.'

'So?' said Pascoe.

'So there's some generous rich men about,' said Dalziel. 'Hospitality, that's the name of the game. I'm on my holidays, I get asked to go and try my hand at a shoot, where's the harm in that?'

'Depends who's inviting.'

'How about Sir William Pledger, that do you? Well, that's who'll be coughing up in the long run, but more directly, it's his general manager, Barney Kassell, who's doing the inviting. And for Christ's sake, lad, make up your mind.'

'About what?' asked Pascoe.

'About your expression. What's it to be – amazement that I got invited or indignation that I accepted? Listen, lad; Sir William Pledger came up from nowt, and he's not forgotten it. It's not your chinless charlies who get asked to Haycroft Grange. It's people with clout. Frogs, Wops, Krauts, maybe, but they can't help that! And the locals too; they don't get asked because of the schools they went to, but because of what they are. The Chief Constable, like I said; and Arnie Charlesworth. There's a mix for you! People who know how to make people jump or money jump, that's what's on the ticket of entry. People who don't get old worrying if they'll manage on their pension, if it's index-linked or not, if they'll still be able to afford their subscriptions, or if they'll have to give up smoking and drinking and eating and breathing!'

Dalziel was speaking with a ferocious earnestness which filled Pascoe with horror. The fat man had always had that healthy respect for money and power which you'd expect of a Yorkshire-bred Scot, but this expression of admiration for the rich and powerful seemed anything but healthy. His only consolation was a feeling that Dalziel was also slyly watching him, gleefully assessing his reaction.

Suddenly the Superintendent let out a long satisfied belch and said, 'One thing. I hope I don't have to wait as long for a refill at Haycroft Grange.'

'Sorry,' said Pascoe, taking his empty glass. 'Fancy another bit of pie?'

'I don't think so. I could mebbe manage a jam buttie, though.'

'What about your diet?'

'I'm sure a trendy bugger like you'll have a bread-bin full of wholewheat loaves. They don't count.'

Pascoe returned to the kitchen. Dalziel's voice drifted after him.

'What about you, Peter? Owt new on this murder?'

'Not much,' said Pascoe, returning with a sandwich made to Dalziel standards, that is, two slices of bread half an inch thick each spread with a quarter-inch layer of butter and cemented together with a good half-inch of homemade strawberry jam.

Dalziel bit into it and washed his bite down with his beer as Pascoe told him about the method of entry, the missing articles, the injuries to Deeks and the boot marks on the bathroom floor.

'So, some local tearaway who's heard rumours about the old fellow keeping money in the house, but doesn't know him well enough to know there's a key hidden in the wash-house, is that it?'

'Seems to fit the bill,' said Pascoe. 'Except that according to his neighbour, there weren't any rumours about money in the house.'

'There's always rumours,' said Dalziel. 'Lovely jam, this.'

'Ellie's mother's,' said Pascoe. 'The stolen property seems the best bet, if he's daft enough to try to flog the medals or the watch.'

'Mebbe,' said Dalziel. 'Anything else going off?'

'No,' said Pascoe hesitantly. 'Except there was another old fellow died the same night.'

'Aye, Peter. I know,' said Dalziel quietly.

'No, I'm sorry, sir. I didn't mean *him*, you know that. This was a man called Parrinder. He had a fall, it seems, broke his hip, cut himself, lay in the wind

177

and sleet for several hours and the exposure and bleeding did for him.'

'Only . . .' prompted Dalziel.

Pascoe launched into a description of the affair, not omitting Hector's sackful of stones.

'I don't know what to do with it,' he said between Dalziel's hoots of laughter. 'I mean, it's evidence in a way. But I daren't send them down to the lab to be looked at when nothing they might or might not find would prove anything about anything! There's nothing to go on, really. I don't know why I'm even talking about it.'

'I do,' said Dalziel. 'You've got one of them feelings, Peter, and nothing short of a cold shower's going to get rid of it! Let's see what we've got. Parrinder goes out late on a nasty wet afternoon. Why? To collect his pension which his friendly neighbours have already offered to collect. Why's he want it now? To buy some rum. Was there nothing to drink in his flat? Where'd he buy the rum? Where'd he collect his pension, for that matter? You'd think he'd go local, wouldn't you? There's a parade of shops with a sub-post-office and beer-off just the far side of Castleton Court, if I remember right. But if he went local, what was he doing walking over the Alderman Woodhouse Recreation Ground which is a short cut into the town centre? And was he going or coming? Of course, you can get all of this sorted out and it'll still not be evidence that he was attacked! The quacks aren't cooperative, you say?'

'Not really. All injuries attributable to his fall.'

'And no evidence of robbery. Pension money intact except for the few quid he'd pay for the rum. It wasn't open, you say?'

'No. The seal was intact or so the doctor said.'

'So he hadn't had a few nips. Better if he had, maybe. Could've kept the cold out a bit longer. And he did speak before he died, but didn't say anything to indicate he'd been attacked.'

'Only *Polly*,' said Pascoe.

'Attacked by a woman, mebbe,' said Dalziel. 'There's plenty as'd pay for the pleasure. No, it looks to me like you've got a sackful of nowt, Peter.'

'So you'd just forget it,' said Pascoe, half-relieved.

'No. I didn't say that,' said Dalziel. 'I'd have a bloody good look at his possessions, see if there's a receipt with the rum, look at the Post Office stamp in his pension book. Mebbe I'd do it in my own time, but I'm like you, Peter. Just plain nosey! So I'd do it!'

They talked a little longer. Pascoe cautiously approached the topic of the road accident, but when Dalziel veered away from it, he didn't press. There was no hint of a specific reason for Dalziel's call and the only one which Pascoe could guess at, which was loneliness and a desire for friendly company, required a mental *lèse-majesté* difficult even to contemplate.

Finally he left abruptly, saying vaguely he had things to do.

An hour later the phone rang. It was Dalziel.

'Just a thought,' he said. 'That old boy, Parrinder, followed the horses you said.'

'So Seymour told me.'

'I was just looking at yesterday's paper. It's got Friday's results in it. Last race at Cheltenham, won by a horse called Polly Styrene – yes, two words. Four to one. Just a thought. Thanks for the jam buttie. You'll make someone a lovely mother!'

The phone went dead and Pascoe went to bed.

The next morning when he arrived at the station, he checked when the Parrinder inquest was to be. It was later that same day, with Inspector Ernie Cruikshank looking after the police side. Pascoe, knowing the man's dislike of CID in general and himself in particular, approached him with caution.

'Bit vague, isn't it? What do you want? Adjournment for further inquiries? That'll have the Press sniffing!'

Pascoe knew this. He could see Ruddlesdin linking this with the other two deaths in a punchy piece about old people being at risk both on the street and in their homes which would have the DCC reaching for his night-stick.

'Try to make it sound very routine,' he said. 'Parrinder's things, anyone looking at them?'

It was not his intention to be anything but conciliatory, but Cruikshank was looking for criticism.

'Listen,' he said. 'If every time some poor old sod dies accidentally we sent his belongings to Forensic, they'd need a fucking warehouse! It's like a fucking Oxfam appeal down there at the best of times with all the rubbish you lot dump on them.'

'Sorry,' said Pascoe. 'I really just meant, has anyone collected them from the hospital?'

Cruikshank exploded.

'They will be collected!' he cried. 'There's no hurry to collect them because there's no one been in any hurry to claim them! You don't see any crowds of mourning fucking relatives or weeping fucking children, do you? But rest assured, they'll get collected as soon as I've got someone to spare to collect them. I'm a bit short-staffed, you see. Why? you ask. Because you lot don't seem to be able to manage without my lads, that's why. Well, that figures, Inspector Pascoe. I put up with that. I even put up with Andy Dalziel fixing for me and a couple of my lads to sit on our arses at the airport all Saturday morning waiting for the Mafia to fly in, which it didn't. But when one of my lads is down to assist you with one case, I don't expect him to be sent off to spend hours gathering old stones which have nothing whatsofuckingever to do with the said case!'

'Good,' said Pascoe, retreating. 'Fine. Look, I'll collect them, shall I, Ernie? All right? Good. Excellent. Thanks a lot.'

*   *   *

181

Half an hour later he was wandering hopefully along the corridors of the City General when he came face to face with Dr Sowden, who was looking so beautifully haggard and weary that any sharp-eyed television director would have snapped him up instantly.

'You look dreadful,' said Pascoe. 'You ought to see a doctor.'

'You look lost,' said Sowden. 'You ought to ask a policeman.'

Pascoe explained his mission and Sowden said, 'You don't give up, do you? I can feel it, you still think there was something odd about Parrinder's death.'

'Maybe. But no reflection on you, Doctor,' said Pascoe. 'Mr Longbottom didn't find anything suspicious and most of my colleagues think I'm daft.'

'An honest cop!' exclaimed Sowden. 'The city may yet not be consumed by fire. Come on, I'm just going off duty, I'll show you where you want to be.'

He stood by and watched curiously as Pascoe removed the dead man's clothes from the plastic storage bag. Carefully he went through the broken glass of the rum bottle and the sodden brown paper in which it had been rewrapped till he came across a receipt.

'A clue?' said Sowden.

'Indeed,' said Pascoe gravely. 'His pension book, money, watch and so on, where will they be?'

'Valuables they lock up,' said Sowden. 'With the

dead, wreckers' laws can apply, even in hospitals.'

Pascoe smiled and removed from Parrinder's raincoat pocket a rolled-up newspaper. Soaked by the rain, it had dried almost into a papier-mâché cylinder which he prised open with difficulty.

'Aha,' he said.

'Another clue?'

'In a way. Evidently before he died he looked up, saw looming over him a dog which one of my men described as being built like a horse, laughed, said *Polly*, and expired. Look.'

He pointed to the list of runners in the 3.55, the last race at Cheltenham. Ringed in blue ballpoint was the horse called *Polly Styrene*.

'Clever old you,' said Sowden.

Pascoe modestly accepted the plaudits on Dalziel's behalf. Things were beginning to make more sense. Here was a real reason for Parrinder's decision to sally forth into the wintry weather. He wanted to place a bet!

'But,' continued Sowden, 'so what?'

'It won, at four to one,' said Pascoe.

'Aha,' said Sowden. 'I think I'm with you. Where, you are wondering, are his winnings? In that bottle of rum, I would suggest. Not to mention in his stomach. He seems to have had a substantial meal not long before he died.'

'You did take a look at Mr Longbottom's findings, then,' grinned Pascoe. 'Just in case, eh? But how much did he win? I wonder how his other selections did?'

He pointed at ballpoint rings in two earlier races, round *Red Vanessa* in the 2.10 and *Usherette* in the 2.45, then he frowned.

'What's up?' asked Sowden, his doctor's eyes quick for symptoms. 'Clue run out, has it?'

'No, it's just that he didn't go out till after three that afternoon, so he would only have had time to back *Polly Styrene* himself.'

'Telephone? Got someone else to place his bets?' suggested Sowden.

'I don't think he was a telephone punter. And if someone had backed it for him, wouldn't they have brought him his winnings too?'

'Perhaps they didn't and he went out looking for them,' suggested Sowden, who seemed enlivened by this detective game. 'Or perhaps he had backed all these horses himself the week before, say. That's possible, isn't it?'

'I think so. Only they seem to have been marked as current selections in Friday's paper. I'll have to find out what kind of gambler he was.'

He went through the rest of the pockets, coming up with nothing except another receipt, this time from the restaurant at Starbuck's, a large department store in the city centre. The main charge was £2.95, which Pascoe remembered from a recent rare visit was the basic cost of the Shopper's Special High Tea. Various smaller items brought the total up to £4.80. This with the rum meant he'd spent £8.75, of which only five pounds had come from his recently collected pension. But how much had he had on him in the first place? Or what if he had decided to place more than his usual fifty pence on *Polly Styrene*, say a couple of pounds, feeling flush because he hadn't touched his pension that week? That would give him eight pounds in winnings which, come to think of it, was just about right. And he celebrates by having a good meal and buying a bottle to keep the cold out. But mocking fate, which likes its victims at their ease and happy, is lurking . . . End of story, Pascoe told himself determinedly, but with no inner conviction.

He collected the rest of Parrinder's possessions from the hospital security officer. A glance in the pension book told him last week's money had been collected at the head Post Office in the city centre on Friday. Good. Everything that fitted was good. He thanked Sowden for his help and would have departed, but the young doctor said, 'That other business . . .'

'Yes?'

'The road accident. Look, I don't want to cause trouble, but I'd just like to be certain that, well, everything's been done that ought to be done.'

'I think I can assure you of that,' said Pascoe gravely.

Sowden's face showed doubt as well as fatigue and Pascoe added, 'I can't say anything more than that, really I can't. I mean, either you believe me or you don't. If you don't, then all you can do is start causing trouble, as you put it. That's your prerogative. And it'll give you something to think about next time a patient complains you've stitched him up with a stethoscope inside.'

Sowden grinned.

'All right,' he said. 'But I'll keep an eye on things if you don't mind. To sweeten the pill, let me buy you a drink next time I cross-question you.'

'You know where to find me,' said Pascoe. 'If I were you, I'd get a few weeks' sleep.'

'And if I were you . . .'

'Yes?'

'. . . I think I'd be telling me to get a few weeks' sleep,' said Sowden, changing direction with a yawn. 'Good hunting.'

'Good sleeping,' said Pascoe.

In the caravan in Welfare Lane he put Parrinder's possessions down in a corner next to Hector's sackful of stones. Wield looked at the new acquisition and raised his eyebrows, producing an effect not unlike the vernal shifting of some Arctic landscape as the sun sets an ice-bound river flowing once more through a waste of snows.

Pascoe explained.

'So that's that,' said Wield. Pascoe sensed an *I-could've-told-you-so* somewhere in there and perversely replied, 'We might as well let Seymour cross the t's and dot the i's. But by himself. You won't believe this, Sergeant, but Mr Cruikshank actually objects to being deprived of Hector under false pretences.'

Wield laughed and said, 'We're all deprived of him today. It's his day off.'

'What do you imagine he does? Moonlights as a road sign perhaps!' mused Pascoe. 'Is Seymour handy?'

'Should be here any minute. What about us, sir? How long do we carry on here?'

'Tired of the gypsy life, are we?' said Pascoe. 'Not much coming in?'

The function of the caravan was to provide an on-the-spot HQ and also attract local witnesses whose energies or faith in the importance of what they had to say might not take them to the Central Police Station.

'Nothing,' said Wield.

'Give it till tonight,' said Pascoe. 'We'll maybe get somebody coming home from work who's been away over the weekend.'

'Coming home from work?' said Wield. 'Well, it won't be crowds round here, that's for sure.'

Seymour arrived. He made a face when Pascoe told him to take Parrinder's possessions and deliver them to Inspector Cruikshank, but brightened up a bit when he was given the off-licence and restaurant receipts and told to go and find out what he could about Parrinder's appearance in those establishments.

'And that doesn't mean sitting around all day sampling their wares,' said Wield, who clearly thought that this was a waste of valuable police time.

'Oh, and Seymour,' said Pascoe, scribbling on a piece of paper. 'Find out what won these races last Friday.'

Seymour took the scrap of paper and studied it carefully.

'He *can* read, can't he?' said Pascoe to Wield.

'Depends. Did you join up the letters?'

With the tired smile with which one greets the wit of superiors, Seymour said, '*Red Vanessa* by two lengths, *Usherette* by a short head. Will there be anything else, sir?'

'Seymour,' said Pascoe, 'you're a racing man!'

'I keep an eye open,' said the red-headed detective modestly.

'Not a good thing in a young CID officer,' said Wield. 'Being a racing man.'

'Temptation, you mean?' said Pascoe.

'Gambling, borrowing, debt,' said Wield.

'Bad company, dirty women, bent bookies,' said Pascoe.

'Any word on Mr Dalziel, sir?' said Seymour.

It was a good but not a wise riposte. Wield's face became Arctic once more after its false spring, and Pascoe's features assumed an expression of mild distaste which those who knew him well did not care to see.

Hastily Seymour gathered together Parrinder's possessions.

'Sir,' he said in a conciliatory tone, 'what about this? Do you want me to give this to Mr Cruikshank too?' He indicated Hector's sack of stones.

Pascoe was sorely tempted. Cruikshank and Seymour – kill two birds with one sack, so to speak! But judgment defeated justice.

'No, leave it. Off you go now. Don't hang around.'

Relieved at getting off so lightly, Seymour made a rapid exit.

Wield, who had recognized the names of the horses from Pascoe's account of his hospital visit, said, 'That explains why he went out, then.'

'Parrinder?'

'Yes. Racing man, makes three selections, sees two of them come up on the telly, he'd be bound to want to chase his luck and make sure he was on the last one. Poor old devil, he must have thought it was his lucky day!'

'Yes, I expect so,' said Pascoe.

It all fitted. Why then couldn't he put it to the back of his mind and concentrate on the Deeks case? Perhaps because there was nothing to concentrate on. Charley Frostick was due home tomorrow, that was the nearest thing to a development, and there seemed little way the young soldier's arrival could help.

As if catching the military trend of his thought, Wield said, 'By the way, sir, Forensic produced this sole pattern from the bathroom vinyl.'

Pascoe studied the sheet of cardboard which Wield handed him.

'Did they have any suggestions?' he asked.

'Size ten, ten and a half,' said Wield.

'Army?'

'Didn't say anything about that. No distinguishing marks, you know, cuts or anything like that. Even the pattern's a bit vague. Wouldn't chance their arm.'

'Well, if they won't, we must!' said Pascoe, eager for some kind of action. 'I'll check it out at Eltervale Camp.'

Wield, condemned to another boring stint in the caravan, said with no overt sarcasm, 'Lunch at Paradise Hall again, sir?'

'No!' said Pascoe. 'No way!'

Chapter 17

'God bless . . . God damn!'

Perhaps fortunately for Andrew Dalziel, the Deputy Chief Constable was neither a vindictive nor a naturally suspicious man. There was no denying that the Head of CID had long been a thorn in his side, if one so broad and solid could be thus described. The Superintendent had made small effort in the past to conceal his contempt for the DCC's intellect, outlook and abilities. The DCC found this a considerable but bearable irritation. He knew his own worth and he had a pretty fair idea of Dalziel's too. It was this ability to separate the Superintendent's manners from his morals that had caused him to pitch the investigation in such a low key. He found it hard to believe that Dalziel, even in panic, would attempt to duck responsibility for any action of his own. So he had set George Headingley to take a close but discreet look at things.

But now there were faint whiffs of something more corrupt than an accident cover-up coming his way. Typically, the DCC's method was to proceed with even greater discretion. Down in the Met they may have lived so long in an atmosphere of suspected corruption that it was probably suspicious for a senior police officer not to be suspected! But up here in the clearer, fresher air of Yorkshire, where the blunt honest burghers knew for certain that there was no smoke without fire, it was still possible for a man's career to be indelibly darkened by suspicion.

So on Monday morning at ten o'clock he found occasion to telephone the regional office of HM Customs and Excise on a question of some necessary statistics for the Chief Constable's annual report, and when this had been sorted out to everyone's satisfaction, he made casual inquiry into the state of the investigation into alleged irregularities in the conduct of A. Charlesworth, Turf Accountant, Ltd.

The investigation had been conducted, he was told.

There would be no proceedings.

Did this mean that there had been no irregularities?

'It means,' said his informant, not without a touch of acidity, 'that there has been no evidence. Mr Charlesworth's records are so clean you'd think they'd been done only yesterday.'

This sounded like good news to the DCC till he incautiously requested complete assurance.

'You mean that Mr Charlesworth has committed no crime.'

There was a pause before the acid voice said carefully, 'I mean that Mr Charlesworth is either the single most conscientious bookmaker we have ever dealt with or that he knew we were coming.'

It emerged that the investigation had been timed to coincide with the final meet of the flat racing season, at Doncaster the weekend before last. Charlesworth's was very much a Yorkshire firm with betting shops all over the county and a large presence at all northern race meetings, so Charlesworth himself would be down at Doncaster on this day and his head office ought to have been particularly vulnerable. Instead they found things here and in all the shops raided in perfect order. Even those natural daily errors caused by human fallibility under pressure were absent. And the painstaking examination, point by decimal point, of his records which had just been concluded the previous week had produced nothing further.

'And when did Mr Charlesworth get the good news?' asked the DCC.

'Oh, he'll just get his records returned some time this week. When we don't slap him in irons, he'll know he's all right.'

'And us: have we been officially informed?'

'I don't think we'd bother unless there were some irregularities,' said the voice.

At least it wasn't a celebration dinner! thought the DCC with relief.

'Though we liaise very closely, of course,' resumed the voice as if sensing a criticism. 'CID knows what we're up to. Your Mr Dalziel insists on that.'

The DCC's heart slipped a notch.

'So we'd probably know sort of casually that the Charlesworth books were in order?'

'Oh certainly. Mr Dalziel was very interested in the whole business from the start. In fact, now I think of it, when we were talking last week on another matter, this investigation came up and he was most sympathetic when he learned that we'd been wasting our time.'

The voice was quite triumphant as if saying *There! you knew all the time!*

The DCC's heart was beginning to pick up speed in its descent.

He said, 'Of course. Mr Dalziel would have been talking with you about your airport check on Saturday morning.'

'That's right. We've got full powers, of course, but we like to make it a joint venture when it's something like this. So I'm afraid we wasted your time as well as ours on this occasion.'

The apology sounded rather like a compliment, but the DCC wasn't concerned with nuances.

He said, 'This was a routine check, was it?'

'No,' said the voice, hardly bothering to conceal its irritation now. 'It wasn't routine, as I'm sure Mr Dalziel's files will tell you. We are not so foolish as to risk irritating William Pledger just for the sake of routine, and very irritated he has been!

There'd been a tip-off that the Van Bellen plane was bringing in a load of heroin.'

'Heroin?' said the DCC faintly.

'Yes,' said the voice. 'But it was clean as a whistle. Clean as a whistle.'

The tone was one of savage disappointment, inviting deep condolence, but the DCC's only response was a subdued farewell as he quietly replaced the phone and sat contemplating the new deeps into which his heart was plummeting.

That Dalziel should have been dining with Charlesworth, whose books had proved clean, and Major Kassell, whose employer's aeroplane had proved clean, was surely not so outrageous a coincidence?

He picked up his phone and dialled Dalziel's number. He whistled quietly to himself as it rang for the usual preliminary minute. But still no one replied. Suddenly he felt the beginnings of anger. Slowly its mists rose, obscuring the idea of coincidence, turning it into a shape, vague and absurd and not to be taken seriously. The phone kept on ringing. Why didn't he answer? He sat back in his chair, listening to the tinny double-noted summons and, quite forgetting that only twenty-four hours before he had been urging Dalziel to make himself scarce, he demanded angrily of the unresponsive air, 'Where, where, where has the bloody man got to?'

But, had the air miraculously responded, it would not have helped the DCC's temper one bit.

*   *   *

'Mr Dalziel, Andy, glad to see you. Barney said you might be turning up and I said, just the job, another English speaker, great. How's your Frog? Never mind. Mostly they speak better English than me, only they don't *think* in English, that's where it shows. I must've met a million foreigners, it's my work, I get on well with 'em, that's my work too, but I've never met one I could make a real pal of, know what I mean? And that's because they don't *think* in English, leastways that's what I put it down to.'

Sir William Pledger was a surprise even for one of Harold Wilson's knights. Short, stout, round and red-faced with huge thick-lensed glasses that magnified his slightly pop eyes, bald except for a few long, ginger hairs which trailed over and indeed out of his jug-ears, he talked in a high-pitched rush, slowed only by his long native Oxfordshire vowel sounds and accompanied by a wild semaphore of both his upper and nether limbs, none of which fortunately was long enough to imperil more than his immediate neighbourhood.

If Dalziel, who had been met at Haycroft Grange by Barney Kassell and driven out in a Range Rover to join the party for lunch, had been self-conscious about his balding corduroy trousers and scene-of-the-crime gum-boots, he might have been put at ease by Sir William's overlarge camouflage jacket and paint-stained grey flannels tucked into a pair of old wellies, which contrasted strangely with the elegant plus-foured tweediness of everyone else.

As it was, Dalziel observed and approved the difference. The top man was the one who didn't need to give a fuck about the niceties.

An early lunch was being taken among the ruins of a building too tumbledown to be identifiable but with sections of irregular stone wall high enough to break the keen north wind. The views were spectacular, the cold collation excellent. Dalziel was introduced vaguely and generally to the six or seven shooters present, most of whom seemed to be foreign.

There was wine to be drunk, but Dalziel gratefully accepted the alternative of coffee with a shot of Scotch.

'Keeps the cold out,' said Sir William. 'Let that lot swill back the vino, mother's milk to most of them, so that's all right, Barney keeps it in bounds, don't you, Barney?'

'That's right,' said Kassell. 'I've developed an eye for that if nothing else. Too much booze and shotguns don't mix. The biggest proportion of accidents happen during the after-lunch drives.'

Kassell looked very much at home in this environment, his face healthily flushed by the boisterous wind which winnowed his hair as though to show how thick it still was. His clothing, though it lacked the evident newness of the guests', gave away nothing in terms of cut and fit.

'Do you get a lot of accidents, then?' asked Dalziel, chewing voraciously at a cold leg of something.

'Not here we don't,' said Kassell. 'But on some of the estates where they let out shooting to syndicates, you can get too many clowns and not enough ringmasters. Result is, often they shoot more dogs than birds.'

'This your first time, Andy?' said Pledger.

'That's right. I said to Barney I fancied giving it a go and he said I should try half a day to see how I liked it. It's good of you to let me come.'

'Always happy to have the law along,' said Pledger. 'Old Tommy Winter's a fair shot, as you probably know. I bet he'd rather be here than burning up on some Caribbean beach. And we usually have one or two of the boys in blue at the other end of the stick too.'

'Sorry?' said Dalziel.

'The beaters,' explained Kassell. 'Of course we can get any amount of casual labour these days, but we like to stick with what we know and can rely on. We get a lot of bobbies using their day off to earn a bit extra. I suppose it's against regulations, is it?'

He smiled faintly as he asked the question.

Dalziel said, 'If it doesn't bother Old Tommy, it don't bother me.'

'Old Tommy' was of course the Chief Constable, who was as unlikely to be addressed to his face in this fashion by Dalziel as he was to address Dalziel as 'Young Andy'.

'Well, I'd better make with the Euro-talk,' said

Pledger cheerfully. 'Good shooting, Andy. Barney will keep an eye on you, I've no doubt. Shall we see you at dinner tonight?'

'I don't think so, Sir William,' said Dalziel. 'I've just come as I am.'

'Pity,' said Pledger. 'Look, if you take to it, you really ought to come again soon, but kitted out for a meal too. I mean, that's the fun of it, isn't it? Not standing around here with the wind whistling among the family jewels, but yakking about it later with your belly full and a noggin in your hand. Barney, you're the only sod who knows what's what. When would be best?'

'Next Friday would suit very well. We're usually a gun or two short on the first afternoon. This lot go back tomorrow. Next bunch arrives on Friday morning, and there's always at least one of the Euros who just wants to lie around after his flight.'

'Splendid,' said Pledger. 'Isn't de Witt coming? He's a Dutch judge, Andy, fascinated by crime. He'd love to meet an English bobby, I know. So that's fixed. Good. Always supposing you don't blow someone's head off this afternoon!'

'Thank you very much,' said Dalziel.

Pledger moved away and Kassell said with the same faint smile as before, 'You've made a hit.'

'You think so? I wouldn't know. Not much to hit by the looks of it,' said Dalziel with the amiable condescension of the large.

'Half of his success derives from no one being

able to believe in him, till it's too late,' said Kassell. 'He could gobble most of this lot up for afternoon tea.'

'And judges? Does he gobble up judges too?'

'The Dutchman, you mean? Rest easy. It's just a question of a patent that's being sorted out in a civil court, that's all. Let's take a stroll, shall we? I have to talk to the beaters.'

They set off together out of the ruins. It was a fine landscape of lightly wooded moorlands rolling like the sea under the boisterous wind which trailed lines of white clouds across a huge sky.

'How was it at the airport?' asked Dalziel.

'All right,' said Kassell. 'How's your bit of bother?'

'Oh, it'll be all right,' said Dalziel. 'Especially now I've got respectable military gents speaking up for me. Thanks for telling Headingley you saw me and Arnie driving off, by the way.'

'I'd hate to see your career messed up unnecessarily,' said Kassell sincerely. 'Now, next Friday, how will it be?'

'You mean, my visit to the Grange?' asked Dalziel innocently.

'Partly. I hope it goes well. I hope our other visitors enjoy themselves too and aren't inconvenienced by any delays on arrival. This holiday of yours, will it keep you out of contact with things?'

'No,' said Dalziel. 'I'll drift in from time to time and suss out what's what. Thursday do you?'

'Fine,' said Kassell. 'Ah, here we are. The workers.'

In a fold of land, out of view of the ruin, the beaters were enjoying their lunch. Their leader approached touching his cap and saying, ''Afternoon, Major.'

Dalziel strolled aside to let the consultation take its course. Strange world, he thought. This lot and the tweedy set back there would spend their day under the same sky, tramping across the same bit of ground. But it was *us* and *them*; this lot working, that lot playing; this lot at the end of the day going home with a few quid in their pockets, that lot going home with twenty times as much out of their bank balance – or someone's bank balance. What did it all signify?

Suddenly his mind was directed from long-term speculation to short-term bewilderment. There were several large stones scattered around this hollow which some of the men used as seats, some as tables. Behind one of these stones some odd life-form was crouching in a vain effort at concealment. His first thought was that someone had brought a pet orang-outang along. But then he realized that the apparently squat and shambling outline was delusory, and recognition came.

'Hector!' he said. 'It's never you?'

Slowly the figure unfolded itself, stretching to its full length: Constable Hector in a lumberjack's jacket, blue jeans and constabulary boots.

'It's my day off, sir,' he said with tremulous bravado.

'The Force's loss is Sir William's gain,' said Dalziel. 'I've no doubt you're doing a grand job. You've got just the right figure for frightening birds.'

'You mean it's all right, sir?' said Hector hopefully.

'Never quote me on it, lad,' said Dalziel. 'But I suppose it's a form of good police training; advancing courageously on a line of armed men intent on shooting you down.'

He turned away, but Hector, slightly puzzled, said, 'Sir, it's the birds the gentlemen shoot down, not us.'

And Dalziel turned back with an expression of ferocious glee.

'I shouldn't bet on it, lad. Not today, I shouldn't bet on it!'

Chapter 18

'Thy necessity is yet greater than mine.'

'That's right. That's right,' said Provost Sergeant Myers. 'Old ammunition boot went out in the early 'sixties. It's all the one-piece moulded now. Only sods who still use studs are those poncy Guards who like to do a lot of stamping around.'

'So this could be a print from a modern Army boot?' asked Pascoe, hot for certainties.

'Could be a print from a modern fucking art exhibition,' said Myers, looking at the smudgy pattern. 'Here. Take a look at mine, take a look at mine.'

He banged his left foot on to the low trestle-table so that Pascoe could make comparison with his sole.

There had been a sense of *déjà vu* when Pascoe was ushered into the guard room. The sergeant was in the same chair by the same glowing stove with Corporal Price and Lance Corporal Gillott apparently drinking the same cups of tea. Pascoe's intention had been to contact the helpful Sergeant Ludlam, but his sense of enclosure, not helped by the suspicious reluctance of the young RP on gate duty to admit him at all, had made him eager to get his business over with as quickly as possible. The trio of NCO's didn't exactly make him welcome but Myers at least seemed disposed to take a professional interest in his query.

'Could be the same,' said Pascoe hopefully. 'Would you mind giving us a print for comparison?'

Myers didn't mind and Pascoe, who'd taken the precaution of bringing along a blank sheet of card and some blacking ink, got to work. The sharp outline so produced could by a stretch, or rather by a smudge, have been the same as the pattern indented into Bob Deeks's vinyl, Corporal Price was confident it was, Sergeant Myers was sceptical and Lance-Corporal Gillott refused to be drawn. The debate, such as it was, was interrupted by the arrival of the orderly officer, a young second-lieutenant who seemed inclined to regard Pascoe as the Forlorn Hope of some terrorist raiding party. Pascoe civilly produced his credentials, but finding himself then treated with the condescension a village squire might offer a village bobby, he became Dalzielish and said, 'Look, laddie, it's getting near my lunch-time. I'd really love to stay and share your rusks, but I ought to be getting back to the grown-up world.' The officer withdrew, nonplussed and offended, and Sergeant Myers regarded Pascoe with a new respect.

'Sorry about him,' he offered. 'He's young. Not licked into shape yet. They're not all like that, the officers.'

'I've only met him and Captain Trott,' said Pascoe. 'Though I did come across one of your former officers recently. Major Kassell.'

'Oh yes. The Major,' said Myers.

There was something in the way he spoke that caught Pascoe's attention. Quickly deciding that Myers was the kind of soldier who would clam up if directly invited to gossip about the regiment with an outsider, he opted for provocation.

'You remember him?' he said. 'He seems to have done all right for himself. Of course, he had the sense to get out and make it in civvy street, didn't he?'

He intended merely to be slightly rude about the Army but by chance the button he pressed won him a jackpot.

'The sense to get out? The sense to get out?' said Myers angrily. 'Doesn't take much fucking sense when the choice is to be court-martialled, does it? At least he had the choice, which is more than others did, you want to ask Dave Ludlam about that, oh yes, you want to ask Ludlam!'

'Yes,' said Pascoe, his mind racing. 'The other day, I got a hint; same business, was it?'

'The very same. CSM he was then, would've been RSM by now, no doubt. Well, if you're daft enough to get caught, that's your bad luck, that's what I tell these lads with their hard luck stories, that's your bad luck. But it should be one law for all, wouldn't you say? One law for all.'

'Indeed yes,' said Pascoe cautiously. 'I dare say there was a lot of it going on?'

'Out in Hong Kong?' said Myers incredulously. 'Never known a place like it. Everyone had a fucking racket, from the police down. Keeping out of the rackets was harder than getting in! What's a few more Chinks, anyway? Place bursting at the seams with them, what's a few more? That's how Dave Ludlam saw it. But it's not right that the same thing as turns a CSM into a private and gets him stuck in the glasshouse should leave a major a major and get him a nice cushy billet in civvy street!'

There was no more. Myers's indignation had taken him as far as he was going. Pascoe drove back to town so rapt in speculation that his doubtfully motivated half-plan to stop for a lunch-time drink at Paradise Hall was completely forgotten.

Dennis Seymour was a pragmatist. An ambitious young man, if he could have impressed Pascoe by performing his appointed tasks and returning with his report in half an hour, he would have done so. But when on learning at Starbuck's restaurant where Tap Parrinder had enjoyed his last meal that the waitress who probably served him wouldn't be on duty till noon, he happily accepted this set-back as an excuse to return and eat there. Meanwhile he went down to the off-licence which was situated only a couple of hundred yards away from the store.

Here he was more lucky. The man in charge recalled Parrinder well.

'Old boy, cheerful sort. I said something about the terrible weather and he laughed and said he didn't mind. No, what he said was *the going suited him fine*, like he was a horse, if you see what I mean. I said it takes all sorts, and he bought a half of rum. I had some of our own brand on offer, but he said no, he'd prefer the very best, bugger the expense!'

'What time was this?' asked Seymour.

'About a quarter past, half past six.'

'You're sure?'

'Real sure. He was just about the only customer I'd had in hours. Friday's usually the big shopping day, but that weather kept them at home till Saturday last week. What's up, anyway? Nothing wrong with the old chap, is there?'

'He had a fall,' said Seymour.

'Poor old devil!'

'Yes,' said Seymour. 'Do you remember how he paid?'

'Yes. He gave me a fiver, I think. That's it. Definitely a fiver.'

'Did he take it out of a wallet? or a purse? or what?'

'I don't rightly know. Well, I didn't see, did I?

He sort of half turned away to get his money out. They nearly all do it, the old 'uns. What's yours is your own business; you don't let any bugger see how much money you've got, even if it's next to nowt! Mebbe *especially* if it's next to nowt!'

Still having plenty of time to kill, Seymour tried a couple of town-centre betting shops to see if anyone remembered an old boy having a winning bet on *Polly Styrene* the previous Friday and was not surprised to be greeted with indifference verging on impertinence. He did however establish that in the form book *Polly Styrene* was a horse that revelled in heavy going, as were *Red Vanessa* and *Usherette*.

At twelve o'clock he returned to the restaurant. To his delight, Parrinder's waitress turned out to be an extremely attractive Irish girl called Bernadette McCrystal with shoulder-length hair almost as red as his own, who seemed to show a pleasing readiness to be impressed by his official standing. He modestly corrected her when she addressed him as Superintendent and again when she got down to Inspector, but when she then replied, 'Oh, I'm really sorry, I'm just a plain ignorant country girl, Sergeant,' he spotted the gleam in her eye and realized he was being sent up.

Promising himself he would deal with this personal matter in a moment, he showed her the receipt and asked her if she remembered Parrinder.

'I think so,' she said carefully. 'Is there maybe something wrong with the old fellow?'

Suspecting that what she meant was that she was not about to say anything which might get Parrinder into bother, Seymour said gently, 'I'm sorry to say he had an accident, probably not long after leaving here.'

'Oh, I'm sorry to hear it,' the girl said, looking genuinely concerned. 'Was it serious?'

'Very,' said Seymour. 'I'm afraid he's dead.'

She pulled out a chair from one of the lunch tables and sat down heavily. The restaurant manageress glared disapprovingly from the other side of the room. Seymour glared back and sat down opposite the girl.

'He was such a nice old fellow,' she said. 'Full of fun. He said he'd had a bit of luck and was sort of celebrating. That's what's so upsetting, there he was all happy with his bit of luck, whatever it was, then he walked out of here and . . . what was it that happened? Knocked down in the street, was it?'

'He had a fall,' said Seymour. 'Did he say what he was celebrating?'

'No. He just ordered the Shopper's Special, a pork chop was what he had, then he said he'd have some soup to start with, and a portion of mushrooms, see you can see it's all down here on the bill. Make that a double portion of mushrooms, he said. I'm very partial and as I've had a bit of luck, I might as well treat myself as there's no one else likely to be treating me. And I'll have a pint of ale with it. We don't serve pints, I said. Only halves; the manageress doesn't like to see a pint pot on

209

the table. Bring me two halves then, he said. It's all one, they'll be rejoined together soon enough!'

'What time was this?' asked Seymour.

'Not long after five,' she said. 'He was here about an hour. We weren't very busy, that awful weather kept people at home, I think, so I had a little bit of a talk with him whenever I went past.'

'But he never said where he'd been or anything?'

'No. He asked me about myself mainly, I got the feeling that the old chap was a bit lonely, well, it's a lonely time, old age, if you're on your own, isn't it?'

'I dare say,' said Seymour. 'You didn't notice how he paid, did you?'

'Why, with money, how else would he pay? He wasn't the type to be bothered with cheques or credit cards.'

'And did you see his money?'

'I did, and a lot of it there was,' she said without envy. 'Part of his stroke of good luck, I supposed. He gave me a pound for myself. Sure and the meal didn't come to above a fiver, not even with his extra mushrooms. I told him not to be daft, but he said it would have been worth it just for the seeing of me across the room, let alone the service, so I took it and said thank you and hoped he'd come back soon with his blarney and all.'

Her eyes filled with tears. Seymour said hastily, 'When you say a lot, what do you mean?'

'I don't know. It looked a lot, that was all.'

'Did he have it in a wallet, or what?'

'No, it was in an old envelope, one of those long buff things. There was an elastic band round it, I recall.'

'An envelope? You're sure it wasn't just a few fivers in a pension book?'

'No! I'm not blind, am I? It was a lot of money and it was in an envelope. Why d'you ask? Oh, the old chap was never robbed, was he? No, that'd be a terrible thing, terrible!'

'No,' said Seymour. 'No, well, we don't know. I'll keep you posted if you're interested.'

'I'd like that,' said Bernadette.

'Good. What time do you come off duty?'

'Oh, is that your game?' she said, rising. 'Well, I'd better get myself *on* duty now or else that old dragon will be giving me a scorching.'

'All right,' said Seymour. 'You can start by serving me. What have you got that'll keep a poor detective-constable on his feet for the rest of the day without turning him into a pauper?'

'*Constable*, is it?' she said with a grin. 'I think you'd better be having the special.'

'What's that?' he said.

'Tripe and onions,' she said. 'I'll see if I can wangle you an extra portion of onions!'

With the extra virtue of one who has been kept virtuous by accident, Pascoe said, 'You've taken your time! Enjoy your lunch?'

211

'Sorry, sir. Some of the witnesses have been difficult to pin down,' said Seymour.

Quickly he reported his findings.

'So. A lot of money. But it can't have been all that much, not at four to one. Not unless he put a lot more on the horse than we imagine.'

'Or he'd rolled it up with the other two,' said Seymour eagerly.

'Rolled it up?' said Pascoe, who understood the term only vaguely, not being a racing man.

'Yes. What I mean is, put his money on all three horses to win in a treble. Now *Red Vanessa* was five to one, so a fiver would give him twenty-five pounds plus his stake on *Usherette*, two to one, equals sixty plus thirty on *Polly Styrene* at four to one equals three hundred and sixty plus the stake. Three hundred and ninety pounds. That's money.'

Pascoe, impressed by the rapid calculation, quibbled, 'Yes, but that means he'd have had to have his bet on in advance, doesn't it?'

Wield, in whom the mention of a relatively large sum of money had roused a spark of interest, said, 'But it makes more sense, sir. I was thinking. He was drinking tea and watching television with this Mrs Escott until nearly half past three, you say? It was always going to be a bit of a rush for him to get into town in time to put a bet on the three fifty-five. But if he'd got the money on a roll-up, surely he'd have sat at home and watched the last race on the telly?'

Pascoe looked at Seymour, who nodded and

said, 'Wild horses wouldn't have dragged him away.'

Wield said, 'So maybe he did just feel his luck running good and go out to put a bet on the last of selections. There's a betting shop in that parade of shops just beyond Castleton Court, isn't there? He'd get there in time.'

Pascoe who, following Dalziel's hint, had checked the local shops in his street directory, nodded.

'Yes. One of Arnie Charlesworth's.'

'But there's no way he could've won all that money, Sarge,' argued Seymour. 'Not on one bet at four to one.'

'Mebbe a little looks a lot to an Irish waitress,' said Wield sardonically. 'There could be hope for you yet.'

Seymour was disturbed to realize how much of his personal response he must have given away in what he'd thought was a carefully neutral account of Bernadette's evidence. Pascoe came to his rescue saying, 'But there's a sub-post-office in that parade of shops too. Why would he place his bet there, then go into town to collect his pension? There's even a local off-licence, so he could have got his rum too.'

'Well, perhaps he collected his winnings, set off home, decided he'd treat himself to a meal and jumped on a bus and went into town,' said Wield tentatively.

Pascoe shook his head, then spoke with sudden decision.

'This is all detail,' he said. 'It'll get sorted eventually. The main thing is, at least we've something to go on. If Parrinder had a bundle of notes in an old brown envelope when he left the restaurant, where are they now?'

'So you think we can be certain this was a mugging?' said Wield doubtfully. 'Why just take the envelope? What was wrong with the money in his pension book?'

'Perhaps whoever did it just knew for certain about the envelope,' said Pascoe. 'You get some pretty odd people hanging around betting shops. Seeing an old guy going out with a big win would be very tempting to some of them. But let's tread slowly. Seymour, you're obviously at home among the bookies. If someone had a win on a roll-up bet on those three horses, it'll be recorded somewhere. Start with the local one near Castleton Court, but I've got no real hopes there. I want you to do the rounds till you find out where it was, *if* it was. Come the heavy if they drag their feet. They've all got something to hide! Once we get confirmation that Parrinder *did* have a little bank-roll, then we can get a proper official investigation under way! Off you go lad. And don't hang about this time, keep away from the colleens.'

'Yes, sir. Thank you, sir. And you have a good day too, sir,' said Seymour as he left.

'Cheeky bugger,' observed Wield.

'But he has the makings,' said Pascoe. 'He definitely has the makings. The future of the Force is in good hands if we train the Seymours up right.'

'Yes, sir,' said Wield.

From where Andy Dalziel was sitting, the future of the Force did not seem to be in quite so good a shape. He was outside Haycroft Grange high up in the passenger seat of Kassell's Range Rover and he could see the lanky figure of PC Hector under the archway of the stable wing where the estate offices were, waiting with the other beaters to collect his day's pay.

Dalziel had refused Pledger's invitation to come into the house for a parting drink. There had been things to talk over with Kassell and there was more privacy out here. But Kassell had been summoned to take a phone call and Dalziel was wishing that he'd accepted Pledger's offer after all.

The truck with its bright cargo of dead pheasants was being unloaded by the stable block. There were getting on for a hundred of them, but only one of them was Dalziel's personal responsibility. He was not a man who cared to do things badly and the degree to which age and hard living seemed to have impaired his coordination of muscle and eye had taken him aback.

A green van bumped into the courtyard. Kassell came out of the house and spoke briefly with the new arrival, a short, squat man in a tweed suit patterned violently in brown and yellow checks. Then Kassell helped himself to a couple of birds from the truck and walked back to his own vehicle.

'Sorry about that,' he said as he climbed in. 'You should've gone inside and sampled Willy's brandy.'

'Plenty of time for that,' said Dalziel. 'What's this?'

Kassell had reached into the back of the Range Rover, got hold of a plastic carrier into which he put the brace of birds before dropping it onto Dalziel's lap.

'To the victor the spoils,' he said. 'All the guns are entitled to a couple at the end of the day.'

'But I only hit one of the bloody things!' protested Dalziel. 'And what the fuck am I meant to do with them anyway?'

'That's up to you. But one thing I learned in the Army was that a perk is a perk. Never turn down a buckshee!'

'What happens to the rest?' said Dalziel.

'We sell 'em,' said Kassell. 'That chap in the explosive suit is Vernon Briggs, game dealer. He claims his firm's motto is *Game for Owt*. He's not unamusing, though he thinks of himself as a bit of a character, which is rather a bore. He pays about a quid a bird and they end up on your plate at places like Paradise Hall at ten times the price.'

'I thought that consumptive lass shot her own,' said Dalziel.

'Mrs Abbiss? Yes, she's a fair shot. We've had her out here from time to time. I intend no *double entendre*. The lady's not for touching, much to the disappointment of some of our foreign guests. Fortunately we usually contrive to keep them happy in other directions.'

'How's that?'

'Oh, they tend to be rather seignorial in their attitude to serving wenches, so we have to make sure that we have the right kind of stuff.'

'Old and ugly you mean?' said Dalziel.

Kassell laughed and said, 'You're very whimsical, Andy. Interestingly, my phone call was from a new recruit. That girl who waited on us, or do I mean on whom we waited, on Friday night.'

'The one who looked like a reject from a punk band?' said Dalziel. 'Jesus!'

'You didn't seem to find her unattractive yourself if I remember right,' grinned Kassell. 'I've noticed her before. She has a certain something. And she was so clearly discontented with her lot on Friday that I had a word with her on the way out.'

'That's why you hung back, was it?' said Dalziel. 'I thought you were fixing yourself a soldier's hello. I didn't realize you were a talent scout.'

'*Pimp*, did you think of saying? No, I don't believe you did. If you had, you'd have said it, wouldn't you?'

'Oh aye,' said Dalziel. 'And is she hired, then?'

'Yes. She hesitated at the possible isolation. I assured her that transport was provided on days off to get the staff to town and back. So we have a new maid. Yes, talent scout, I like that. Always on the lookout for talent.'

'Like me,' said Dalziel.

'Yes, I'm glad I spotted you. With Arnie's help, of course. To get back to what we were talking about, you're perfectly satisfied with our arrangement?'

'For the time being,' said Dalziel cautiously.

'Subject to review, you mean? Well, we can't ask fairer than that. If you won't go to Willy's brandy, let's at least wet our deal with his equally excellent Scotch.'

He produced a silver-plated flask from the door-pocket, unscrewed the cup which doubled as a stopper and poured the contents into it.

'There's only enough for one,' protested Dalziel.

'You have it,' urged Kassell. 'You've got further to go than me.'

'To get to the next drink, you mean?'

'That too.'

The two men looked at each other in silence for a moment.

'Cheers,' said Dalziel. And drank.

Chapter 19

'Je m'en vais chercher un grand peut-être.'

Tuesday was a day of short tempers.

Dalziel had at last received the DCC's urgent summons. The two men were closeted together for over an hour. Dalziel emerged shaking his head angrily as though pushed to the edge of even *his* superhuman tolerance, and when George Headingley tapped cautiously at the DCC's door five minutes later, the scream of *Come in!* echoed round the station like a sergeant-major's *Shun!* across a parade ground.

Dalziel meanwhile had kicked open the door of Pascoe's office like a man leading a raid, but for once found his assistant in a mood to match his own.

'Come in, do,' growled Pascoe. 'That's the door sorted. What'd you like to demolish next? The window? Or the desk? Sir.'

'What the hell's up with you?' demanded Dalziel.

'Nothing.'

'Is it the Deeks killing? Pull in half a dozen kids off the streets and kick it out of them. They'll likely know something.'

'No, it's not that,' said Pascoe. 'Though we're getting nowhere there either. It's this other business.'

He explained to Dalziel about Parrinder. The truth was that after the discoveries of the previous day he had been rather over-jubilant in assuring Inspector Cruikshank that the famous Pascoe hunch had been correct and the Parrinder 'accident' could almost certainly now be regarded as a mugging. The trouble was that, since then, Seymour had not been able to trace a single sighting of Parrinder at any betting shop nor to get anyone to admit having paid out on a roll-up involving those three horses. Even the pay-outs on single bets on *Polly Styrene* offered few possibilities, the customers either being known, or their descriptions not fitting.

'So you started crowing before you'd got to the top of the midden,' said Dalziel, not without satisfaction. 'And now you're thinking mebbe there never was an envelope full of money to be stolen, mebbe Seymour's Irish waitress was dazzled by the sight of the poor old devil's pension money!'

'Something like that.'

'Well, better make absolutely sure before you start eating Cruikshank's humble pie. You want information, always go to experts. Let's see what we can do.'

He picked up the phone and dialled.

When it was answered he said. 'Arnie there? Tell him it's Andy. Just plain Andy, that's right, you can remember that, can you, love? Well done! Hello? Arnie? Yes, it's me. Listen, one of my boys is interested to know if an old lad called Parrinder collected last Friday on a roll-up on . . . what were them horses called?'

Pascoe told him. The information was relayed.

'Aye, that's all we've got. You'll check around? Grand! About twelve o'clock; no, someone will call at your flat, that'll be best. Can't have you seen hobnobbing with the fuzz too much, can we? Yesterday? Oh aye. Bloody marvellous. I only hit one of the bloody things and it wasn't the one I was aiming at. But I got two given. Listen, Arnie, like to buy a pair of pheasants? What? . . . You too!'

He replaced the receiver.

'There you are,' he said. 'Midday at Arnie Charlesworth's flat. If there's owt to know, he'll know it.'

'Well, thank you, sir,' said Pascoe uncertainly.

'Nothing wrong, lad?' said Dalziel softly. 'You don't object to visiting Arnie, do you? I mean he's not persona non grata or owt, is he?'

'No, nothing like that,' lied Pascoe. 'I was just thinking, I can't make midday myself. Charley Frostick, that's Deeks's grandson, is arriving from

221

Germany then and I want to be there to talk to him. But I'll send Seymour. He's been dealing with the Parrinder business mainly and making not a bad job of it.'

'Aye, he's not bad,' agreed Dalziel. 'And could be Arnie'd prefer a youngster. But you'll have to start paddling your own feet in this puddle sooner or later, Peter. Detection's like copulation, you can't manage it properly once removed. Now, important business. Your Ellie's a dab hand with a pheasant if I remember right. I've got two of the buggers. Two quid apiece. Or I'll take three for the pair. How's that? An offer you can't refuse, else Ellie'll skin you alive when I tell her.'

'I don't think so, sir,' said Pascoe.

'No? Oh, I've got it,' cried Dalziel. 'She's not come back yet! No wonder you're in such a miserable bloody mood!'

Pascoe grinned sheepishly, acknowledging there was some truth in this. Ellie had received no comfort at all from her visit to the doctor. The ageing process was impossible to reverse, difficult even to delay. The only direction was down. Her father had underlined this pessimistic prognosis by slipping into the past again and setting off for the work he'd retired from years earlier. Ellie had resolved to stay on longer.

'I can't just leave Mum,' she said. 'I've got to be sure she can cope.'

Past observation had suggested to Pascoe that Mrs Soper was able to cope very well with most things, not least a bossy daughter. Wisely he kept this observation to himself. But he was far from happy, though he was not about to discuss just how far with Andy Dalziel.

Sergeant Wield, quietly at work among the files in the corner, removed the pressure by addressing the fat man.

'Sir,' he said. 'About them pheasants. I'll take them, if you like.'

'Wield, I always knew you were a man with a nose for a bargain,' said Dalziel. 'They're yours. I've got them in the car. Four pound, we said.' He held out a huge hand.

Wield produced his wallet and said, 'Three pound the pair, I think it was, sir.'

'*Three?* Oh, that was a special discount for Inspectors whose hunches are all falling apart.'

Wield did not move; his fingers had withdrawn three pound notes from his wallet and he regarded Dalziel's hand unblinkingly.

'Christ,' said the fat man. 'I'd best take the money before he tells me what he's seeing there.'

He whisked the notes out of Wield's fingers.

'I'll leave them at the desk downstairs,' he said. 'Now I'm off. I've got things to do even if you buggers haven't!'

After he had left, Pascoe sat in thought for a while. The fat man was right. He'd interested himself in this Parrinder business without making the slightest direct contact with the case after his first casual view of the body at the hospital. Delegation is the better part of seniority, maybe; but it could be the worst part of detection.

He glanced at his watch.

Charley Frostick was due home from Germany at twelve o'clock. Pascoe had little real hope that the young soldier could help him, but he was planning to see him anyway. Give him half an hour to say hello. And that would give Pascoe plenty of time to call at Castleton Court and take a look at Tap Parrinder's background and neighbours for himself. He instructed Wield to get hold of Seymour and send him round to see Charlesworth.

'He's the only one who understands the language as far as I can see,' he said.

On his way out he bumped into George Headingley.

'How's it going, George?' he asked.

'I'm not sure,' was the reply. 'You seen the fat man this morning?'

'Briefly.'

'How was he?'

'Much the same as ever. A bit bad-tempered till he conned Wield into buying two dead pheasants. Why?'

'I've just been in with the DCC,' said Headingley. 'He's told me to wind up this accident investigation. He says he'll be taking care of things personally from now on.'

'Oh,' said Pascoe, taken aback. 'And what do you make of that?'

'I don't know. Except that junior officers aren't

allowed to investigate senior officers, are they? I mean, not properly *investigate*. I reckon something's changed, Peter. I reckon Andy Dalziel must be in very serious trouble, and I doubt if it's just poaching!'

Mrs Jane Escott at first looked blank when Pascoe on introducing himself mentioned DC Seymour. Then her eyes lit up and she said, 'Of course. How silly of me. The young man with the red hair!'

'That's him,' said Pascoe.

'And you're his boss, are you? I hope it's not about pulling the alarm cord. It was an accident. Anyone could have done that,' she said earnestly.

'No,' said Pascoe, puzzled, but determined not to be diverted. 'It's about your neighbour, Mr Parrinder.'

'Oh yes. Poor Tap. Do they know when the funeral will be yet?' she asked, her eyes filling with tears.

'No, not yet. May I come in, Mrs Escott?'

'What am I thinking of? Please do. Would you like a cup of tea?'

'No, thanks,' said Pascoe, following her into the neat living-room which had the heating turned up to what he found was a rather uncomfortable level.

He sat down in an armchair in front of a low coffee table. Scattered across the table was a heap of loose change with perhaps a dozen piles of coins stacked alongside it, according to denomination.

On the floor by the table was a pouch handbag of old soft leather.

'I'm sorry about this,' said Mrs Escott. 'I don't know how, but I always end up with so much change these days.'

'Me too,' said Pascoe. 'It wears holes in my pockets. It's the paper money I can't keep hold of.'

She opened the handbag and started to sweep the money into it.

'No, don't,' said Pascoe. 'You were counting it up. You'll have to start all over again.'

'It doesn't matter,' she said, completing the job and letting the bag drop to the floor with a dull thud. 'Now, please, Inspector. How can I help you with poor Tap?'

Pascoe took her over her story again.

'And he was watching the racing on television?' he asked.

'That's right,' she said.

'You'd watched races with Mr Parrinder, Tap, before?' Pascoe continued.

'Sometimes,' she said.

'And did he get excited when he watched? I mean, was he bothered about who won?'

'Of course he was!' she said sharply. 'There's not much point otherwise.'

'Even when he hadn't got a bet on?'

'Oh yes. He'd pick the horse he would have backed and shout at that one. Of course, it was even more exciting if he had some money on.'

'You were there from two till nearly half past three,' he said. 'So you'd see the two-ten and the two forty-five races.'

'I expect so. I didn't pay too much attention.'

'Did he have any money on those?'

'No.' She was quite definite.

'You're sure?' he pressed. 'Even though you didn't pay much attention?'

'I paid a lot of attention to Tap,' she reproved. 'The horses he was shouting for didn't even get a place, I recall, and he said what a good thing it was he hadn't been able to get out and make a bet.'

Pascoe concealed his disappointment and said, 'He always went out to make a bet, did he?'

'Oh yes.'

'Never telephoned?'

'I don't think so. He always talked about the betting shop. I've never been in one myself and he used to laugh when I told him I had this picture of a sort of old-fashioned general store with assistants wearing white coats.'

She laughed at her own silliness and Pascoe laughed with her.

'Well, thank you very much, Mrs Escott,' he said, rising.

'Have I been any help, Inspector?' she asked earnestly.

'Yes, very much,' he said, with all the false sincerity of a man who has just seen the last remnants of a promising theory knocked down.

'I'm so glad. Sometimes I forget things. It's just

old age, Mr Pascoe,' she said sorrowfully. 'But it can be so annoying.'

'Your memory seems fine to me. Just one last test. You can't remember the names of the horses he was shouting for on Friday, can you?'

His mind was toying with the absurd idea that Parrinder might have wished to keep his real selections secret from Mrs Escott and picked some rank outsider for his pretended support, though why he might have wanted to do this was as yet beyond even hypothesis. He had brought Parrinder's paper with him and he took it out now, ready to prompt Mrs Escott if necessary by reading the runners.

But it wasn't necessary. Her eyes lit up and she said triumphantly, 'Yes, I can. The first one was a horse called *Willie Wagtail*. It was such a funny name it stuck in my mind. In the second race it was *Glaramara*.'

'Well done,' said Pascoe, looking down the list to check the betting forecasts.

He looked again. He went through the card for the whole afternoon. There were no such horses running that day.

But as his eye ranged over the racing page, it did pick up the name of *Glaramara*. He still had to search to locate it, but there it was, in the small print of the alsorans after the result of the 2.40 at Wincanton on Thursday afternoon. *Willie Wagtail* was an also-ran in the previous race on the same day.

He looked at the old lady's smiling, happy face

and said gently, 'Yes, that's very good, Mrs Escott. Thank you. By the way, you don't happen to remember what the weather was like that afternoon when you watched television with Mr Parrinder, do you?'

'Why, yes,' she said, looking puzzled. 'Friday, you mean? It was bright but blowy. I remember saying to Tap that the sun looked warm enough from inside but there'd be precious little warmth in it if you went out. But he did go out, didn't he? And there was no need, no need at all. Especially not in the dark. It's so frightening these days if you're old, Mr Pascoe. All these muggings you hear about. I try never to be out after dark. Why did Tap go, Mr Pascoe? Why did he go?'

Pascoe folded the newspaper and put it in his pocket. His theory was coming back together, but he felt little joy in it.

'I don't know, Mrs Escott,' he said quietly. 'Thank you again for all your help. Thank you very much indeed.'

When Pascoe arrived at the Frostick house on Nethertown Road he was greeted by much the same sounds as had sped him on his way on Sunday. The argument died down as he rang the doorbell. An anxious-looking Mrs Frostick opened the door and ushered him into the living-room where he found Mr Frostick, red-faced and clench-fisted, glaring at a limb-entangled couple in an armchair. The tangle consisted of a young man in private soldier's uniform whom Pascoe took to be Charley Frostick, with Andrea Gregory, in or out of a mini-skirt, coiled sinuously about his person. There was, Pascoe felt, more of provocation than passion in her pose. It was aimed at fuelling the wrath of Frostick Senior rather than the desires of Frostick Junior, who was looking both physically and mentally rather uncomfortable under the girl's embrace.

The pause in debate lasted only until Frostick saw how unimportant the interrupter was. He nodded dismissively at Pascoe, then picked up the silver thread of his oratory with all the ease of a Cicero.

'Bloody mad's what I say, and bloody mad's what I mean! That's what you'll be if you let her get you hitched. You're just getting a start, you've your whole life ahead of you, your career, everything!'

'He's got me too,' said the girl. 'He wants me! We're in love! And he's old enough to make his own mind up, right, Charley?'

Charley looked miserable. Left to a man-to-man heart-to-heart discussion with his dad, he might well have been able to admit the sense of the elder Frostick's viewpoint. But Andrea with a sharp sense of timing had made sure she precipitated the crisis before the young man could be forewarned, and now the father's vehemence only served to provoke a macho I'll-not-let-my-self-be-pushed-around response.

But at the same time Pascoe sensed even in Andrea's stage-managing another dimension of play-acting which he didn't quite understand.

'Old enough!' sneered Frostick. 'He'll need another hundred years till he's old enough to deal with your sort, flashing everything you've got at him, that's all you bloody know.'

'Is that right? I've never noticed *you* looking away from whatever I've got to flash, Mr Frostick,' retorted the girl.

Then suddenly Charley was on his feet and Andrea was sprawling alone in the armchair.

'Will you both belt up!' commanded the young man. 'I've not come home to get yelled at and ordered around by *anyone*. I get plenty of that in my job, and I'll not put up with it here, all right? I've come home for me granda's funeral, that's what, and I think it's time we were showing some respect.'

Even in his brief period away from home, some process of maturation had taken place which surprised the others, Pascoe could see. Andrea recovered quickest and said, 'You tell him, Charley!'

Her fiancé spun round and said, 'And that goes for you too, girl. He was good to me, was Granda. If it weren't for him being so generous, you wouldn't have that ring on your finger, so show some respect, will you?'

Andrea stood up. She was wearing less make-up today, perhaps in anticipation of the extra mobility of expression circumstances were likely to require.

Rather than anger, what showed now was triumph. The explanation of that sense of play-acting was imminent, Pascoe realized.

'Here, if it's this old ring you're worried about, you take the bloody thing,' she said viciously, pulling it off and chucking it at the young man. 'I've got better things to do than go and live in some crummy married quarters with a private!'

Charley was dumb-stricken but his father, unable to believe this turn of fortune, said, 'You've changed your tune! What's happened? Found yourself some money, have you?'

'You could say that. I've got myself a job,' she said. 'A good job. Out at Haycroft Grange, that's that big house out beyond Pedgely Bank.'

'Haycroft Grange! What'll you be doing there?' demanded Charley.

'Helping out,' said the girl. 'Serving at table, and so on. There's a lot of important people gets there.'

'You mean, domestic service? You'll be a maid?' said Frostick in disbelief.

'I'll be assistant to the housekeeper,' retorted Andrea. 'And I get my own room and a colour telly too. You reckon nowt to me, don't you, Mr Frostick? Well, let me tell you this, I only did my job at Paradise Hall so well that one of the customers there noticed me and it was him that got me this job.'

'You didn't say owt about this on Sunday!' said Frostick.

'I didn't know I was going till last night,' said Andrea.

'I get it!' said Frostick. 'So now you've got yourself fixed up, you don't need to shove yourself off on Charley here any more. Christ, Charley lad, I hope you can see what a lucky escape you've had.'

'Oh shut up, Dad!' the young man burst out. With a last glance, part accusing, part amazed, at Andrea he turned away and rushed from the room. They heard his footsteps going upstairs.

'See you then, Mr Frostick,' said the girl, with a provocative pout. She left too. Pascoe said, 'Excuse me,' and followed her.

He caught up with her just outside the front door.

'You know who I am, Miss Gregory,' he said, with a smile which won a response compounded equally of distrust and dislike.

'Yeah, what do you want?'

'This job you've got, was it Major Kassell who got it for you by any chance?'

'That's right. What about it?'

It wasn't so much aggressiveness, he decided, as an inability to respond other than in terms of her own self-interest. What about it, indeed? So Major Kassell, knowing they were short-staffed out at Haycroft Grange, had suggested to this girl that she might care to apply. But why, for God's sake? Pascoe could imagine the kind of waitress she was. Her one talent was probably provoking men. Takes a big tip to get a big tip.

He said, 'Listen, love, I just want a few answers, that's all. I'll get 'em here, or I'll come up to Haycroft Grange for them if you prefer.'

The threat was mild but effective. She responded instantly.

'Yes, it was him, the Major. He gets in a lot to Paradise Hall. Said to me a week or two back, if ever I needed a job, they were always looking for staff at Haycroft Grange. Well, I thought, no wonder, stuck out there in the middle of nowhere. I mean, Paradise Hall was bad enough but at least there was the bus or you could thumb a lift.'

'What made you change your mind?' asked Pascoe.

'I needed a job, didn't I? Anyway, he told me there was regular transport laid on for the staff. So I thought, why not give it a whirl? I'm starting tomorrow so I can get to know the ropes before the next lot of guests come at the weekend. That's what it is mainly, see, these rich men coming up for the shooting.'

She spoke with real respect. No wonder Kassell had hired her! The rich would get real service. But what did that make Kassell? Added to the information supplied by Sergeant Myers, it made him a lot less than a perfectly respectable witness. Not that it mattered too much now that Mrs Warsop had changed her mind.

'On Friday night, did you notice the other people with Major Kassell?'

'Yeah,' she said. 'There was that bookie, Charlesworth. He gets in a lot. And this big fat bloke, pissed out of his mind. He looked a real villain! Is that who you're after?'

'No, no,' prevaricated Pascoe hastily. 'Just a general question. I was really just interested in the restaurant and the clientele generally.'

'Here, it's not old Abbiss you're after?' said the girl, with sudden malice. 'I could tell you a thing or two about his fiddles. You want to be looking at him and that old dyke from The Towers, that's what you want to be doing.'

'From The Towers?' said Pascoe, suddenly alert. 'You mean Mrs Warsop?'

'That's right. She brings her little fancy girls along, rubs knees with them under the table, it makes me sick!' said Andrea viciously.

'Bad tipper, is she?' said Pascoe disapprovingly.

'Tip? *Her?* You never see her money. Signs her bill, like she was important. But Abbiss, he never sees her money either.'

'What are you trying to tell me, Andrea?' said Pascoe gently.

But the girl had gone full circle and was now back to her original instinctive distrust.

'Nothing,' she said. 'I've said nothing. It's nothing to do with me any more. I'm off now.'

She stepped over the fence into her own garden. From the house a plaintive wail arose.

'Teeny! Where's my biscuits?'

'Thank Christ I'll be away from that!' she said half to herself.

'I'll see you again some time, Andrea,' promised Pascoe.

'Will you?' she said, turning on him a crooked, not unattractive smile. 'Perhaps.'

'Perhaps,' agreed Pascoe. 'Perhaps.'

Chapter 20

'All my possessions for one moment of time!'

Dennis Seymour was inclined to regard this consultation with Arnie Charlesworth as a slight on his own detective resources. Having spent several hours trudging round all the possible, and some pretty improbable, betting shops, he resented the implication that Charlesworth could cover the same ground with a few telephone calls. Worst of all would be, of course, if Charlesworth proved to have succeeded where he had failed.

No. He corrected this. It'd be a blow to his *amour-propre*, but the worst thing of all would be if this investigation which he had begun to regard as very much his own should finally grind to a halt.

Charlesworth lived in the highest of a quartet of flats carved out of a tall Victorian terraced house near the town centre. It was somehow curiously depersonalized, feeling more like a hotel suite than a permanent residence. The only personal touches were a set of racing prints on one of the lounge walls and a framed photograph of a group of young men in rugby kit, with one of them holding a large cup.

When Seymour introduced himself at the door, Charlesworth had regarded him with cold assessing eyes before letting him in. Not a man you could get close to, thought Seymour. There was something reserved and watching about him, a mind calculating the odds and at the same time sardonically amused at the absurdity of the race.

'Drink?' said Charlesworth.

'I could manage a beer,' said Seymour, sitting on a rather hard armchair.

Charlesworth poured him a lager. He took nothing himself.

'Cheers,' said Seymour, taking a sip. 'Did you have any luck, sir?'

'Luck?' said Charlesworth as though it were not a word he was acquainted with. 'In the whole of this city there was only one bet placed which linked those three horses last Friday, and that was for a hundred pounds, and the punter concerned is well known by name and in person.'

'Ah,' said Seymour. 'No luck then.'

'How old are you, son?' asked Charlesworth.

It was an unexpected question, but Charlesworth was not the kind of man whose unexpected questions could be ignored.

'Twenty-three,' said Seymour.

'And you like your work?'

'Yes, sir.'

'Ambitious?'

'Yes, sir.'

What was all this about? wondered Seymour. Was he being sounded out for a bribe? The story of Dalziel's troubles, suitably embellished, was all over the station by now. According to this, the bookie had the fat man in his pocket; was he now looking to invest in the future?

If so, should not Seymour perhaps be flattered by being singled out as a prospective high-flier?

'I had a son,' said Charlesworth abruptly.

'Sir?'

'He was twenty-three when he died. Nearly. Another week and he'd have been twenty-three.'

'I'm sorry,' said Seymour helplessly. He finished his beer and made as if to rise, but something in Charlesworth's hard, set face told him that he was not yet excused.

'You interested in racing? Apart from professionally, that is?' asked Charlesworth.

'Well, yes. I like to go when I get the chance. And I like a bet,' said Seymour, glad to re-enter the realm of casual conversation, even if it might lead to some kind of offer which he hoped he'd have the strength and the sense to refuse.

'It's a mug's game,' said Charlesworth dismissively. 'Punters are mugs. Bookies can be mugs as well, but it takes another bookie to do that.'

Seymour laughed, deciding this must be a joke, but Charlesworth didn't even smile. Seymour wasn't sure what the subject was but he decided to change it.

'Nice prints,' said the young detective. 'Worth a bob or two if they're genuine.'

'They're what they look like,' said Charlesworth ambiguously. 'That's the most you can say about anything, isn't it?'

'I suppose so, sir,' said Seymour, using his interest in the prints as an excuse to rise and study them more closely, with a view to making an early exit.

'I had a Stubbs once. You know Stubbs?'

'I've heard of him,' said Seymour. 'That'd be really valuable, wouldn't it?'

'I let my wife take it,' said Charlesworth. 'She liked it. My son liked it too. So when we divorced, I let her take it.'

Seymour wandered round the room, showing great interest in long stretches of light green emulsion paint, till he arrived at the team photograph.

'Is this your son here?' he said, stabbing his finger at the youth holding the cup. 'I can see the resemblance.'

'No,' said Charlesworth. 'That's me.'

Seymour looked more closely. There was no writing on the photograph, but now he looked, he could see that the cut of the shorts, not to mention the hair, suggested a distant era.

'Rugby, isn't it?' he said.

'Yes. The Mid-Yorkshire cup,' said Charlesworth.

'Hold on,' said Seymour, peering even more

closely. One of the figures in the back row, a large solid young man, well-muscled and with the grin of a tiger, looked familiar.

'That's never . . .' he said doubtfully.

'Your Mr Dalziel? Oh yes,' said Charlesworth. 'We go back a long way.'

'My God!' said Seymour, delighted. 'He hasn't changed much. I mean, he's put on a lot of weight, but you can still see . . .'

'He's changed,' interrupted Charlesworth brusquely. 'We all change, given the chance.'

'Yes, sir,' said Seymour. 'Well, thanks again for your help. I'd best be getting back. It's a pity, but I think we'll just have to give up on this one; I reckon it was always a long shot . . .'

'You give up easy, son,' said Charlesworth.

'Sorry?'

'There's no record of this bet, so what you decide is that this bet wasn't made. Is that the way Andy Dalziel teaches you to think?'

'I'm not sure what you mean,' said Seymour. 'I mean, if there's no record . . .'

'That means there's no record. It doesn't mean there was no bet.'

'I see,' lied Seymour, resuming his seat.

Charlesworth tossed him another can of lager and smiled. It wasn't much of a smile, but there was something of genuine feeling in it, a promise of spring in a wintry sky.

'Two reasons why there should be no record,' he said. 'One: the bookie "lost" it. Now this

241

sometimes happens with some bets, with some bookies. There's a ten per cent tax on all bets. So you can see the incentive to "lose" a few: not only do you cut down on your income tax, you get to keep the ten per cent as well.'

'But,' said Seymour, 'surely there's no point in a bookie "losing" a winning bet, if you follow me. I mean, what he pays out he'll want to keep on record, won't he?'

'That's right,' said Charlesworth approvingly. 'Mr Dalziel'd be proud of you. So what's the second reason a bet might not be recorded?'

'Because,' said Seymour, screwing up his face in concentration, 'because it wasn't placed with a regular bookie!'

'Right.'

'You mean, this particular bet might've been placed with a street-corner bookie?'

'There's a lot of them about. Pubs, clubs, factories, offices; the betting shops drove them out of business to start with, but the ten per cent tax has given them new life. Tax-free betting's very attractive to the regular punter. This old boy of yours was a regular, was he?'

'I gather so,' said Seymour. 'But it doesn't help much, not unless we can lay our hands on the joker concerned.'

'If it's a street-corner job, then you'll be pushed,' said Charlesworth.

'What's the alternative?'

Charlesworth shook his head sadly.

'Things are slipping in this town,' he said. 'Time was, we paid the police to do police work.'

Seymour decided the time had come to exert his authority. He was fed up of being treated as 'the lad'. And what the hell was Charlesworth but a jumped-up bookie anyway, and probably bent at that?

'Look,' he said. 'If you know anything, you've got to tell me. All right? I mean, it's your duty.'

It came out much more weakly than he'd intended. Charlesworth suddenly laughed.

'You really know how to lean on people, son,' he mocked. 'All right. I give in. Thirty-two, Merton Street. Down the ginnel back of Inglis's hardware shop. Take a couple of mates in case you need to kick the door down. And don't say I sent you.'

It was curious but this last injunction carried more weight than a whole anthology of threats, bargains or appeals.

At the door, Seymour began to say thank you but Charlesworth grunted, 'Don't thank me till you know what you've got, lad.'

'All right!' said Seymour. 'Shall I come back and tell you if it's been worth it?'

He didn't know why he made the offer except that he had a sense of responding to some unspoken request.

Charlesworth's cold eyes examined him closely as if searching for sarcasm. Seymour did not exactly feel threatened but he certainly felt glad none had been intended.

'Come if you like,' said Charlesworth. 'Why not? Come if you like.'

Rather to Seymour's disappointment there was no need to kick down any doors. The front door of 32 Merton Street opened at a push. Instructing PC Hector that no one was to leave, Seymour and Sergeant Wield entered a narrow entrance hall smelling of cabbage and cat. A toilet flushed and a man emerged from one of the several inner doors. He nodded in a friendly fashion and, opening another door, ushered them into a smoke-filled room.

Here there was a pleasant social atmosphere. A scattering of comfortable-looking chairs faced a raised television screen on which horses were being walked around a paddock. In one corner a girl was dispensing drinks from a small domestic cocktail bar. In the opposite corner behind a rather larger bar with the protection of a metal grille, a man and a woman were taking bets. There were between twenty and thirty people in the room. It was a scene which Seymour recognized from the old black-and-white pre-war American thrillers he sometimes saw on the box.

'In you go, lads,' urged their polite acquaintance, a grey-haired man in his sixties. 'This your first time? His booze is a bit pricey, but it don't stop at three o'clock, that's the main thing, ain't it?'

'I suppose so,' said Seymour, glancing uncertainly at Wield. The sergeant had authorized the raid in Pascoe's absence, but assured the young detective that it was still very much his show.

'In fact,' said Seymour to the grey-haired man, 'we're the police.'

'Pardon?' he replied, cupping his hand over his ear. 'You'll have to shout.'

'Police,' shouted Seymour. 'We're policemen.'

'I shouldn't let it worry you,' said this amiable old fellow. 'They're not choosy here.'

Seymour glanced again at Wield whose craggy face gave no sign of the earthquake of mirth going on beneath it.

'Who's the gaffer here?' demanded Seymour.

'Gaffer? That'll be Don you want, him at the counter. I warn you, he's not keen on credit, but if you really are bobbies, that'll probably be all right.'

'Thanks, dad,' said Seymour.

He pushed his way towards the betting counter. There was some protest as he went to the head of the queue waiting to be served by a benevolent white-haired man with a ruddy farmer's face.

'You Don?' said Seymour.

'That's right.'

'This your place?'

'Right again.'

'Police,' said Seymour, producing his warrant card.

'Oh aye? That's buggered it,' said Don calmly. 'Just give us a moment, Officer. Mavis, love, it's police.'

The woman by his side slid off her stool. She

was plumply middle-aged, with a stolid expression which didn't change as she gathered up trays of cash from a shelf beneath the counter.

'What's she doing?' asked Seymour.

'I don't know. What are you doing, Mavis?' asked the man.

She did not reply but turned, unlocked a door behind her and went out.

'Hey, stop!' cried Seymour. 'Where's she going?'

'I don't know,' said the man. 'It's a free country.'

Seymour looked in vain for a way to get behind the counter from this side.

'If you just wait there, I'll come round, shall I?' said Don helpfully.

'No! I mean ... look, don't move. I'll come round to you ... no ...'

'Look, lad, if I was going off somewhere, I'd have gone by now,' said Don. 'This is all my stuff in here; I'm not going to go and leave this lot to nick it, am I?'

It sounded reasonable.

'All right,' said Seymour.

He returned to Wield who was leaning against the door, blocking any attempt to leave, though to tell the truth most of those present were more concerned with the television where the horses were just coming under starter's orders.

'He's coming round,' said Seymour.

'Is he?' said Wield.

'Should I go and see if Hector stopped the woman?'

246

'You don't imagine Hector's suspicions would be aroused by the sight of a woman carrying a pile of cash trays, do you?' said Wield. 'Anyway, she'll likely have gone off another way. Mind you, it's just a precaution.'

'Precaution?'

'Aye. Fifty quid fine's the most they'll get for this lot, I should think.'

'Bloody hell,' said Seymour in disgust. 'It's hardly worth our bother, is it?'

'Listen, son,' said Wield in what passed for his friendly tone. 'Never forget the object of the exercise, right? That's the first rule.'

Behind him the door opened against his back and the venerable white head appeared.

'Shall I come in?' asked Don.

'No. We'll step out,' said Wield.

In the smelly entrance hall, the ugly sergeant put his ruin of a face close to the other man's open, honest features and said softly, 'This is an illegal betting shop you've got here, Don. No, listen. It's also a fire risk. You've boarded the windows up, haven't you? Only one door. Bit of panic in there, caused by something like a police raid, say, and there could be a lot of damage. I don't just mean people. I mean, people mend. But fixtures. Furniture trampled, television smashed, bottles broken, bar pulled down; ruined; I've seen it.'

'Oh aye,' said the man. 'But there isn't any panic.'

'No,' said Wield. 'Let's keep it that way shall we?

247

Friday afternoon last. A win-treble. *Red Vanessa* in the two-ten at Cheltenham, *Usherette* in the two forty-five . . .'

'And *Polly Styrene* in the three fifty-five,' completed Don. 'Aye, I remember that. Three hundred and ninety quid it cost me!'

'Three ninety?' said Wield. 'You remember the punter?'

'An old boy. Calls himself Tap, I don't know his real name. He's in a lot, fifty p. stuff mainly, chances a quid now and then if he feels lucky. He hadn't been in all week, might've been saving up for this one I reckon. He puts a fiver on. Well, they're all fair horses, good on heavy ground, but there's plenty of good competition and over the sticks in the rain's always a bit of a lottery. But it's his lucky day. We all deserve one, don't we? Here, it's not him who's put the bubble in, is it? Why'd he do that, now?'

'No,' said Wield. 'It wasn't him. When you paid him out were there a lot of customers about?'

'A few,' said Don. 'Hold on. He's never been robbed, has he? Is that what this is about?'

'Mebbe,' said Wield. 'Tell me about the other customers.'

'Listen, I'll tell you what I can,' said the man. 'But I'm not daft. An old boy wins that amount, I take a bit of care. If he wants the world to know that he's got it when he's got it, that's his business. But when I saw the bet come up, I got his winnings counted out in tenners and fivers, put 'em in an old envelope. He was fly too; he hung back till the end of the pay-out queue. It was the last race, so most people had drifted off. *Then* he comes and collects.'

'You mean he didn't count it?' said Wield disbelievingly.

'Oh aye, he stood there and went through it. But still in the envelope, you understand. He was excited, I could see that, but he wasn't going to shout it out from the rooftops.'

'Right,' said Wield. 'But some people have sharp eyes and sharp ears, so we'll need to be knowing who was about.'

'I'll try my best,' said the white-haired man. 'But what does Tap himself say? I mean, it's him that's lost the money, isn't it?'

'More than money,' said Wield quietly. 'He's lost a lot more than money.'

'What? Oh bugger,' said the white-haired man feelingly. 'The poor old sod.'

He fixed Wield with his patriarchal eye and said earnestly, 'It's not worth it, is it? What's the point of money if it brings you that kind of trouble? It's just not worth it.'

Wield said to Seymour, 'Hark at him, lad! You didn't know you were raiding a charitable institution, did you? Get Hector and take the names and addresses of all them refugees in there.'

And to Don he said, 'You come along with me, Dr Barnardo. You're nicked.'

Chapter 21

'I have opened it.'

Charley Frostick sat in the passenger seat of Pascoe's car and stared morosely out of the window at the passing scene.

'How do you like the Army, Charley?' inquired Pascoe.

'It's all right,' grunted the youth.

Pascoe sighed. He could see that the War Office might well rate the social graces a little way below rifle practice, but surely someone there acknowledged that a young soldier might want to *talk* to the occasional stranger before shooting him?

But now Charley, who was basically a nice lad and not unappreciative of Pascoe's kindness in rescuing him from the hotted-up emotionalism of his home by his offer to run him round to Welfare Lane, roused himself from his lethargy and resumed, 'It's right enough. I've got some grand mates and you can have a bit of a laugh.

It's a bit boring sometimes, some of the things they make us do; but most things are sometimes, I reckon. And it's better than being out of work. I was pig-sick of that. In the end it was either the Police or the Army and I didn't fancy running into bother with my old mates.'

'Rather shoot strangers, eh?' laughed Pascoe.

'I don't want to shoot anyone,' protested Charley with great indignation.

'Sorry,' said Pascoe.

'Except mebbe the bastard who killed my granda. I'd shoot him soon enough, no bother.'

He glared defiantly at Pascoe, who said gently, 'Everyone feels like that when someone they love's been hurt, Charley. But it just means that you get yourself in bother and probably leave someone feeling the same way about you.'

Charley didn't look as if he accepted this argument and said grumblingly, 'Any road, you've got to find the bastard yet, haven't you? Have your mob not found out anything yet?'

Pascoe tried to look as if he were bound by a vow of silence but he was all too conscious that he had very little to be silent about. The possible boot prints were too vague to be a significant clue. Fingerprints abounded, but none that showed up in the records, and the process of elimination of all those whose prints were legitimately in the house was slow and likely to be inconclusive. It was his personal view that their best, if not their only, hope of making an arrest would be if the killer attempted to sell the medals or the watch.

'Charley, I was asking your mam about money. She was able to give us a good idea of what things had been stolen, but money's more difficult. I mean, you've got to have some idea how much there was there for a start.'

'What did Mam say?' asked the youth.

'She didn't know of any cash there might be lying around, any more than what you'd expect, I mean. But someone said something about your grandfather helping you out, when you wanted to buy an engagement ring . . .'

'I paid him every penny back after I signed on!' exploded the young soldier angrily. 'Every penny! Anyone who says different is a liar!'

'Yes, I'm sure they are, Charley,' said Pascoe placatingly. 'It's just a matter of where the money came from, that's all.'

'He weren't badly off, my granda,' said Charley. 'He had money in the Building Society, did you know that?'

'Yes. I've seen his book,' said Pascoe. 'That'd be a help too. When was it you got engaged, Charley? There've been a few withdrawals in the past year and it'd be useful to see whether he went along and drew the money out to loan you for the ring, for instance. How much was it, by the way?'

'A hundred quid,' said Charley. 'I were on the dole and there was no way I could manage that amount. But it were the ring that Andrea wanted.'

His voice had the flatness of withheld emotion. Jesus Christ! thought Pascoe angrily as he considered the mentality of a girl who could demand a hundred pound engagement ring from her boyfriend on the dole. He must put it to Ellie, though he could guess her response. It was men who created the marriage-obsessed, pretty-stone-greedy girl; they shouldn't complain when she went over the top. On the other hand, he asked himself, who was it who created this poor lad soft enough to let himself be browbeaten into giving her the ring?

'Your grandad must've thought a lot of you, to lend you that much money, Charley,' he said. 'And he must have thought Andrea was all right too.'

'No,' admitted the young man miserably. 'He only met her a couple of times, didn't like her much at all, I could see that. When I told him I wanted to get engaged before I joined up he laughed and said I'd soon have girls all over the face of the world.'

'But he still made the loan.'

'Yes,' said the young man. Then he added with a rush, 'I never told him it was all for the ring. I let on I wanted some clothes and things so I could smarten myself up for my Army interview. At home I tried to let on it were just a cheap ring but Andrea made sure everyone knew how much it cost, so I had to tell them where I'd borrowed the money else they'd have thought I nicked it!'

He spoke with the bitterness of misunderstood youth, but with something more too. It was a bad time he'd been through, Pascoe knew. His grandfather's death, his broken engagement.

He said gently, 'Will you try to make it up with Andrea?'

The young man thought, then said, 'No.'

It didn't sound a definitive negative. The qualification when it came surprised Pascoe by its honesty and to some extent its maturity.

'What I mean is, no, I'll not be chasing after her. I mean, when I'm away from her, I think about her, but, you know, well, just like *that* mainly. And if she came after me, I expect I'd make it up because when we're together, you know, by ourselves . . .'

He stopped speaking but his stumbling words and now his silence were more eloquent than any literary erotica of the power of sex.

'She's an attractive girl,' said Pascoe.

'She is that. I used to slip out from the camp sometimes when she were at that hotel – it's only a couple of miles down the road – we weren't supposed to stay out at night, not during training, but I'd still go and she'd let me in at the back. It were daft really, I could have got into serious bother, but I knew this lad on the gate. Later, when I'd passed out, we were allowed to stay out. I'd still get back late sometimes even though it were so close. And often I'd be fair worn out on the square or at the range!'

He spoke with a mixture of pride, bewilderment and awkwardness. He was glad, Pascoe guessed, to have someone to talk to who was sympathetic but also a stranger, and official with it. He did not doubt that Charley had indulged in his fill of sexual boasting in the company of his fellow soldiers, but that was miles away from this stumbling analysis of the strange ambiguities of body and spirit.

'I'd not really thought of being married to Andrea, do you understand that?' he continued. 'Even when we got engaged. I mean, I couldn't think of her as a wife, somehow, not like me mam, you know, in the house and taking care of things and all that . . . no, I couldn't see that . . .'

They had arrived at Welfare Lane. The police caravan had gone and there was nothing to distinguish No. 25 from its neighbours. After Charley's visit, Pascoe could see no further reason for keeping the house sealed. Mrs Frostick would want to start the sad job of sorting out her father's belongings. There had been no will, so the whole estate – money, goods and the house itself – would pass to her as the only child. Pascoe had no doubt that she would see Charley right, but the boy wasn't going to get the old pocket watch that had always been promised him. Not unless the gods decided to be kind.

He didn't open the car door straight away but sat for a moment in case Charley wanted to unburden himself further, but the youth quickly opened the passenger door and got out, perhaps because he felt that there had been quite enough self-examination for one day, perhaps because Mrs Tracey Spillings had appeared at the kerbside and was peering through the windscreen.

'Hello, Charley,' she said. 'You're looking grand. It must suit you, all this open air life. I was right sorry about your grandad. He could be a miserable old devil when he wanted but he never did nobody any harm and we've had some good times. All these years we've been neighbours and I never thought it'd come to this. It's a terrible business, Charley. I hope they get the bugger as did it, but they run rings round the police nowadays, don't they? You've got the best one of the bunch here, I reckon, but that's not saying too much. You know who was first round? Mrs Jolley's nephew from Parish Road, that Tony Hector, looks as if he's been washed and stretched. Then there was another, you've never seen such a face! When first I saw it, I thought they'd caught the killer, he looked ripe for anything! How are you, lad?'

'I'm fine, thanks, Mrs Spillings,' said Charley, looking slightly shell-shocked.

'And your mam and dad? And that lass you're engaged to? All all right?'

Charley glanced at Pascoe and said, 'Aye, they're OK.'

'Good. You'd like a cup of tea,' asserted Mrs Spillings without fear of contradiction.

'No, thanks,' said Charley boldly. 'But don't let me stop you from having one, Mr Pascoe. In fact, I'd as lief have a look round the house by myself to start with.'

Pascoe who had slid away to unlock the front door regarded the boy with mute congratulation. Such tactical skill must surely predicate a knapsack full of field-marshal's batons.

'That's right,' approved Mrs Spillings. 'You come along with me, Mr Pascoe.'

She seized his arm and Pascoe for the first time in his life knew what it must feel like to be nicked.

But as he entered No. 27, a second and perhaps stranger phenomenon occupied all his attention.

The house was in silence.

Without the waves of broadcast decibels beating against it, even the wallpaper seemed almost peaceful, like a coral reef after a tropical storm.

'Where . . . ?' began Pascoe.

'Mam?' said Mrs Spillings. 'Aye, it is quiet. She's gone.'

'Gone? Oh, I'm sorry,' said Pascoe sitting down heavily and feeling the usual English middle-class inadequacy in matters of commiseration.

'What? No! You silly bugger!' roared Mrs Spillings. 'I don't mean *gone*. I mean she's gone away. She were booked down to go to The Towers this Friday, but this vacancy came up unexpected and Betty Day, the matron there, she got in touch to ask if she'd like an extra few days. I've known Betty Day for years, her dad was Eric Day who used to have the fish shop in Brahma Street and her mam was a Spurling out of Otley. They washed their hands of her by all accounts when she married Eric, but they changed their tune when Betty

257

came along. She's a grand lass – lass! she must be nearly forty now! Mam's been going to The Towers for years, and I was right pleased when Betty took it over last year! Mrs Collins who ran it before were all right, but she was ancient herself and letting things slide. Betty's making a world of difference. And Mam loves it there and it's a bit of a break for me. Gives me a chance to really bottom this place!'

There were signs everywhere of an enthusiastic November spring-clean about to be commenced.

'A bit of a busman's holiday,' said Pascoe wryly.

'Busman's? Oh aye! I see what you mean. No, I've never minded cleaning, it comes easy to me. But talking of busmen, I'd better get a move on. It all happened so sudden there was half a dozen things Mam forgot to take. Nowt that she can't do without, mind you, but they like to make a fuss! I'm sorry, lad, but can you make your own tea?'

'You mean you're going out there on the bus?' said Pascoe.

'Well, I'm not walking, love!' said Tracey Spillings cheerfully.

Suddenly she eyed him speculatively.

'Of course, if you were happening to be passing that way in that fancy motor of yours, it'd save me a trip and I could make you that tea after all.'

Cheeky cow! thought Pascoe without any real indignation. In fact, he found himself thinking, why not? He'd been wondering intermittently what, if anything, he should do about Andrea's insinuations concerning Mrs Warsop and her former employer. *Pass them to Headingley* was the obvious answer, except that Headingley had been warned off the Dalziel affair and was likely to respond to any new information with an answer even more obvious.

Now, nudged by the coincidence that Tracey Spillings's old mam had clearly been slipped into the space vacated by Philip Westerman, Pascoe found himself unable to resist the temptation to meddle. The kind of bother Dalziel seemed to be in clearly went a lot further than just the question of his involvement in Westerman's death.

'All right,' he said. 'You're on. I'll take them.'

'Could you? That'd be grand! It'd really save me half a day,' said Tracey Spillings. 'Mind you, it's just like a man. Do owt to get out of going into the kitchen!'

She bustled off to make the tea. With her temporary departure, Pascoe became aware just how unfortunate Mrs Spillings Senior's listening habits had been for poor old Bob Deeks. With no masking roar of TV soundtrack, the noises made by Charley Frostick as he moved around next door were quite clear. Tracey Spillings would surely have recognized a pattern different from her old neighbour's usual one and just as surely, being the kind of woman she was, gone to investigate.

He listened carefully, gauging that Charley was upstairs now, probably in the bathroom. There was a distant crash, as of something falling, not too heavily, but with a strangely hollow noise.

Pascoe rose from his chair and moved quietly out of the house. Charley had left the front door of No. 25 ajar. He went in, through the living-room and up the stairs. The bathroom door was open.

Charley was on his hands and knees by the bath. The fibreglass panel which boxed in the end had been removed. It was probably the noise of this as it fell back against the ceramic lavatory pan that had attracted Pascoe. Charley was reaching beneath the bath. He grunted with effort, or more likely with achievement, for now he withdrew his arm.

In his hand was a cardboard shoe-box. Still with his back to the door, he took the top off.

Pascoe took a quiet pace forward but not quiet enough. Charley spun round in alarm and more than alarm, for there were tears on his face. The box fell out of his grip. Across the patterned vinyl floor fluttered a skein of five-pound notes.

'I just wondered if it were still there,' said Charley. 'No one had said anything about it and I just wondered.'

They were sitting downstairs drinking the tea which Mrs Spillings had brought round on discovering Pascoe's departure. Her volubility did not mean she was insensitive to atmosphere and she had withdrawn without demur when Pascoe had thanked her firmly and promised he would collect the stuff for The Towers before he left.

'No one would say anything about it, unless they *knew*,' Pascoe pointed out reasonably. 'Who did know, Charley?'

'What's it matter?' asked the young man. 'It didn't get nicked.'

'Which probably clears anyone who knew,' offered Pascoe.

Charley considered this.

'Oh yeah. I get you,' he said. 'Well, no one knew, as far as I'm concerned. I never told anyone.'

'And how did you know? Did your grandfather tell you?'

It would have been easy for the young man to lie, and for a moment perhaps he considered it. But to his great credit in Pascoe's eyes, he decided against it and said, 'No. It was when he lent me the money for the ring. He told me to wait a bit, then he went upstairs and I heard a noise, it must've been the panel coming off, you've got to spring it and it sort of flies out, so I went half way up the stairs, just far enough to see he was all right.'

'And you saw him replacing the panel, and then he came down with your money?'

'That's right,' said Charley. 'It'll be me mam's money now, won't it?'

'I expect so,' said Pascoe. 'You should have told me about the possibility of its being there before, Charley. You realize that?'

'Yeah, all right. But I wasn't going to nick it, if that's what you're thinking.'

Pascoe believed him. The tears on the boy's face

had been provoked by the presence in the box of several envelopes containing the cash and money orders with which Charley had conscientiously paid off his debt. Such a fond relationship as this had clearly been could not have led to theft.

'We'll say you showed me where it might be hidden, all right?' he said. 'There's about two hundred quid in notes, plus the money orders. Want to check?'

Charley shook his head.

'It'll be kept safe down at the police station for the time being, but your mam will get it all, never fear. Now, is there anything else you want to tell me or show me?'

Charley shook his head.

'OK,' said Pascoe. 'Let's be getting you back. Your mam can have the keys now, I think. You've got the front door one, haven't you? Oh and while I think on, here's the back door key. The one from the wash-house.'

He dug into his pocket and produced the key he'd found in the old boiler in the wash-house.

Charley took it and looked at it, puzzled.

'This isn't it,' he said.

'Isn't what? The back door key? Why do you say that?' asked Pascoe.

'I'm not saying it's not the back door key,' said Charley. 'But it's not the one Granda kept hid in the wash-house.'

'No?' said Pascoe.

He went into the kitchen, the youth following.

'What about this one?' he said, holding up the key which had been in the lock beneath the broken window.

'Aye, that's it. That's the one out of the wash-house,' said Charley.

'Are you sure?'

'Of course I'm sure. That's the way I always came and went, see. Look, it's older and muckier, isn't it? And it's got a number on and this one hasn't.'

It was true. The two keys were readily distinguishable. But did it matter? Charley had been away from home for a few weeks after all. Perhaps the old man himself had swapped the keys round.

Yet if he hadn't, what might it signify?

Much, perhaps, if only he had time to sit and ponder it. Much.

Chapter 22

'If this is dying, I don't think much of it.'

Pascoe's hopes of finding a small square of pondering time vanished when he was greeted at the station with news of the raid on the unlicensed betting shop.

'So he did have money? A lot of money? Great!' he declared, much to the delight of Seymour, who hoped that he was in for a large helping of undeserved credit to compensate for the great dollops of undeserved criticism which were ladled on to a detective-constable's plate with monotonous regularity.

But this was not to be. As Pascoe recounted his interview with Mrs Escott it became clear that he did not hold Seymour innocent of blame.

'So she just lost a day,' said Wield.

'That's right. A possibility you would expect a young detective to admit, who had just been warned that the old lady was having memory problems.'

It had been a mistake to let on that Tempest, the warden, had made any comment on Mrs Escott's mental decline, realized Seymour miserably.

'They're not what they used to be, young detectives,' observed Wield.

'You'll need proper statements now, you realize that?' Pascoe said. 'The waitress who served him, the man in the off-licence.'

Seymour brightened up. His attempts to blarney a date out of Bernadette had failed the previous lunch-time, but he had high hopes that a second assault might weaken resistance.

'Something still puzzles me,' said Pascoe. 'Here's an old lad come into a bit of money, and he's got the spirit and the gumption to lash out on a good meal and a bottle of booze to take home. Now why, on a night like that, does he set off to walk home? Money in his pocket, he could afford a taxi! Or, if that seemed too extravagant, you'd think at the very least he'd catch a bus. A No. 17 would take him from the town centre right to those shops behind Castleton Court, wouldn't it? And how often do they run? Every quarter of an hour, isn't it?'

He looked questioningly at Wield and Seymour. Wield had the face to abide such questions; Seymour felt challenged. He had no answer, but his mind was stimulated to a suggestion offered in hope of a consolation prize.

'Sir, shall I go back and see Mrs Escott again?' he asked.

'For a statement, you mean?' said Pascoe in surprise. 'A statement of what, for God's sake? She can't remember!'

'No, sir,' contradicted Seymour. 'She remembered the wrong day but she remembered it very well. Now, she might still have seen Parrinder on the Friday, mightn't she? Perhaps now she's had time to puzzle it over, something might have come back to her.'

Pascoe doubted it. His own gentle probings had produced a puzzled appreciation that the old lady might have got something wrong, but he had not felt it worth while to risk distressing her by going too hard. And now that 'Tap' Parrinder was definitely placed in the betting shop from 1.45 to 4.30 P.M., he couldn't see what positive contribution any further memories of Mrs Escott could make. On the other hand, he appreciated Seymour's eagerness to regain what he felt as lost credit.

'Worth a try perhaps,' he said. 'But go easy, very easy. She's old and confused. And make damn sure you've got all those statements first!'

After Seymour had gone, Wield looked at Pascoe with something which might have been a smile fissuring his lips.

'He's a good lad,' he said.

'Yes, I know,' said Pascoe. 'He did well to get Charlesworth to cooperate, though I expect he's as keen as anyone to see these illicit shops closed.'

'So it clears the way for his own fiddles, you mean?' said Wield.

'Perhaps, though he was looked at recently and he came out clean.'

'So I believe. Did you know he was such an old chum of the Super's?'

Again that immediate and suggestive association! It was going to be very difficult to prevent Dalziel's friendship and Charlesworth's fortune from going together like fish and chips.

'No, but it does give Mr Dalziel a good reason for dining with him, doesn't it?' he pointed out.

'Aye, but then you'd think he'd have put Mr Dalziel on to this illegal betting shop racket, wouldn't you?' said Wield, who seemed determined to play devil's advocate.

'It was Mr Dalziel who put us on to Charlesworth, remember? I suppose a bookie has got to be careful about fingering others in the same line, even when they're bent. Could be that friend Don will turn out to be financed by some legit firm who might not take kindly to Charlesworth shopping them. Seymour will keep his mouth shut there, I hope.'

'Oh yes. He didn't really want to tell me! I think he rather liked Charlesworth, and *he's* certainly taken a shine to Seymour from the sound of it.'

'Yes,' said Pascoe thoughtfully. 'There was a son, I recall. It was in the local rag a few years back. He seemed bent on raising a bit of hell with his dad's hard-earned cash and ended up getting himself killed in a car smash. He'd be almost Seymour's age.'

'And build too if he took after his dad. And mebbe colouring if he took after his mam.'

Pascoe looked at Wield in surprise.

'You know her?'

'I saw her once in court. Speeding offence. Not long after the lad died. And not long before she and Charlesworth separated. Big red-haired woman. I got the impression she was chasing her lad the best way she knew how. I often wondered if she ran out of steam before she caught up with him.'

Pascoe shook his head glumly. This dying was enough to get a man down. He could just about cope, as everyone had to, with the idea that the car or perhaps the blood clot which was to knock him over was already speeding on its way. But the thought of what his death might mean to Ellie and to Rose was unbearable. Though is that real altruism or just disguised egotism? he asked himself. After all, the pension's not bad, and there's a bit of insurance, and that supercilious, bow-tied historian at the college has always fancied Ellie, and Rose would have lost all memory of me by the time she was two . . .

This morbid train of thought was interrupted by the arrival of Inspector Cruikshank.

'Seems you were right, then,' he congratulated Pascoe, with the smile of a candidate who has just lost his deposit.

'Yes, well, it's got to happen sometimes. Law of averages,' joked Pascoe, careful not to crow in the face of this attempt at magnanimity.

'That's right,' said Cruikshank. 'Oh, by the way, in the caravan that came back from Welfare Lane, there was this bag of stones. Hector told me they were the ones you got him to collect from the recreation ground. I thought, that's Inspector Pascoe! So much on his plate, he's bound to overlook a thing or two. So I've sent them down to Forensic for testing. On CID authority. That all right then?'

Pascoe looked at him with horror, imagining the reaction of the irascible little Scot in charge of the laboratory to the arrival of several dozen stones, unlabelled, all piled together in one bag, with a request for careful and almost certainly non-productive examination.

You rotten sod, Cruikshank! he thought. You wouldn't have dared pull such a stunt if Dalziel had been around!

'Thanks a lot,' he said to Cruikshank. 'Mr Dalziel will be so pleased to find uniformed and CID working so well together. I'll make sure he knows exactly how much you've cooperated, Inspector!'

Which in the circumstances was the best he could do.

Dennis Seymour was also doing his best, but Bernadette McCrystal was more than a match for him. To the vast disapproval of the dragon supervisor, he had insisted that taking her statement was a matter of such urgency that it brooked no delay. Now, in the supervisor's own office, with the statement signed and sealed, he had turned to more personal matters.

'Why won't I go out with you, is it?' she asked. 'Time was when a girl didn't have to offer reasons, but times change and here's three to be going on with. One, you're a policeman and I've got me reputation to be thinking of. Two, you're a Protestant, and I've got me religion to be thinking of.'

'And three?' prompted Seymour.

'Three, I like dancing, *real* dancing I mean, and you look a clumsy, awkward sort of a fellow and I've got me feet to be thinking of.'

'Hold on!' he protested. 'I'm a black belt at the old ballroom.'

'Black belt? That's judo, isn't it?'

'Yeah,' he grinned. 'I'm not so hot on the entrechats, but you won't half fly around the floor.'

She laughed and said, 'All right. I'll give you a two-dance trial. Where are we going?'

'I'll leave that to you,' said Seymour, delighted. 'I'll just choose where we're starting from. The lounge bar at The Portland, eight o'clock tonight.'

'That's a posh kind of place,' she said thoughtfully.

'I reckon you're a posh kind of girl,' said Seymour gallantly.

'Then you're on. Now I'd better get back to cleaning them tables, else she'll be grinding her false teeth to pumice.'

Outside the department store, Seymour stopped to take in a deep breath of wintry air. He felt well satisfied with life. Just as (oh, how these untimely thoughts came sneaking in!) 'Tap' Parrinder must have felt, close to this very spot last Friday. Money in his pocket, food in his belly, nothing to bother him except to decide which off-licence to buy his rum in.

In fact, it occurred to Seymour for the first time, he had a choice of two close at hand. Turning left about a hundred yards along on the opposite side of the road was the off-licence he'd actually used.

But if he'd turned right instead, the very next shop to Starbuck's was a wine and spirit store.

And if his plan had been to walk back to Castleton Court, taking the short cut across the Recreation Ground, then that was the way he should have gone.

It was probably simply explained. Perhaps this wine shop had been closed on Friday evening. It was easy to check. Seymour strolled along and looked at the listed opening hours, then went in to double-check.

No, it had been open.

Perhaps it was a question of choice, or of price? But a glance at the shelves showed the same brand of rum that he'd purchased at the other place, and five pence cheaper at that.

As Seymour made his way to the other off-licence, he recalled Pascoe's puzzlement that a man with money in his pocket should choose to walk home in that weather. Fifty yards further in this direction there was a taxi-rank. Perhaps

Parrinder had determined to get a taxi, but after buying his rum changed his mind. Perhaps there was no taxi free and, impatient of waiting, he had set out on foot.

The man who'd served Parrinder couldn't help. He signed his statement but was unable to say which direction the old man had turned as he left the shop.

Seymour thanked him and walked on to the taxi-rank. His reception swung between opposite poles in the first minute, from being greeted as a customer to being recognized as a cop, but it soon settled at cautious cooperation when the cabbies realized he was not inquiring into their peccadilloes.

It was a quiet time of day and there were seven of them there, all of whom had been on on Friday afternoon, but none of them recalled Parrinder.

'We hardly ever got back here,' explained one of them. 'It was a filthy afternoon; folk who'd never dream of taking a cab normally were flagging us down. You'd no sooner dropped one lot than there was someone else pushing in.'

So probably the rank had been empty and old 'Tap' had made the fatal decision to set off walking.

But Seymour was bent on thoroughness today. No more questions left unasked! He was not going to have Wield's Gothic eyebrows arch up in disbelief or, worse still, Pascoe's leanly handsome features stretch in faint puzzlement as one or the

272

other asked, 'But you didn't actually talk to *all* the cabbies?'

A comprehensive list of those who might have been around on Friday was provided by the now very friendly seven who took him into their shelter and gave him cups of tea, the whiles vying with each other to provide the most remarkable reminiscence of cab-life. An hour later Seymour was awarding the palm to the perhaps valedictory coupling of groom and best man on their way to church, with as a close second the story of the couple who kept the taxi with its meter running outside a bank which, unbeknown to the driver, they were robbing, only later to be caught by the police having a fierce argument about the size of the fare, when a little man called Grundy appeared with a terrible cold which his colleagues told him in plain unadorned terms to keep to himself.

But Grundy when questioned about 'Tap' Parrinder replied instantly, if throatily, 'Yeah, I remember him. Old boy, full of the joys of spring, he were. Told me to drive him to Castleton Court.'

'That's the one,' said Seymour, now very puzzled. 'You didn't see what he did when he got to Castleton Court, did you?'

'No, I didn't,' snuffled Grundy. 'Mainly because I wasn't there.'

'You weren't there?'

'We never got to Castleton Court, see?' proclaimed the catarrhal cabbie. 'I was driving steadily along through the rain when suddenly he yells out,

'All right! Stop here! This'll do!' so I stops, and out he gets, there was eighty-five p. on the clock and he gives me a quid and that's the last I see of him.'

'You don't know why he changed his mind?'

'I don't know. I thought maybe he just realized how much it was costing him. Could be it was his last quid, poor old sod. If he'd said something, like, I'd have run him home all the same. It wasn't a night for putting a cat out.'

He sneezed violently. Seymour averted his face in a hopeless attempt at evasion.

'And where was this?' he asked.

'Where he got out, you mean? Right outside the Alderman Woodhouse Recreation Ground.'

Seymour knew he was putting his health at grave risk by getting into a cab driven by a man with a cold like Grundy's, but when a bout of sneezing almost had them on to the pavement, he realized that germs might be the least of his worries.

It was with great relief that he got out at the spot which Grundy assured him was as near the point of Parrinder's departure as made no difference.

As an exercise in reconstruction in the event it didn't seem to have very much point. Grundy repeated his story without alteration. He also pointed out that, as stated, there was eighty-five pence on the clock, and looked significantly at his passenger.

Assuring him that he would later want a full

statement, Seymour paid up. The cab drew away, leaving him in the gathering dusk looking into the uninviting gloom of the recreation ground. But it was not as uninviting as it must have been two hours later in last Friday's weather. What had possessed the man? he wondered.

He entered the ground, determined to see his reconstruction through to the end. Pascoe and Wield would not be able to claim he had left any stone unturned! The cliché reminded him of Hector and his famous sack. A joke it had seemed at the time of collecting, and a waste of time too. But now, with the certainty of assault and robbery of an old man looming large in his mind, there seemed little to laugh at. And indeed, as he walked slowly across the recreation ground and the few figures still visible seemed very distant, and the lights beginning to glow along the roads at the park's edge were like camp-fires in some vague valley seen from a perilous hill, he found himself wishing for the company even of a twit like Hector.

A few minutes later he had made the crossing without the experience of either assault or inspiration and his remembered fears made him feel ashamed.

Castleton Court lay not far ahead. It seemed a good opportunity to pay another visit to Mrs Escott, though later reflection had brought him to much the same conclusion as Pascoe: i.e., that it was not likely to prove of any profit.

Still, he told himself with the good-natured perception of a favourite grandchild, a visit would most likely be welcome, be rewarded with a hot drink against the chill November air and Grundy's germs. Also it occurred to him that the old lady might well need cheering up if she herself had realized her error of recall.

He let his big, cheerful, reassuring smile slide across his face as he pressed the doorbell, but when no reply came to a second and prolonged pressing, the smile faded.

Oh well, he thought, she was probably out shopping. Try again later.

He turned away, then on impulse turned back and went to Mrs Campbell's door. Here again he thought he was out of luck, but just as he was giving up the door opened cautiously on the chain and Lucy Campbell's bold, handsome face appeared.

She recognized him instantly, which was surprisingly flattering.

'It's Mr Seymour, isn't it? How are you?'

'Well,' he said. 'Look, I'm sorry to disturb you, but it's Mrs Escott I was looking for. She's not at home and I just thought she might have popped in here.'

'No, no,' said Mrs Campbell. 'I saw her a little earlier this afternoon coming in. She looked a little *distrait*, I recall, hardly even looked at me when I said hello. But she's been like that, off and on, recently, poor dear.'

'And she went into her flat?'

'Oh yes. And shut the door rather emphatically.'

There was a pause while they both reflected.

'I think I'd better get the warden,' said Seymour finally.

'Please, wait a moment,' said Mrs Campbell.

She closed the door to undo the chain, then opened it wide.

'Come in,' she said. 'Mr Tempest is in fact visiting me. He's been repairing a window-catch and I asked him to have a cup of tea.'

Mr Tempest was in fact standing in front of the fireplace, an expression of some uneasiness on his round, open face. There was no tea in sight.

Seymour wondered why Mrs Campbell had felt it necessary to put the chain on the door before she opened, then blushed furiously as the outrageous explanation presented itself.

Not at their age! his suddenly puritanical young mind protested.

But Mr Tempest's unease was quickly redirected when he heard Seymour's story.

'She's likely just gone out again, or mebbe having a nap, but we'd best just check,' he said, producing his master key.

The living-room was empty. Seymour looked into the kitchen while Tempest opened the bedroom door.

'Oh Christ!' he heard the warden choke out.

He pushed past him into the room.

Across the bed surrounded by a scatter of pill bottles lay Jane Escott. Her eyes were wide open and staring, but it was not possible to tell if she were alive or dead.

Chapter 23

'There is treachery, O Ahaziah.'

Approached at night through an avenue of skeletal trees which Walt Disney might have designed, The Towers was a sinister sight, more suited to the incisive antics of venereal vampirism than to the careful cradling of reposing age. Their crenellated teeth snatching at a wild November moon, the ungainly asymmetric structures which gave the house its name impressed Pascoe with that sense of foreboding frequently enjoyed by heroines of Gothic romance as they approached some three-volume test of their nerve and their virtue.

All it needed, thought Pascoe, was for the old brass-studded oaken front door to creak open at his approach and a corpse-like figure to glide forward and beckon him in.

He set his foot on the doorstep. The door swung slowly open with a small but indisputable creak and there indeed was a figure, if not corpse-like, at least at an advanced stage of rehearsal of that condition.

It glided forward and spoke.

'Are you the undertaker's man?' it asked in a querulous tone. ''Cos if so, you're not wanted. She's got better.'

'Thank you, Mr Wilson,' said Miss Day's patient and kindly voice. 'I'll look after this. Oh hello. It's Mr Pascoe, isn't it?'

'That's right,' said Pascoe, shaking the matron's hand and looking after the retreating Mr Wilson who in the light of the hallway now appeared as simply a white-haired old gent with a glissading style of ambulation caused by a dilapidated pair of carpet slippers.

'What was all that about?' he asked.

'Mr Wilson? Oh, one of our ladies was taken ill. A bad bout of indigestion was all it was, but she looked very poorly for a while. Another of our lady guests has a distant cousin in the undertaking business and at the slightest sign of decline, she's off to the telephone, presumably to assure the poor man that if he turns up here with a coffin, there'll be work for him to do!'

'And Mr Wilson?'

'He hates her. He's convinced that she's been in his room at night measuring him up.'

She laughed and Pascoe joined in.

'Don't get the impression we're all as odd as that, Mr Pascoe,' she said. 'Most of them here are just plain, straightforward people, whatever that means! But they're all at the time of life when the cracks begin to show. Usually it doesn't matter. Sometimes, though, it can be very painful.'

'Yes, I know,' said Pascoe soberly, thinking of Mrs Escott.

The news of her attempted suicide had been one of the things which had delayed his visit here. When Seymour had rung in from the hospital, he had felt incredibly guilty. It was irrational, he knew. He and Ellie had often discussed the putative right of individuals to determine when they died and though he was not quite so emphatic about it as Ellie, they generally agreed that such a right existed. So Mrs Escott, becoming aware that senility was creeping up on her, had decided to exit with dignity. Only, she hadn't exited. And Pascoe was left with the memory of the apparently content and cogent woman he had spoken to, happily unaware till his interference that she had managed to forget a whole day.

'I'm sorry to call so late,' he began.

Miss Day interrupted him with some exasperation.

'It's only eight-thirty, Mr Pascoe. We don't sound lights out at nine, you know. This is neither a hospital, nor a nursery, nor an army barracks!'

'Sorry, sorry,' said Pascoe. 'What I really meant was that I hope old Mrs Spillings hasn't been creating because her things didn't turn up earlier.'

He held up the bag which Tracey Spillings had given him.

'No, not a word. She's settled in front of the telly and hasn't moved. Thanks, I'll see she gets it. Was that all, Mr Pascoe? You're just a messenger boy?'

'From each according to his ability, Miss Day,' murmured Pascoe.

'I'm sorry,' she said. 'I didn't mean to be rude. I know from old experience that when Tracey's around, people find themselves doing odd things!'

'Yes, she does rather take over, doesn't she?' grinned Pascoe. 'But while I'm here, I'd quite like a word with Mrs Warsop, if she's around.'

'Sorry, you've just missed her. She went out about half an hour ago. Can I help?'

Something about the way in which she made this offer caught Pascoe's attention. Years of playing the rapier to Dalziel's bludgeon in the interrogation room had developed in him a keen ear for the nuances of response. Often there was a rigid barrier between what a witness was willing to volunteer and what he was willing to reveal under questioning. The interviewer had to be alert to these tonal signals which said *ask me this and I shall reply, but if you keep silent, so shall I.*

He said, 'Is there somewhere we can talk for a moment?'

She led him into an office made homely by chintzy curtains, Constable reproductions, and a pair of wing-chairs set round a coffee table. It all smacked of a conscious care to put any of the residents who visited her here at their ease, a theory empirically confirmed when he sat down and found that the cushion was several inches higher than expected to facilitate sitting and rising for old limbs.

He guessed that Mrs Warsop's office would be designed on different lines.

'Miss Day,' he said, 'how long have you been doing this job?'

'At The Towers? Nearly a year now. I've been with the social service department a lot longer of course, since I left school in fact, if you count training periods. I was running one of the residential homes in town before this job fell vacant.'

'Were you asked to come here or did you apply?' wondered Pascoe, letting his instinct direct the questioning.

'Oh, I asked. It surprised some people, but I think it's a good thing to move around in any field, don't you? I know that you've got to stay in one job long enough to be able to do it right, but if you stay too long you risk becoming complacent, don't you agree?'

She spoke earnestly. Pascoe nodded, certain he was on the right track.

'Your predecessor here, had she been here a long time?'

'Miss Collins? Oh yes. Donkey's years! Much longer and she'd have been older than some of the residents!' she laughed.

'And Mrs Warsop?'

'Seven or eight years,' said Miss Day. 'I think

she'd been bursar at some girls' boarding-school before, so in some ways it must have been a change for her too.'

'So you had to slot in with many old and well-established routines, I suppose?' said Pascoe.

'Yes. Well, you don't go rushing in like a mad thing, do you? You take your time, change what needs to be changed gradually.'

'Quite right,' approved Pascoe. 'You are in over-all charge, are you? Or do you and Mrs Warsop rank equal in respect of your different areas?'

'No. On paper I'm in charge. But after eight years Mrs Warsop is naturally rather possessive of her side of things.'

'Possessive,' said Pascoe. 'Or protective, perhaps?'

'Protective?'

'Defensive. Miss Day, you and I are both public servants and both sensible of the need to tread carefully.' Pascoe hesitated, then plunged. 'Let me ask you a hypothetical question. If there were anything not quite right in the financial management of The Towers, would you be certain of your ability to detect it?'

The woman gave this careful thought.

'Sooner or later, yes,' she said. 'But probably later. And always at the risk of giving sufficient warning for any mismanagement to be halted and the tracks leading to it obliterated. I'll be honest, Mr Pascoe. I've got big plans or at least big hopes. I want to be helping to shape policy about our whole approach to caring for the elderly before I finish. So I've got to move carefully until I'm sure. And I'm far from sure. Look, can I be completely frank?'

Pascoe nodded. Words might be dangerous.

'I don't much like Mrs Warsop. I know it. I don't know why. I don't think it's anything to do with her being, well, *gay*, though that seems a silly word for her, but *lesbian* sounds sort of critical, I always feel. Anyway, I don't think that's it, though it might be part of it. There's none of us quite as liberal as we like to think, is there?'

'No,' said Pascoe, interested at this unsolicited (though as yet unsupported) confirmation of part of Andrea Gregory's Parthian malice.

'But that's irrelevant to her job here, of course. Though it might have been a bit of a strain in a girls' boarding-school. Miaow! Excuse me, Mr Pascoe. But when you're like me, biggish, pushy, and unmarried in your late thirties, you get used to people regarding you as butch. Whereas once you get the *Mrs* tag, even if it's just a label left over from an eighteen-month marriage and a relieved divorce, society offers sympathy and assistance. All right. So men see you as an easy target, but at least they don't see you as a dangerous competitor!'

'To return to Mrs Warsop,' said Pascoe gently, feeling the time had come for a nudge before Betty Day talked herself out of talking. 'What you're saying is, you suspect a fiddle, but also suspect your own motives in suspecting. Right?'

She looked at him steadily for a moment and then nodded her head.

'You've hit it precisely,' she said. 'And you, Inspector. What's *your* interest in all this?'

'Just interest, so far,' he said. 'A long way from a formal investigation. A vague allegation, a supportive circumstance, and now your own gut-feeling, if you'll excuse the phrase. There's a long way to go, Miss Day. So, for starters, why not tell me about this possible fiddle?'

The approach to Paradise Hall was by no means as Gothic as that to The Towers but the white face and shadowed eyes of Stella Abbiss would not have been out of place in a Transylvanian castle.

She had seen him hesitating at the dining-room door and after a short delay while she finished serving a table, she came to join him.

'I don't expect you want to eat,' she said.

Pascoe sniffed the rich odours drifting from the kitchen.

'Alas,' he said. 'A light purse develops simple tastes. A loaf of bread. A flask of wine.'

She frowned and said, 'Is it me or Jeremy you want?'

Pascoe did not reply. His eyes had moved away from that face, so sensual with suffering, into the dining-room. It was half full, not bad for so early in the week, he guessed. But what really took his attention was the presence of Doreen Warsop. She was seated at a table for two in front of one of the windows. Her companion was a young woman with frizzy blonde hair who was indulging in the disgusting habit of smoking between courses. Not that she'd had much of a course if the pile of food on her plate was to be completely abandoned. Probably eight or nine quid's worth there, assessed Pascoe. There were probably hungry people in Chinese takeaways who'd be glad of it. He got the impression that Mrs Warsop, who was persevering with her pheasant with truffles, did not take kindly to having smoke puffed in her face.

He said, 'He's in the kitchen, is he?'

'Yes. Very busy. Like me.'

There were in fact two girls serving, one of them looking suspiciously young. Pascoe tried to recollect the law on children's working hours, but quickly abandoned the attempt. His purpose here was vague and delicate enough already without risking unnecessary diversion.

'Right, I'll go through,' he said.

'Is it a raid?' demanded Jeremy Abbiss as Pascoe entered the kitchen. 'Pray God it's a raid and I can abandon this devil's kitchen for a simple monastic cell!'

'What's up? Have you got the *zabaglione* gang in again?'

'What? Oh. You remembered! No, in fact, things would be fine, only our idiot girl from the village is being assisted by her even less gifted sister. She keeps getting lost between here and the further tables!'

'Worse than the girl you fired, is she?' asked Pascoe idly.

'Infinitely, though it grieves me to say it. At least dear Miss Andrea had all her marbles, it was just her morals and motivation that were in doubt.'

'Morals? You were concerned for her essential purity, no doubt?'

'No!' laughed Abbiss, chopping a tomato with incredible speed. 'I do not set myself up as an arbiter of private pleasures, though I must say I draw a line at some things. There was this bloody soldier she used to bring back, spent all night here sometimes; well, that was pretty cheeky, but when I came down early one morning and caught him taking a final soldier's farewell across the reception desk, I felt that things were getting out of hand! When I remonstrated he didn't even stop, just told me over his shoulder to get lost! I mean, really!'

Pascoe grinned at the thought of young Charley's youthful energy. He probably had to run all the way back to camp too, in an exhausted state! Still, a sergeant-major's wrath is straw to the fire in the blood.

'But it wasn't the screwing, as long as she didn't do it in the dining-room and frighten the customers; it was the way things tended to fade away around her. Half a bottle of Scotch here, a couple of quid there, nothing startling, nothing provable. And she acted as if she wasn't really employed here at all, but just doing a favour by helping out.

Enough's enough. At last we quarrelled beyond repair.'

The infant idiot came in, allowed Abbiss to present her with a bowl of salad, then looked around hopefully for the door.

Abbiss ushered her out, rolling his eyes upward in mute appeal.

'So, tell me, Mr Pascoe,' he resumed. 'Why have you come to see me? More questions about your fat friend?'

'Indirectly,' said Pascoe. 'You remember last time we talked, I mentioned Mrs Warsop.'

'Who?' asked Abbiss, now at work on a cucumber. There was, Pascoe noted, coincident with Mrs Warsop's name, a slice a couple of millimetres thicker than the others.

Encouraged, he pressed on.

'The bursar at The Towers. I'm sure you know her. In fact she's dining here tonight. Shall I perhaps call her in?'

'I don't think we need disturb the customers,' said Abbiss primly. 'What about her anyway?'

'At first she was certain she'd observed Mr Dalziel driving his car away. Later she became unsure.'

'A woman's privilege.'

'I tend to seek less sexist explanations,' said Pascoe.

'Such as?'

'Perhaps someone persuaded her to change her mind.'

'Good lord. You mean the portly gent bribed her?' said Abbiss in mock amazement.

'I doubt it,' said Pascoe.

'Because he's a policeman and water doesn't flow uphill?'

'Because Mr Dalziel is not by nature a briber,' said Pascoe calmly. 'As for Mrs Warsop, she doesn't look like a lady who's short of money. Eating here twice in five days, for instance. It is only twice, is it?'

The door from the dining-room opened and Stella Abbiss came in. She had a trayful of plates in her hands. She set it down by the sink and made no move to go out again.

'Precisely what are you trying to say, Inspector?' asked Abbiss. His face had lost a bit of colour. Another half-hour teasing this man and I could make them a matching pair, thought Pascoe. But now he was convinced of the truth, he was tired of the game. There would be specialists to work through records and accounts and unravel the woof and warp of the fraud. He felt almost sorry for Abbiss. It probably didn't amount to all that much, though any saving must be tempting when margins were narrow.

On the other hand, it was his sad experience that fiddling was zymotic; it would be no surprise to learn that every area of Abbiss's business dealings had been tainted.

'It is my considered opinion,' said Pascoe carefully, 'that you suggested to Mrs Warsop that it might not be a very clever idea for her to get in bad with the police by pursuing her claim that Superintendent Dalziel was driving the car. She admits she did not know that Mr Dalziel was a policeman until after she had spoken to the Press. Suddenly your hotel must have seemed very full of the Law, Mr Abbiss. The quickest way to get rid of them must have seemed to be to get Mr Dalziel off the hook. Hence your advice. But why should you be worried and why should Mrs Warsop be advised by you? Could it be that the pair of you have a business relationship you would prefer not to come under the risk of scrutiny? Could this be why she gets to eat here so regularly and is able to sign her bill?'

'She gets an account like anybody else,' protested Abbiss.

'In which case your records will show this, as will her own cheque-stubs and bank statement.'

'But often she pays by cash anyway,' tried Abbiss desperately.

'You mean she often pays her restaurant bill by cash? How often?'

'For Christ's sake, how am I expected to remember something like that?'

'Well, we'll just have to consult your staff about that, shan't we?' said Pascoe. 'See what *their* memories are like!'

Suddenly Abbiss's expression changed to one of shocked enlightenment, his chopping knife rose in the air and came hissing down on a capsicum which it clove apart with such violence that the halves shot off the table. One hit the floor. The other, Pascoe caught in an instinctive reaction.

'It's that little cow, isn't it? That's why you were so bloody interested in talking about her! It's really coming to something when a slut like that who gets the push for dishonesty should be allowed to blacken other people's names! The poxy little whore, if I ever get my hands on her . . .'

It was interesting to detect a definite strain of Mersey-side emerging in Abbiss's speech under emotional pressure.

Pascoe put the capsicum half on the table.

'Good night, Mr Abbiss,' he said courteously.

He went to the dining-room door and peered out. He was uncertain yet whether he ought to talk to Mrs Warsop too at this juncture. As he looked, the frizzy-haired girl who was listening with a bored expression to what looked like a lengthy remonstration from her companion suddenly stubbed her cigarette out in the other's pheasant, rose and left the dining-room. After an agitated moment, Mrs Warsop followed her.

That made up Pascoe's mind. A wise cop didn't get involved in domestics if he could help it.

Stella Abbiss followed him to the front door.

'What happens?' she asked.

He looked at her and shrugged.

'Out of my hands,' he said.

'Does it have to be?'

She spoke flatly but there was no possibility of ambiguity.

Pascoe looked sadly at this pale, shining woman with her cloud of black hair and her dark tragic eyes which were yet sharp enough to have penetrated his fantasies. Did she honestly believe they were realizable? His gaze moved behind her to the reception desk against which Abbiss had discovered Charley Frostick socking it to Andrea. He nodded.

It occurred to him that this was certainly ambiguous.

He said firmly, 'Yes, it has to be,' and went out into the car park.

Chapter 24

'Pluck up thy spirits, man, and do not
be afraid to do thine office.'

At seven o'clock the following morning Pascoe was
roused by the telephone. When he answered it, the
familiar foghorn at the other end made him think
for a moment that all was as it had been and he
was merely receiving another urgent summons to
another urgent case.

'Peter,' said Dalziel. 'You still in bed, you lazy
bugger?'

'Where else?' he yawned.

'You alone?'

'Ellie's still not back,' he answered regretfully.

'Oh aye. But are you alone?'

'Ha ha,' said Pascoe, waking up now. 'Sir, to
what do I owe the . . .'

'Peter, I hear you're piling a bit of trouble on
Paradise Hall.'

'Do you? Now, how on earth . . .'

'Forget it, Peter.'

'*What?*'

'Forget it.'

'But . . .'

'Peter, I'm still in charge, aren't I? I mean, they haven't made you commissioner and me the tea-boy, have they?'

'No, of course . . .'

'Then forget it. That's an order. All right?'

Pascoe was amazed. He said, 'As a subordinate, I suppose it's all right though I'll need to think about it. As a friend . . .'

'A friend. You want for us to talk as friends?' said Dalziel.

'Yes, sir. If you'll make the effort, then I will.'

'All right,' said Dalziel. 'Then *please* forget it.'

The phone went dead.

It rang an hour later just as he was getting ready to leave. This time it was Ellie.

'I rang last night,' she said.

'I'm sorry. I was a bit late.'

'Too late to ring me?'

'No. Well, yes. I didn't want to disturb you.'

The truth was he'd had a drink when he got home, switched on the ten o'clock news and awakened in the armchair with a crick in his neck, a nasty taste in his mouth and the TV switch-off tone in his ears.

'How is everything?' he asked.

'Pretty bloody,' she said in a worryingly flat voice. 'He went off last evening, just disappeared.

I found him outside the library. It was quarter to nine. He said he was waiting for it to open at nine.'

'Poor old devil,' said Pascoe, genuinely distressed at his father-in-law's confusion, but also with a slight sense of comedy. This vanished rapidly with Ellie's next remark.

'Peter,' she said hopelessly. 'I don't know what to do.'

This was truly horrifying, more shocking far than the vagaries of senility. With a sudden flash of insight, he appreciated that Ellie was to his personal life what Dalziel was to his professional, a bulwark of certainty, often wrong, it was true, and frequently in need of diplomatic redirection, but always high on self-assurance and low on self-doubt.

She went on, 'He's not going to get any better, I can see that now. And as he gets worse, he's going to need more and more looking after and I'm not sure Mum can cope. She just seems to want to sit and play with Rose all day and pretend that nothing's happening. Peter, what am I going to do?'

Well, here's your chance, boy, here's your big moment, thought Pascoe. The perfect soap-opera situation: the modern, independent, feminist wife is at last forced to appeal to the big strong man in her life for strength and guidance; he is silent, but even his silence is reassuring; the hunter-provider, fleet of foot and rational of thought, is about to pronounce.

He said, 'Christ knows. I mean, it's pretty much of a mess, isn't it? I mean, I can see what . . .'

He took a deep breath, exhaled, blowing the remnants of hunter-provider out of his system, and said, 'Why don't I pop down and suss things out on the spot, so to speak?'

'Peter, could you? That'd be bloody marvellous! When?'

Heady with rapturously-applauded decision and suddenly filled with a huge need to see Ellie again, he said carelessly, 'This afternoon? Why not? I'll stay overnight, but I'll have to be up at the crack to get back here for slopping-out time.'

They spent a few more minutes promising an exchange of delights which left Pascoe feeling weak with desire and he needed another two cups of caponizing coffee before he felt able to go to work.

Getting away after lunch proved easier than mature reflection on the way to the station had suggested it might be. Like nearly all working detectives, he had no shortage of back-time; what was rare was the front-time to take it up in. Today, despite his two murders (the death of 'Tap' Parrinder now being acknowledged officially as a likely unlawful killing) there occurred one of those lulls in which everything possible to do was being, or had been, done and nothing remained but to wait hopefully for a break and catch up with the paperwork.

There was also a pleasing absence of brass about

the place, and with Sergeant Wield and George Headingley happy to watch the shop for him, Pascoe felt no pangs of conscience at baling out after lunch in the CID's usual city haunt, The Black Bull.

He bought Wield and Headingley a third pint, contenting himself with a pre-driving tomato juice, and told them of his visit to The Towers and Paradise Hall the previous evening. He also told them of Dalziel's injunction, which he had obeyed though not without misgivings.

Wield interrupted his story during his description of Doreen Warsop and her companion at the restaurant.

'You're not saying that being lesbian means she's more likely to be a crook?' he said mildly.

'Well, no,' said Pascoe. 'I didn't mean to imply that.'

'It sounded like you were offering it as supportive evidence, that was all,' said Wield.

'Not intended, except in so far as treating her friends to expensive meals for which she didn't have to pay is supportive,' said Pascoe, rather irritated by what felt like an attack on his liberal convictions.

Wield nodded his acceptance. Such gentle forays as this were the nearest he ever came in his professional life to declaring his own homosexuality. When he first joined the Force, there had been no debate about concealment. But time and times had changed things, and now, though he did not delude himself that coming out would not still harm his own career, he felt a growing dissatisfaction with the path of secrecy he had chosen, and now these minor skirmishes tended to feel like acts of cowardice rather than courage.

When Pascoe finished his account, there was silence. He neither invited nor desired them to comment on Dalziel's intervention. His reasons for telling them he freely acknowledged; should it ever come to an inquiry, it might stand him in good stead to produce albeit secondhand support for his contention that he was obeying legitimate orders. He felt something of the same kind of self-revulsion in this as Wield was feeling after his little defence of Mrs Warsop. But he also had a career to consider and a wife and family to provide for. His loyalty to Dalziel was strong but there were loyalties which had to be stronger.

Seymour came into the pub as he was leaving. Rather to Pascoe's surprise, he said he had just come from the hospital.

'I don't think Mrs Escott can really have anything useful to tell us,' Pascoe said gently.

The young constable flushed and said, 'I just wanted to see how she was, sir.'

Pascoe thought: Of course, he talked to her first, and he found her. He feels guilty.

His own guilt had rapidly been overtaken by a tide of other emotions closer to home. Compassion was a small flame, needing care and attention

and protection from the wind. Perhaps the professional carers' first object was to preserve what
they sensed as precious in themselves.

What should a policeman's first object be, then?
To remain honest, perhaps. But being compassionate helped.

He said, 'Quite right, Dennis. Well done. How is
the old lady?'

Seymour said, 'Just the same. Out of danger
from the pills she took, but still in shock from
the experience and Dr Sowden says that can be
just as dangerous.'

'Sowden?' Pascoe smiled. 'Well, she's in good
hands. Keep me posted, lad.'

Lad! he thought as he left. I'm beginning to talk
to them as if I were Dalziel!

Seymour bought himself a pint and a pie and sat
some distance from Wield and Headingley. Rela-
tions in the CID under Dalziel were easy and open,
which meant that detective-constables could with
no offence given or taken be told to sod off if their
company was not desired. At the present moment,
the Sergeant and Inspector were cautiously analys-
ing what Pascoe had just told them about Dalziel's
intervention, a conversation they would certainly
not have continued in Seymour's presence. But it
was his own depression as much as his diplomatic
sensors that made the young detective sit apart.

His previous night's date had not gone well. The
gloom of discovering Mrs Escott and getting her to

the hospital and hanging around till she had been pumped out was still on him. He had begged off going dancing, attempting an explanation which sounded self-indulgently prima-donna-ish even to his own ears. Bernadette had been sympathetic enough but made it quite clear as she brought the evening to an early though friendly close that their short acquaintance did not include access to her shoulders for crying on, still less any other part of her anatomy for any other purpose.

He couldn't blame her. He knew what a dull companion he had been and he hadn't even bothered to suggest another date, being so certain of her negative response. Today he should have been off duty but he had gloomed around all morning, visited the hospital when he might simply have phoned, and drifted by instinct into The Black Bull, where he felt quite unable now to distinguish between feeling sorry for Mrs Escott and feeling sorry for himself.

'What's up with you, then? Too much beer last night?'

It was Wield, who had sat unnoticed on the chair opposite. Headingley was disappearing through the door.

'No, not really, Sarge,' he said.

'You did well yesterday,' said Wield. 'Mr Pascoe was very pleased with you.'

'Was he?' said Seymour, brightening up a little.

'I just said so,' said Wield. 'If you want to hear

it again, you should have got it on tape. Isn't this your rest day?'

'Yes, Sarge.'

'Well, at least you're getting a bit of rest,' approved Wield. 'Not like most of 'em, moonlighting away like mad. You had any more thoughts?'

'About what?'

'About why a man with three hundred quid in his pocket should suddenly decide to get out of his taxi in a sleet storm and walk the rest of the way home?'

'Well, I did think about it a bit,' said Seymour. 'I don't know. Mebbe someone was following him, someone who saw him pick up his winnings, and he was trying to shake 'em off, or something.'

Wield considered this.

'You watch a lot of television, do you, Seymour?' he inquired.

'If you can think of anything better, Sarge, I'm listening,' Seymour was stung to retort.

Wield shook his head.

'Not yet, but I'm working at it. Well, I'd best be getting back. We're checking up on everyone we can trace who was in the betting shop on Friday afternoon. It's a weary business.'

'I'll give a hand if you like, Sarge,' volunteered Seymour.

The sergeant smiled wintrily.

'I don't know what this police force is coming to,' he said. 'Mr Pascoe gives himself half a day off and you give yourself half a day on. But I'll not come between a martyr and his crown. You want to help, you'll be very welcome. On one condition.'

'What's that, Sarge?'

'Contact that girl of yours and find out whether it's still on or you've parted for ever. There's enough misery in the world without me having to look it in the face all afternoon!'

Coming from Wield, whose face even in the fullness of joy was not a sight to dwell on, this might have seemed an unjust reproach. But Seymour, whose nature was not a brooding one, took it as a spur to action.

There was a telephone in the entrance hall of the pub. He rang, asked for the restaurant, got the dragon, requested that Miss McCrystal should be brought to the phone. She demurred. He became official, told her that the case was a serious one and a piece of clarification from Miss McCrystal essential.

'Hello?' said Bernadette. 'You'll get me shot!'

'I'm sorry. Look, I just wanted to say, sorry I was such a drag last night.'

'That's true. So you were,' she said not very encouragingly. 'How's the old lady?'

'Sorry?' ——

'You've been to see her, I hope?' said Bernadette threateningly.

'Well, yes. I went to the hospital this morning. She's not very well, I'm afraid.'

'The poor old soul. Right, listen now, *my* old

lady's glowering like the heart of a peat. Is it about tonight you're ringing?'

'Well, yes . . .'

'Then you're in luck. Wednesday's old-time night at the Eldorado. I'll see you outside at eight. Can you manage that?'

'Well, yes . . .'

'And you'll need a tie. You've got a tie, have you?'

'Yes, somewhere . . .'

'Then eight it is. Goodbye now, Chief Inspector.'

She put the phone down.

Wield watched Seymour return into the bar and did not need more than the young man's expressive face to tell him all was well. He tested his own memory and knew that such joy as this he had never known. Love there had been, and on occasion high delight, but always qualified by the demands of secrecy and, in his conventional and restrictive youth, the taint of guilt.

'Will you have another beer, Sarge?' said Seymour, eager to spread his joy.

'Some other time, lad,' said Wield. 'There's work to be done. We'll have it later. Pleasure's best if you've had to wait, right?'

Which could be the story of my life; with a bit of luck; he thought as they left the pub together.

Pascoe and Ellie too had to wait for their pleasure. Even with the early hours kept in the Soper household, it seemed an eternity from their first embrace until they were at last alone in the narrow confines of Ellie's childhood bed. Neither of them complained about the narrowness, though Ellie was concerned for various reasons about the speed and violence of her husband's orgasm.

'Hey,' she said. 'It's a good job I caught you, wasn't it? Another day away, and God knows what you'd have been up to! Who's been tickling your fancy these past few days, then?'

It did not seem a ripe moment to mention, even jocularly, the consumptive queen of Paradise Hall, so Pascoe murmured, 'I missed you.'

'Almost,' she agreed. 'But you'll get another chance in the *repêchage*. There is going to be a *repêchage*, isn't there?'

'We try to please,' said Pascoe.

They lay in silence for a while and thoughts of the outside world and its time drifted back into Pascoe's mind. From his point of view it had been a delightful day. Besides Ellie's unconcealed joy at seeing him, there had been Rose's delighted gurgles of recognition. As for his parents-in-law, they had seemed much the same as always. In fact, on the same principle which soothes away toothache at the dentist's or engine squeaks at the garage, Mr Soper had been alert and cogent all evening. Ellie had scarcely referred to the situation, being in the unenviable position of wanting Pascoe to see for himself while at the same time not really wanting anything to happen for him to see.

'Penny for them,' said Ellie.

'Is that your best offer?' evaded Pascoe.

Before Ellie could press him further, there came a knock at the door.

'Ellie! Ellie!' called Mrs Soper's voice.

'Jesus!'

Ellie snapped the light on and headed for the door, grabbing the coverlet for cover en route. Pascoe followed, slipping into his dressing-gown.

'What's up, Mum?'

'He's gone,' said Mrs Soper.

'Gone. Oh Christ. Peter, get the car out. How long ago, Mum?'

'No, it's all right, you don't need the car, I think he's just gone down into the garden. He said he heard a noise and thought that someone was trying to break into the greenhouse.'

'Right,' said Pascoe, relieved that it was perhaps after all a case for the police rather than medical investigation. 'I'll get down there and take a look.'

'What at?' demanded Ellie. 'He hasn't got a greenhouse. It's twenty-five years since he had a greenhouse.'

This changed matters slightly, but the principle of rapid descent held good. Pascoe ran quickly down the stairs, through the kitchen and out of the back door. The cold night wind struck his thinly covered flesh like a water cannon, making him gasp. He could see a figure moving around at the bottom of the garden and he headed towards it, hoping the old man had had the time and sense to put on more clothes than he had.

Behind him he heard Ellie say sharply, 'Mother, you stay there.' He went quickly forward. Archie Soper, his father-in-law, was standing still now, peering intensely into a small patch of shrubbery. He had an old raincoat draped around his body and was carrying a walking-stick in his right hand.

'Archie,' said Pascoe. 'For God's sake . . .'

The old man turned with surprising agility. His face showed no recognition.

'There you are!' he cried. And swung the stick at Pascoe's head.

He managed to duck and raise his arm to ward off the blow, but only at the expense of taking a painful crack on the elbow. But now Ellie was here, crying 'Dad! Dad!' and putting her arms around the old man whose ferocity dissolved into confusion as he let himself be led back towards the house.

Inside the kitchen, Ellie bustled around, checking that her father was all right, putting the kettle on, disappearing into the lounge to stoke up the fire, returning to say that it was much warmer in there and helping her father out of the kitchen with a command over her shoulder to bring the tea through with lots of sugar as soon as it was ready.

Madge Soper had stood around making vague reassuring noises at her husband during all this and now she obediently began to warm the teapot. Her behaviour seemed at first sight to confirm Ellie's assertion that she could no longer cope.

This had surprised Pascoe. She was nearly ten years younger than her husband and had always seemed a perfectly competent if rather self-effacing person.

He touched his elbow and winced.

Mrs Soper noticed and came across to him.

'Oh Peter, did he get you with that stick? Let's have a look. He didn't mean it, he just gets confused. All those years since the greenhouse blew down and now he remembers it! It's not cut. There's nothing broken, is there?'

Pascoe pulled down his sleeve. There was going to be a bruise, but nothing worse.

'Has he attacked anyone before?' he asked.

'Oh no! I mean, he was looking for a burglar, wasn't he? And he saw you. He wouldn't recognize you, you see. I mean, if it'd been me, he'd have recognized me. I was around when he had the greenhouse, after all. You weren't.'

'Where's that tea?' came Ellie's voice from the lounge. 'Do get a move on!'

Pascoe and Madge Soper smiled at each other.

'She's really in charge, isn't she?' said Pascoe.

'Yes, she is,' said Mrs Soper. 'She was always the same from a girl. Not bossy, you know, but she knew her own mind. But I needn't tell you any of this, Peter! And I'm not complaining. She's been a tremendous help these past few days. I'm afraid I've just sat back and let her get on with it while I've looked after little Rose! But I'm glad she came so she could see for herself how things were.

Ellie's never been a girl for taking things on trust. She's always had to see for herself. I warned the doctor she'd want to see him and he said he didn't mind. He's very good.'

'You warned him?'

'Yes. I mean, he'd told me everything there was to know about Archie and how he'd go on, but Ellie needed to hear for herself.'

Pascoe looked at her thoughtfully and said, 'How long's Archie been like this, Madge?'

'Oh a long time,' she said vaguely. 'It's getting worse slowly, and it won't get better. But it's funny what you get used to, isn't it? And most of the time, he's still his old self. Well, that's what he is, isn't it? His *old* self. Himself, but old, I mean. It happens to us all, one way or another, Peter.'

'Well, all I can say is, he's in very good hands,' said Pascoe.

'We both are, Peter,' she said gently. 'Him and me. We both are.'

Pascoe had nothing to say. He put his arms gently round his mother-in-law and drew her close.

From the lounge came another cry.

'Have you two gone to China for that tea?'

Pascoe and Madge smiled at each other.

'Better get to work,' said Pascoe, 'or your evening off will be stopped.'

Later, as he and Ellie lay once more in bed, she said, 'What were you and Mum doing in the kitchen?'

'Talking about you, what else?'

'About me? Not Dad?' she said indignantly.

'Archie too. But there's not much need for Madge to talk about Archie. She knows all about him, after all. Mind you, by the same token, there wasn't much need to talk about you either.'

'That sounds pretty reductive,' said Ellie.

'I don't think it was meant to be,' said Pascoe. 'But we've got to be careful not to reduce people by cramming them in the limits of our understanding, haven't we?'

Ellie mused on this and in the musing, both she and her husband were overtaken by drowsiness and brought to the edge of sleep.

Then Pascoe awoke with a start.

'Jesus Christ!' he said.

'What?'

'I've just thought of something.'

'Not before time,' she grunted, rolling towards him.

It was not what he'd had in mind but a few moments later his mind had room for little else.

'Oh God, I'll never get up in the morning,' he murmured.

'Never mind. Be brave and do your very best,' whispered Ellie.

Chapter 25

> 'I am dying like a poisoned rat in a hole.
> I am what I am! I am what I am!'

'Yes, I'm sure,' said Dalziel. 'I've checked with Customs and with the Squad. Aye, I was careful, what do you think? You're all right tomorrow, that's definite. Yes, I'm looking forward to that. Grand!'

He replaced the receiver and turned round.

Standing in the open doorway of his office were Pascoe and Wield.

'Well, look who's here!' he said. 'Bill and Ben, the Flowerpot Men! Eavesdropping in pairs now, is it?'

'Sorry, sir,' said Pascoe. 'I didn't realize you were in.'

'Well, I am, but just passing through. What do you want?'

'I was after the "fence" file. Sergeant Wield thought you had it last.'

'Did he? Well, he knows more than I do,' said Dalziel, pulling open desk drawers in a desultory fashion. 'What'd I be doing with it, any road? Oh.'

He paused, reached in, pulled out a tattered string-bound cardboard file, looked accusingly at Wield.

'Who put this in here?' he demanded.

Pascoe took the file and said, 'Thank you, sir.'

'What do you want it for anyway?'

'Just to refresh my mind on Edwin Sutton, Antiques,' said Pascoe.

'Oh, *him*. Started on the knock ten years back. Soon got sick of working for the shop dealers, so became one himself. No previous, but got done two years ago for having a few bits of silver from Lord Boldon's house that'd been done a couple of weeks before. Managed to persuade some moronic magistrate that it was all a case of genuine error! Since when, a close eye has been kept, but he's boxed clever and prospered. He's got two or three outlets now and Christ knows how many inlets. Why?'

'The medals stolen at the Welfare Lane killing may have turned up,' explained Pascoe. 'Sutton just rang to say that one of his assistants had bought some yesterday and when he, that's Sutton, spotted them this morning, he remembered the list we circulated and thought he'd better give us a call. The name rang a bell. I thought there'd been some trouble there once.'

'And you were right, as always, Peter,' compli-
mented Dalziel. 'So Sutton's playing the honest
citizen, is he? I wonder what's got into him.'

'Perhaps *honesty*, sir?' suggested Pascoe. 'Perhaps something happened to him on the road to
Damascus.'

'Oh aye?' said Dalziel. 'It'd need to be a long
fucking road, and the first thing I'd do is breathalyse the bastard. Any other leads?'

'No, sir,' said Pascoe.

'Well then, you'd best be off. Oh, by the way,
Peter.'

Pascoe turned back, Wield kept on going.

Dalziel said, 'That Warsop woman. What do you
reckon?'

'I reckon she's been fiddling the household
accounts at The Towers for years. Much easier
to do it with goods than with money. She pushes
her budget to the limit, buying everything that her
books show so that they'll stand up to the annual
audit, but then she pushes as much of the stuff as
she can to Abbiss. This means stretching things at
The Towers, though we'll probably find there's a
bit of swapping goes on. For instance, she buys
good meat. Abbiss buys scrag end. They swap.
At Paradise Hall they get gourmet's delights, at
The Towers they get gristle. Warsop and Abbiss
split the difference. Do the same with everything,
soap, linen, crockery and cutlery even, and it all
mounts up.'

'Aye,' said Dalziel, nodding. 'Clever.'

It was hard to tell whether he was commenting on Mrs Warsop's dishonesty or Pascoe's hypothesis.

'I haven't pursued the matter, sir, as per your instructions,' Pascoe said formally. 'Though I did mention it, and your instructions, to George Headingley and Sergeant Wield.'

'Covering yourself, lad?' said Dalziel. 'Well, well. I've taught you a trick or two, you can't deny that.'

'No, sir, I can't,' said Pascoe.

He stood and waited. Dalziel looked at him reflectively and scratched his Adam's apple, deep buried in the massy column of his neck.

'You got something to say to me, Peter?' inquired the fat man gently.

'No, sir,' said Pascoe. 'Except, well, look, are you in some kind of trouble?'

'What kind of trouble would that be?' inquired Dalziel. 'Any road any troubles of mine aren't your concern, lad. Not so long as you keep yourself covered. Right?'

If it was meant as a reproach, nothing in Dalziel's tone or demeanour showed it.

Pascoe said, 'If I need any more instructions, where shall I find you?'

Dalziel said, 'Who knows, lad? I'm on holiday, remember. Except this afternoon. If you want me this afternoon, you'll find me down at the coroner's court. I've got to give evidence at an inquest, remember?'

*   *   *

Seymour had been much happier this morning. Last night had gone well even though his Terpsichorean prowess had suffered under scrutiny, particularly in the tango where a tendency to self-parody was bitingly criticized.

'You're not mocking it because you think it's funny,' she analysed. 'You're mocking it because you think *you're* funny doing it. And you're not so far wrong, at that, but that's mainly because you *think* you are. Now if you'll just let yourself go and stop imagining the whole world's got you in its sights, you'll do fine. And while I'm putting you to rights, your reverse turn leaves a little bit to be desired. It's only in the swimming baths that they do the tumble turn; on the dance floor it's just a little matter of shifting your weight, are you sure you're not still wearing your copper's boots?'

Normally Seymour would not have accepted such affronts from anyone under the rank of detective-inspector, but as all Bernadette's criticism ended up in demonstration which involved him in once more putting his arms round this slim, warm body, he found himself submitting to his humbling with as good a grace as any religious novice.

His euphoria, however, had not survived long. Pascoe had summoned him soon after his arrival and given him as odd a set of instructions as he'd ever received.

And this was why he was now in Jane Escott's flat, poking around and looking for anything that might come under the famous general heading of 'blunt instrument'.

In fact there proved to be remarkably little. Blunt instruments are not so plentiful as criminal fictions would have the public believe. But he had found the one specific item mentioned by Pascoe and as he hefted it in his hand, an appreciation of the trend of Pascoe's thought began to seep unpleasantly into his mind.

It was a pouch handbag on a long strap for carrying over the shoulder. It was full of loose change and very heavy. And on one side the soft brown leather held a small, faint, darker stain.

Not even Charley Frostick had been able to be exact in his description of his grandfather's medals, but the ones Edwin Sutton showed to Pascoe matched the imprecise details pretty closely.

Edwin Sutton was a rough diamond whom prosperity, expensive clothes and a toupee too perfect to pass for real had not been able to smooth. Invited to dine at the Palace, he would have been down on one knee in no time, not out of patriotism but examining the table bottom and making deprecating comments prior to trying an offer.

At least, such was Pascoe's assessment. But his main attention was concentrated on Paul Moody, the assistant who had purchased the medals. Moody was a personable young man, quite well-spoken, and reasonably knowledgeable. His honesty was harder to judge. Did a man in Sutton's position hire people for their honesty or their crookedness? From which did he have more to fear?

But the question was irrelevant in the present circumstances. Moody was merely a witness who, honest or not, was under orders to cooperate.

'Ordinary sort of fellow,' he said. 'About twenty-five. Medium height. Stocky. Light brown hair, a bit of a moustache. He was wearing one of those lumberjack jackets, sort of green tartan. He said the medals had been his uncle's. I didn't pay much heed. I mean, it's not like something really valuable when you need to establish ownership and all that, is it?'

Sutton nodded approval.

'But when I saw them this morning, I remembered the circular, Inspector,' said Sutton. 'You're a bad boy, Paul, you should've remembered the circular too. Perhaps you'll pay more heed another time.'

'Yes, Mr Sutton.'

'How did he talk?' asked Pascoe.

'He didn't say much,' said Moody. 'And most of that was monosyllables. Accent? Ordinary. Like most people round here.'

'When you made him your offer, what did he say?'

'He said, *Is that all?* and I said I couldn't do any better and I didn't think anyone else would, but he was entitled to try. And he said no, he'd take it.'

'And how much was *it*?'

'Five pounds,' said Moody.

Five pounds. The price of Bob Deeks's death. What Hitler's Panzers had not been able to do, some mindless thug had achieved for the sum of five pounds.

It wasn't much, and it was a very small sum indeed for Edwin Sutton to pay to buy himself into the CID's good books. This was clearly his motivation. At this price good citizenship came very cheap. Pascoe looked at his smiling face with concealed revulsion.

'I hope this helps you clear up this awful business, Inspector,' said the dealer. 'It's a terrible world, isn't it? Terrible.'

'Yes. Thank you for your help. Much appreciated,' said Pascoe.

'No more than my duty. That's what I always tell the youngster here. You meet with some dicey characters in our line of business, it's part of the game, isn't it! But when in doubt, call for the Law. Always cooperate with the Law and you can't go far wrong. Isn't that what I tell you, Paul?'

'Indeed it is, sir,' replied the young man.

'I'm glad to hear it,' said Pascoe. 'Mr Moody, could you call in at the Central Police Station at, say, two o'clock to look at some photos and help with an Identikit picture? I'm sure Mr Sutton, being so civically minded, won't mind filling in for you for an hour or so!'

On his way back to the station he was very silent in the car.

'What now, sir?' asked Wield.

Pascoe yawned. He'd got back on time this morning, but only with a double effort of will, the first to wake up and the second, having woken up, to drag himself away from the sleep-soft warmth of Ellie's body.

'We'd better show the medals to the Frosticks, I suppose.'

Wield glanced at his watch.

'I'd leave it till later, sir. The funeral's today. They'll be getting ready, then afterwards there'll be the family back at the house, that sort of thing.'

'Yes, of course,' said Pascoe.

Bob Deeks's funeral. Philip Westerman's inquest. And with luck (though could you call the invocation of another tragedy luck?) the solution of 'Tap' Parrinder's death.

He said, 'I didn't much care for Edwin Sutton.'

'No, sir.'

'I don't believe in his conversion to the good citizen. What say you, Sergeant?'

'It doesn't seem likely, sir,' agreed Wield.

'No. People don't change much on the whole. Not by choice. Sometimes when they can't help it, perhaps, but even then, deep down, they'll be the same. Wouldn't you say, Sergeant?'

'I'd say so,' said Wield. 'Except that circumstances . . .'

'Yes?'

'Well, mebbe we don't always know what other people really are. Or even ourselves, not till circumstances force us to know. Or admit.'

Pascoe brooded on this for a moment, then shook his head in irritation. Dalziel was right – too much brooding and you grew hair on your mind! This metaphysical sensibility which fused thought and feeling was of little use to a working cop. Thought and action was the only possible union even if it had to be a shotgun wedding.

He said savagely, 'Do me a favour, Sergeant. When Moody comes in to look at the pics, try to find out from him when Sutton will next be away, preferably far away, on a buying trip.'

'Sir?'

'And then we'll go in, remind anyone who objects of Sutton's publicly declared eagerness to help the Law, and turn his fucking shop inside out!'

The day which had dawned bright as Pascoe drove north from Lincolnshire had turned sullen by noon and by mid-afternoon the wind gusting down from over the Pennines was driving flurries of snow to sprinkle the moorland plain. Bob Deeks's mourners had a cold time of it as the keening blasts saw to it that there was not a dry eye to be found about the graveside.

Afterwards Charley dropped behind his parents as they returned to the cars and spoke with Mrs Gregory, whose usual careworn appearance was not materially affected by the weather.

'Andrea all right, is she?' asked the young soldier.

'Yes, Charley. I think so,' said the woman. 'She's moved to her new job, she's living in, you knew that? She would've been here today, Charley, pay her respects and all that, but it'd be awkward, her just starting, and they have different people coming most weekends, important people from the sound of it, and they have to clear up after the last lot and get ready for the next. I'm sorry about you and her, Charley, I always thought how nice it'd be, when the pair of you were little, but, well, it's not to be, and mebbe after all it's for the best.'

'Mebbe,' Charley agreed.

When they reached the car, he didn't get in.

'Come on, Charley,' said his father. 'Let's get this heater going before we all freeze to death!'

'You go on,' said Charley. 'I fancy a bit of a walk.'

'Charley!' protested Mrs Frostick. 'You'll catch your death.'

'I'm in the right spot then,' said her son. 'No, I'll be all right, Mam. I just don't fancy all them cups of tea and people chatting and all that. I'll have a bit of a blow and see you later.'

He shut the door on further argument.

'Alan, can't you make him come?' demanded Mrs Frostick of her husband.

But he looked not without pride at his son's retreating figure and said, 'Let the lad be, Dolly. He's lost a lot these past few days. But he'll be all right. Give him time, he'll be all right.'

*   *   *

Dalziel and Arnold Charlesworth came out of the coroner's court together and met the icy blasts with the indifference of strong men, which was more than could be said for the thin figure of Sammy Ruddlesdin who came panting up behind them.

'Happy with the verdict?' he yelled into the wind.

'Happy? A man's dead. How should that make me happy?' said Charlesworth.

'I meant, do you think it was a fair verdict?'

'Death by misadventure,' said Dalziel. 'That's what they said. And that's what it was.'

'And will the police be taking any further action, Mr Dalziel?' yelled Ruddlesdin.

'Who against?'

'Against the driver.' He paused, perhaps significantly, perhaps just to catch his breath. 'Against Mr Charlesworth.'

'Not for me to say, Mr Ruddlesdin,' said Dalziel. 'But you heard what was established. Mr Charlesworth hadn't been drinking, wasn't speeding, and was driving on the correct side of the road. Coroner said that no blame could be attached. You did hear that?'

'Yes, I heard it.'

'Right, then. Now why don't you sod off, Sammy, before them drips from your nose freeze to your toe-caps?'

The two big men walked away together.

'He still doesn't believe you, Andy,' said Charlesworth.

'When the Press starts trusting me, then I'll know I'm in trouble,' said Dalziel. 'Here, talking of trouble, what did you say to young Seymour to put him on to Merton Street? You must be slipping. I thought you'd just check it out yourself.'

'I gave him the address,' said Charlesworth calmly.

'You what?'

'You heard, Andy.'

'I heard, but I didn't believe. Why?'

'Christ knows. Mebbe I liked the lad. Mebbe I'm turning honest. You know me as well as anyone, Andy. You know that since our Tommy died, I've not found much to get excited about. Mebbe I'm after something new.'

Then he smiled faintly.

'And any road, that greedy bugger Don's been ripping me off for as much as gets saved in tax. It's not worth the candle, Andy. With a bit of luck, it'll frighten a lot of the other do-it-yourself clowns off and us honest bookies will be able to turn an honest copper.'

'I'm not sure I like your choice of phrase,' said Dalziel.

'Beggars can't be choosers. Fancy a warmer at my place?'

'You still have some?'

'Why not? I didn't give it up for all the world, Andy. It was just that Tommy used to tell me it was as bad as the stuff he was on, and when I surfaced after his death I remembered, and I just stopped wanting it after that. Now, well, if ever I want it again, I'll take it.'

'Christ, if it's like this tomorrow, you'll want it,' said Dalziel, looking up at the lines of snow streaming horizontally beneath the lowering grey cloud. 'Will we be expected to go out in this?'

'You're no sportsman, are you, Andy? Good shooting weather this, sorts the men out from the boys. More important is, will the weather be too bad for all those important people to fly in?'

Dalziel shrugged.

'One thing I've learnt, being in regular employment. Pay's the same whatever the hours.'

'Is that so? I wouldn't know, being in the risk business,' said Charlesworth.

'Risk? Bookies take risks like the Queen Mother takes snuff,' mocked Dalziel. 'Not often and behind locked doors. Let's get to that drink before I freeze up, Arnie. There's bits of me I've only seen in a mirror these past few years and I don't want our first face-to-face to be with them lying on a pavement!'

And the snow swirled madly in the light of Pascoe's headlamps as he parked his car as close as possible to the hospital door early that evening. A sign told him that this space was reserved for consultants. He recalled that Sherlock Holmes had called himself a consulting detective. What was good enough for Sherlock was good enough for him.

Seymour was waiting for him in the entrance.

324

He carried with him the lab report on Mrs Escott's bag. It had come in while Pascoe was out at the Frostick house. Charley had still not returned from his post-funeral walk, but Mrs Frostick had given a positive identification of the medals. Suspecting that his evening might be busy and knowing from experience how easily the time could slip away, Pascoe had headed for home to have his first hot meal of the day and ring Ellie.

He had been very tentative in his hints that Mrs Soper's passivity might be as much due to her daughter's energetic authoritarianism as to her own incapacity, but he knew that Ellie was very sharp to sniff out meanings.

He also knew that she was reluctant to accept alternative judgments until she had pragmatically tested them, but, once having made the test, she was scrupulously honest in reporting her findings.

'Hi,' she said. 'You got back all right?'

'Just about. It was the thought of the headlines that kept me going. *Policeman arrested for driving under the influence of sexual exhaustion.*'

'Oh yes. And *Unsatisfied wife gives evidence!*'

'That's not what you said this morning!' he protested.

'That was this morning. Still, I've just got to wait till Saturday.'

'Saturday?' he said neutrally.

'Yes, Saturday. Rose was a bit fractious this morning, so I took her firmly under my wing and kept at a safe observing distance from Mum and Dad. He was generally OK, but when he showed a slight tendency to want to mow the lawn, she took him very firmly in hand. I had a talk with her at tea-time. She says she's been very glad of the rest and will be delighted if any time in the future I feel like spelling her. Also if she feels she can't cope, she'll be in touch with the speed of light. I believe her. In fact I think I got a faint whiff of not-being-too-sorry-to-see-the-back-of me.'

'I can't believe it,' he said.

'You smug swine,' said Ellie. 'Look, the problem's not going to go away, you do understand that, don't you, you-who-understand-everything? And it'll get worse.'

'It's life we're talking about, isn't it?' said Pascoe, with a pessimism which was meant to be comic but didn't entirely come off.

The phone had rung again as soon as he replaced the receiver. It was Wield with news of the lab report.

'I'll meet you at the hospital,' Pascoe had replied. Then, changing his mind, had added, 'No. Send Seymour with it. Familiar faces might help.'

And faces didn't come much more unfamiliar than Wield's, he thought unkindly as he replaced the telephone.

He read the report quickly as they made their way up to the ward. There they met Dr Sowden.

'My God,' said Pascoe. 'Do you run this place single-handed?'

'It sometimes feels like it,' said Sowden. 'What is it this time? Come to pay me off?'

'Pay you off?' said Pascoe in puzzlement.

'I read about the inquest in the evening paper. You will note I didn't go along in person.'

'Doctor,' said Pascoe. 'If you feel you had something to say, you should've gone along and said it. What happened anyway?'

Sowden looked abashed.

'You don't know? Your fat friend got off. No, sorry, that's not the way to put it. Death by misadventure, with no one querying that Charlesworth was the driver.'

'Wrong, Doctor,' said Pascoe softly. 'A great deal of querying has been done.'

'But not publicly?'

'Publicity you want? Next time someone complains you've stitched a glove inside him, let's hear you demand publicity. Even if you come out innocent, you don't come out clean.'

Pascoe spoke with a vehemence which sprang from doubt rather than certainty. Sowden seemed to accept his argument, if rather grudgingly, but his antagonism was re-awoken when Pascoe explained his present purposes.

'Let me get this straight,' he said. 'You're saying that the old gent who died from exposure and shock after he broke his hip was attacked – well, you've tried that before, Inspector. I must give you credit for sticking to your guns! But this latest, that he was attacked by a seventy-five-year-old woman, his neighbour and friend, who left him there to die! This is something else.'

'Read that,' said Pascoe, handing over the lab report.

Sowden scanned it. Briefly it stated that on the side of Mrs Escott's bag there were faint traces of human blood and tissue.

'So what does that prove? That she'd cut herself at some time, most probably. It happens. It happens a lot more frequently than old ladies turning to mugging, I should think.'

'Not mugging,' said Pascoe. 'She thought she was being mugged. She was terrified of being out after dark. At the same time she'd started rambling, losing her grip on time and place. Only intermittently at this stage before returning to complete normality, except for some memory lapses. Her friends were worried about her. The old worry greatly about their own. Who else understands the problems like they do? So imagine what "Tap" Parrinder felt when, being driven home in a taxi with a full belly and three hundred pounds' worth of winnings in his pocket, suddenly as they pass the Alderman Woodhouse Recreation Ground, he glimpses his friend Jane Escott going in.'

'Of course!' said Seymour. 'That's why he jumped out so suddenly!'

'Yes. He runs after her. Perhaps she hears him and starts running away in terror. He catches up, seizes her shoulder. She turns, swinging with her shoulder-bag heavy with all her hoarded change, catching him on the temple. He goes down and she goes on running, running, not stopping till she is safely at home, taken there by instinct, getting undressed, going to bed with her heart still pounding, and finally falling asleep to awake on Saturday morning with all memory of the Friday gone, and Thursday substituted in its stead.'

'You have a persuasive narrative style,' said Sowden. 'You should try fiction.'

'No,' said Pascoe. 'Fiction's full of bright, perceptive, open-minded young doctors. I couldn't screw myself up to that pitch of invention.'

'You will permit me to criticize your thesis medically, I take it?' said Sowden with heavy sarcasm.

'Why? You're not a geriatrician, are you?' said Pascoe. 'From what I can make out, the old are either dead or dying by the time they reach your hands. Look, it's possible. I've checked it. I talked with your Mr Blunt earlier today.'

This introduction of the respected head of geriatrics clearly impressed Sowden.

Pascoe pressed home his advantage. 'Her mind had even more reason to repress the memory as she learned about Tap's death. She couldn't permit herself to associate the two things, could she? And it was only when my questioning forced her to recognize the missing day that she realized what she'd done and decided to crash out. I'd no idea, of course. All I wanted was to clear the decks about Parrinder's movements and her evidence conflicted with the rest.'

'It's still only a theory,' said Sowden stubbornly.

'And will remain so until I talk to Mrs Escott,' said Pascoe. 'Is that possible?'

The young doctor slowly nodded.

'You can talk to her. For a moment anyway. I doubt if she'll reply. Poor woman.'

'Thanks,' said Pascoe.

'Hold on, though!' said Sowden suddenly. 'You said that Mr Parrinder was carrying a lot of money? And that went missing? Now Mrs Escott might just turn out to have struck out at him in her terror and panic, but you're not telling me she robbed him too!'

Seymour said, 'Yes, sir. I was wondering about that, sir. I mean, it doesn't seem likely, does it?'

'No,' said Pascoe. 'What does seem likely is that a man on the dole with a wife, kids, and a seven-foot dog that must cost a tenner a week at least to feed, might be sorely tempted if an old envelope full of ten-pound notes suddenly appeared at his feet. I suggest when we finish here, it might be worthwhile having another chat with your Mr Cox, Seymour.'

Pascoe was horrified to see the change in Mrs Escott. She had looked her age before, but in a healthy, well-nourished fashion. Now she looked like age itself, with hollow cheeks, thread-like lips and eyes sunk almost out of sight into the funnels of their sockets.

'Mrs Escott,' said Pascoe softly. 'I'm Inspector Pascoe who came to talk to you about Tap. Mr Seymour's with me. You'll remember him, I think. He saw you too about Mr Parrinder. Listen, Mrs Escott, what I want to say is we know what happened, and we know it was an accident, and there's nothing to worry about, nothing at all. We all know what happened and nobody blames you. Believe me, Mrs Escott. Nobody blames you.'

There was no response either of sound or movement. Pascoe looked up and caught Sowden's eye. It was good to see that the doctor's face was sympathetic, but it was sympathy based on the expectation of utter failure.

Well, perhaps it would have to be one of those cases where the likelihood of an explanation was strong enough for the case to be shelved, but not certain enough for it to be closed.

'It's all right, Mrs Escott,' he said gently. 'We're going now. Good night. Sleep well.'

As he straightened, she spoke in a voice distant and strange but perfectly clear, like the piping of a bird in some lonely spot.

'Nothing . . .' she said. 'All nothing . . . dreams . . . awful dreams . . . the rain . . . footsteps . . . hitting him . . . Tap's face . . . hitting him . . . then running . . . like a girl again . . . but not happy like a girl . . .'

Suddenly she seemed to gain strength and for the first time there was expression on her face and the voice was traceable to the moving mouth.

'Awful dreams,' she said loudly. 'But true. Have they always been true? All of them, always? It's not . . . it's not . . . it's not . . .'

And then she was gone again. Gone where? Back to the world of the awful dreams? Pascoe wondered.

He walked away from the bed and out of the ward. Sowden caught him up and put his hand on his arm.

'Don't forget that drink some time,' he said. 'We can't keep on meeting like this.'

'Can't we?' said Pascoe, then took a deep breath and managed a smile.

'I won't forget,' he said.

Chapter 26

'I am about to take my last voyage,
a great leap in the dark.'

The Cessna taxied to a halt at the end of the short runway, the door opened, and steps were wheeled against it, and the passengers began to disembark.

There were seven of them, five men and two women. Barney Kassell was there to greet them, bare-headed despite the blustering wind which caught at his silky grey hair and streamed it over his brow and eyes to the bridge of his prominent nose.

He greeted them all by name as they descended, some fairly formally, as with the distinguished Dutch judge and his stout wife, a couple of the men very familiarly.

'Helmuth! Jacques!' he cried to the last pair out. 'How nice to see you again.'

'And you. But where is the fine weather Willy promised us?'

'This is it,' grinned Kassell. 'You should have seen it yesterday. I began to doubt if you'd make it. I hope you've brought your winter boots. There's a lot of snow lying up on the moor. Jacques, where is your lovely wife?'

The Frenchman smiled and said in a low voice, 'Busy with family matters this weekend. I hope that you will be able to help me not to miss her too much, my friend.'

'I think we can promise our usual high standard of service,' said Kassell. 'On you go. Usual formalities, won't take long.'

The luggage was being unloaded almost as fast as the passengers. Kassell looked up at the aircraft. The pilot had appeared at the door. He smiled down at Kassell and gave a little nod of the head.

Kassell turned and followed the new arrivals to the clubhouse of the local gliding club, in the doorway of which stood a Customs officer, quietly observing the approaching passengers.

He remained there till Kassell reached him.

'Just by yourself this week, Mr Downey?' said Kassell. 'Not the full treatment like last time?'

'Everyone's got to take their turn, Major,' said Downey.

'I know. And quite right too,' approved Kassell. 'Sir William was delighted to hear about it. A man with his kind of contacts really hates it if people believe he's getting preferential treatment! Strange, isn't it?'

The formalities were quickly over and the party installed in two Range Rovers.

'Let's be on our way,' cried the Frenchman who for a man whose banking interests 'earned' him more than he had ever bothered to work out was greedier of 'freebies' than any other visitor Kassell had ever welcomed to the Grange. 'I feel that this is going to be one of the great weekends!'

'If,' said Mr Cox, 'I get sent to one of them open prisons, will they let me take Hammy?'

Mr Cox had not been at home the previous night. A neighbour told Seymour that the whole family was away visiting relatives in Leeds and wouldn't be back till late, probably after midnight. Pascoe knew as well as any policeman the psychological advantage of an early morning arrest, but he felt that this particular case didn't warrant it. So Mr Cox got a good night's sleep and in the morning Pascoe's consideration was proved to be deserved, for when Cox opened the door to Seymour and Hector (taken along to provide diversion for the dog) he nodded sadly and went upstairs without speaking and returned wearing his coat and carrying a brown envelope.

'It's all there,' he said. 'It had fallen out of his pocket when he fell, I suppose. When I saw all them notes, I just stuck it in my jacket, just for safety. Then when I heard he was dead, I didn't say owt. And when no one else said owt about any missing money, well, I began to wonder if I hadn't best hang on to it.'

Hammy had accompanied them to the station. There had been no debate. Seymour was not about to argue with a dog which even an upright man, not dying and in daylight, might be forgiven for mistaking for a horse.

Pascoe doubted if it would come to prison for Cox, but it wasn't up to him.

'Get a statement, put the fear of God into him, then send him home till we need him again,' he said.

'On bail, you mean?'

'Who needs bail with a dog like that?' asked Pascoe. 'Can you imagine him fleeing the country with Hammy in tow?'

Hector showed surprising stubbornness when Seymour tried to wish the taking of the statement off on him.

'I'm off duty in an hour,' he said.

'So it probably won't take that long,' said Seymour. 'Anyway, what's wrong with a bit of overtime? You've not got anything urgent to do, have you?'

'Yes, I have,' replied Hector surprisingly.

'Oh,' said Seymour, taken aback. 'In that case . . .'

The one thing about Hector was that you always knew if he was lying. It was something about the way the rather pointed tips of his ears went bright red and he started stammering like a loose sash-window in a high wind. When he told the truth, on the other hand, he merely looked gormless. As now.

Seymour had finished taking the statement and was seeing Cox and, more importantly, Hammy, safely off the premises when Charley Frostick walked in, looking very smart in his uniform.

'Is that Inspector Pascoe around?' he demanded of the desk sergeant.

'Could be, colonel,' answered the elderly sergeant to whom inferiority of rank negated the need for his customary courtesy. 'What's your business with him?'

'Private,' said Charley.

'Well, it wouldn't be *general*,' quipped the sergeant, grinning broadly in self-applause.

Seymour intervened.

'It's Mr Frostick, isn't it? I'll look after this, Sarge.'

On their way upstairs, he ascertained that all Charley wanted to do was have a look at his grandfather's medals. Pascoe agreed to see the youth straight away and Seymour left them together.

'Your mum identified them,' said Pascoe, spreading them out on the desk. 'You weren't around.'

'Yeah. I know. I just wanted to take a walk by myself. It really gets me, thinking that the bastard that did that to Granda is walking around free somewhere. I'd like to get my hands on him, me and a few of my mates, just for five minutes . . .'

A look of rage settled on the young man's face, but not altogether convincingly. It was, Pascoe suspected, conventional, an expression learned to please instructors during bayonet practice or whatever aggressive equivalent the modern army went in for nowadays. Here it was a macho mask for the deeper feelings of grief and pain which had sent this likeable young man in search of solitude after yesterday's funeral. Not that he wouldn't be capable of taking a swing at his grandfather's killer if confronted by him, but who wouldn't?

The boy examined the medals, the stage rage fading from his face as he touched the faded ribbons and ran his fingers over the embossed metal.

'You didn't get the watch, then?' he said.

'No,' said Pascoe. 'I gather that had Mr Deeks's name on. The medals are anonymous. Your grandfather never had them engraved.'

'Never saw no need to,' said Charley. 'He knew they were his, and he said no one else mattered 'cos you had to win your own medals. But I'd like them, specially if his watch never turns up. He always said I was to have the watch; that was useful, he said. But I'd like the medals.'

'They'll be returned to your mother eventually,' said Pascoe, removing the medals and putting in their place the Identikit picture made up with Mr Moody's help. Moody had not been a good witness and the picture was even less convincingly human than usual.

'This remind you of anyone?' he asked.

'Yeah,' said Charley.

'Really. Who?'

'One of the Kraut gardeners in Germany. And he's a bit like that Scottish sweeper, him who played in the last World Cup.'

With a sigh, Pascoe removed the useless picture and asked, 'When do you go back?'

'Tonight.'

'As soon as that?'

Charley nodded and said, 'To tell the truth, I could've stayed till Sunday, but now with the funeral over and all, well, there's nothing to keep me. Don't get me wrong, it's grand seeing me mam and dad again, but you can't be sitting around the house all the time, and I'd as lief get back to me mates.'

'No mates around here any more?'

'Well, yeah, I suppose so. Only it's not the same, is it, not now I'm in the Army. I could put on my civvies, I suppose, and go round some of the old places, but it'd just be me talking big and telling them how bloody marvellous it was in the Army, and likely there'd be a bit of aggro. I could always go to the depot and see some of the boys there, but if I'm going to do that, I might as well be back with me real mates in Germany. There's always a lot going off on Saturday night, you can have a right good time over there.'

Pascoe smiled, liking Charley more and more and thinking he'd done well to get out of the clutches of the anorectic Andrea.

'You'll be able to chase the Fräuleins with a clear

conscience now,' he said, testing the strength of the separation.

'Eh?'

'Now you're not engaged.'

'Oh. Yeah, that's true, I suppose.'

He didn't sound too convinced.

Pascoe probed further, thinking Ellie would be amused at his interest, but also just as keen to know.

'Have you seen Andrea again?'

He thought for a moment he was going to be told, quite rightly, that it was none of his sodding business, but Charley settled for shaking his head.

'Right, then,' said Pascoe, feeling it was time the interview came to an end.

'She's started her new job,' said Charley abruptly. 'Her mam told me.'

'At Haycroft Grange?'

'Yeah. She'll like it there. Married folk. Like there was at that Paradise Hall.'

'She didn't seem to like it there much.'

'I think she did till she got the sack. It was me as didn't like her being there.'

'Why? It was handy for the camp, surely.'

'Yeah, there was that all right. No, it was just the idea of her sleeping there, you know. She just laughed and said there was nothing to worry about, the owner was an old poof.'

'Oh? A *married* old poof,' corrected Pascoe.

'Yeah, I know. But she said it didn't make any

340

difference. She thought he was still as queer as a clockwork orange.'

'And what did you think?' inquired Pascoe, maliciously amused at these descriptions of Jeremy Abbiss.

'Me? I never met him.'

Ah, but he met you, thought Pascoe, recalling Abbiss's description of catching them *in flagrante* across the reception desk.

But hadn't Abbiss said that words were exchanged?

He said carefully, 'You mean that when you used to visit Andrea at Paradise Hall you never encountered Mr Abbiss, the proprietor.'

'No, never laid eyes on him,' said Charley. 'I made sure of that, didn't I? Andrea said it was all right, she was entitled to use her room the way she liked, but I didn't want any trouble, not with me still doing my training and all that.'

He rose to his feet and awkwardly held out his hand.

'Cheerio, Mr Pascoe,' he said. 'I hope you get the bastard. It's not a right way to end up, not after living all them years, is it?'

'Perhaps after all those years it doesn't make too much difference, Charley,' said Pascoe gently. 'But rest assured, we'll do our best.'

He sat for a little while in deep thought after the boy had left, then summoned Wield.

'Sergeant,' he said. 'How do you fancy a little trip to Paradise?'

Chapter 27

'It will end as it began, it came with a
lass and it will go with a lass.'

Once more Pascoe arrived in the kitchens of Paradise Hall while a meal was in full swing.

'Oh no!' cried Abbiss. 'Not you again. And this time you've brought the public hangman!'

Wield did not change expression. Why should he, thought Pascoe, when the one he wore normally did so very well?

It was interesting to see that Abbiss seemed to have recovered completely from the trauma of Pascoe's last visit. He must have received promises of immunity which were very potent. Oh, Dalziel, Dalziel, what are you playing at?

Pascoe said, 'Last time we talked, you said that one of your complaints against your former employee, Andrea Gregory, was that she brought a soldier back to her room. You also said you caught them *in flagrante delicto* early one morning.'

'Ah, you liked that picture, did you, Inspector?' mocked Abbiss. 'Want an action re-run, is that it?'

'When was this, sir?' asked Pascoe patiently.

Perhaps it was the courtesy of the 'sir' that did it, but Abbiss began to take things seriously.

'When? I'm not sure precisely. Last week some time.'

'Last week? Not a few weeks ago?'

'Oh no. Not long before I gave her the push.'

Pascoe felt angry with himself. He had made assumptions, which as Dalziel put it, was posh for making cock-ups. The mention of a soldier had automatically made him think of Charley Frostick and he hadn't seen any reason to check on dates.

He said, 'And it was definitely a soldier?'

'Oh yes,' said Abbiss. 'Fully kitted out from beret to boots, with the minor modification that his pants were pushed down over his buttocks, the better to apply himself to little Miss Andrea who was wearing her nightie round her neck.'

'Could this have been the man, sir?' inquired Pascoe, handing over the Photofit picture.

'Maybe,' said Abbiss doubtfully. 'I mean, it doesn't really look like anybody, does it? I *think* he had a moustache. On the other hand if you gave me a picture of his backside, I could give you a positive identification straight away! There was a rather interesting bite-mark on his left buttock, I seem to recall.'

It conjured up for Pascoe a picture of a very

unusual identity parade. But in fact he hardly had enough to go on to ask for a normal identity parade. The point was that Andrea Gregory had been putting it about a bit, and she had shown a kind of loyalty to Charley by putting it about among the large number of lonely soldiers who at any one moment were inmates of Eltervale Camp.

Just how significant did this make the print on the vinyl floor of Bob Deeks's bathroom which might have been from an Army boot? And could those stab marks on his neck and shoulders possibly have been made by a bayonet?

There was little to go on, but too much to ignore. Andrea herself was the best source of information, but he could imagine those painted lips closing to a thin red line when asked to betray herself.

'Come now, Inspector,' said Abbiss. 'Don't look so baffled. Surely there can't be all that many NCO's of the British Army with teeth marks on their left buttocks. Is it yourself you want him for, or is he a present for a friend?'

'An NCO?' said Pascoe. 'You're sure he was an NCO?'

'Oh yes. There was a stripe on his arm. Just the one, that makes him a lance-corporal, doesn't it?'

'That's right. Anything else about him? Colour of hair, build, anything at all?'

'I don't really know. Good athletic action, I'd say. Brownish hair. Like I say, I think he had a moustache. Oh, and there was one rather odd thing – those webbing belts they wear. Well, his was white.'

Into Pascoe's mind there leapt a picture of a ramrod-straight man with a mousy moustache and watchful eyes, whose friendship with Charley Frostick had perhaps led him to cover up the young man's nocturnal ramblings.

Lance Corporal Gillott of the Mid-Yorkies' regimental police.

'Thank you, sir,' he said, turning on his heel and leaving the kitchen.

There was a public phone in the hallway. He rang the station and got Seymour.

'Pick Moody up and bring him out to Paradise Hall,' he ordered. 'Don't take no for an answer.'

He rejoined Wield.

'Let me buy you a drink while we're waiting, Sergeant,' he said, leading him into the bar where Stella Abbiss was serving a customer. 'And if you're hungry, they do a nice cold game pie.'

The woman heard him and turned her big dark eyes on him with something in them which might almost have been contempt. She thinks I've been fixed! thought Pascoe. And while she might have understood passion, she reckons nothing to greed.

'You're out of luck today, Inspector,' she said in her low deep voice. 'For you, game pie is definitely off.'

Moody sat sulkily in the front seat of Pascoe's car as he drove towards Eltervale Barracks. He had not been pleased, as he put it, to be dragged away from his work, but Pascoe was in no mood to be conciliatory.

It was his intention, however, to tread carefully in his dealings with the military and not to risk provoking any of that protective closing of ranks by which army units traditionally protected their own. It was his intention to talk first with the camp CO and then to arrange for Moody to see Lance-Corporal Gillott while he himself remained unobserved.

It didn't work out quite like that.

As they approached the camp gates, a trio of men in fatigues and carrying spades came doubling out. Presumably they were a work detail of men under arrest. And escorting them was the upright, poker-faced figure of Lance-Corporal Gillott.

'That's him!' cried Moody. 'That's the man I bought the medals from.'

He wound down the window in his excitement. Gillott did a classic Ealing Comedy double-take, then with a reaction speedy enough to impress the most demanding of training instructors, he grabbed a spade off one of the prisoners and hurled it at Pascoe's car.

The windscreen crazed. Moody shrieked, Pascoe slammed on the brake and the car, though already slowing, spun on the road surface still treacherous from the previous day's sleet and snow, scattering the working party in panic.

And Gillott was away down the road, head

back, knees pumping high, wisely (so he must have thought) not heading back into the trap of the camp with its high soldier-proof perimeter fence.

What he was heading towards was Seymour's car which drew in to the side of the road. Seymour made to get out, but Wield in the passenger seat restrained him. And as the sprinting corporal drew level with the car, the sergeant leaned across and flung open the driver's door. There was a fearsome impact and the door slammed shut with a violence that set the inmates' eardrums vibrating.

'Now you can get out and pick him up,' said Wield. 'Good arrest, son. It'll look well on your record. And it'll be something to impress that little Irish girl of yours with next time you go dancing. Might make her forget the pain.'

Gillott was incredibly verbose for one who had appeared so taciturn. It was stopping him talking that was difficult, but with Moody's identification and the discovery of Bob Deeks's pocket watch hidden in his locker, he saw little hope in silence. Not even his bruised ribs inhibited the flow, the main current of which was directed at washing as much blame towards Andrea Gregory as possible.

'It was her idea. She said he was an animal. She said all old people were animals. She said they were crazy, smelly and nasty. She said she'd want to be put down before she got like that. We'd been drinking. I'd been driving the sergeant-major to the station in town and I had his car. I thought: Sod going back straight away. No one'll miss me. So I gave Andrea a ring. I'd been stuffing her rotten ever since that wet boyfriend of hers went to join the battalion. We went for a drive. She brought a bottle of Scotch along from the restaurant. We stopped and had a drink and a fuck and some more drink. I said if I had enough money I'd buy myself out of the Army. She said she knew where there was a few hundred lying around for the taking. I said where? She said at Charley's grandad's. She said that when they got engaged Charley had left her outside the back of his grandad's. He went in and came out not long after with a century in cash. He bought her that flashy ring. She said she knew where the back key was kept hid. What she didn't know was where the money was hid and he wouldn't tell us. We looked everywhere. The old man just kept on looking at my uniform and saying "Charley" all the time. It got on my wick. Was there some money, eh? Was there really some money? Or was it all for nothing?'

Pascoe had come as close as he ever had to striking a prisoner at this point.

He said as much to Wield as they sped towards Haycroft Grange to pick up Andrea Gregory. Wield had offered to take his car as Pascoe's was temporarily out of commission but Pascoe had said, 'No. Full panoply of the law, I think. I don't want the Sir William Pledgers of this world thinking that we can be relied on to be nice and discreet for their sake.' Thus he and Wield were sitting in the comfortable back seat of a large white squad car with the Mid-Yorkshire insignia emblazoned proudly on the sides.

'Christ, they took risks, didn't they?' said Wield.

'They were both half-cut from the sound of it,' said Pascoe. 'But with that din coming from Mrs Spillings's house, and the other side empty, they weren't in much danger of being overheard. And Andrea had her wits about her enough to realize that using the outside key might be a giveaway. She spotted the duplicate key on the kitchen table. According to Gillott, it was her idea to stick one of the keys in the inside of the lock and smash the window to make it look as if someone had broken in.'

'But she put the wrong key back in the shed.'

'Yes. I should have spotted the implications of that sooner, but there's been a lot of distraction these past few days.'

The two men fell silent. Dusk was beginning to settle over the undulating landscape, flecked white with snow which the wind had blown into the folds and pleats of the heathered moor. The uniformed driver was consulting a road map and driving with one hand.

'You're not lost, are you, Pearson?' asked Wield.

'No, sir. It's just that we turn off somewhere along here down an unclassified road and I don't want to miss it.'

'How about up there, at the top of the rise, where the green van's turning?'

'Yes, that'll likely be it,' agreed the driver.

They turned off the B-road on to a narrower but still well-metalled track which meandered down into a riverless valley. Distantly they glimpsed the chimneys of Haycroft Grange against the snowy hillside opposite. The green van ahead was either in difficulty or the driver did not trust his brakes as the road steepened.

'For God's sake,' said Pascoe impatiently as their speed dropped to under twenty. 'Can't you get past him, Pearson?'

Wield glanced at the Inspector, thinking he had rarely seen his temper so ragged. The Sergeant's instinct rather than his detective powers sought out the reason. It occurred to him that Pascoe, despite his comparative youthfulness and liberal modernism of outlook, would have done very nicely as an English gent in one of Wield's much loved Rider Haggard novels. His belief in the equality of women still turned to disappointment at the discovery that they could equal men in baseness as well as achievement. And his loyalty to Andy Dalziel must be very much at odds with his strict code of fair play and honesty.

Plus, of course, the fact that he was clearly missing his wife and daughter.

Pearson replied defensively. 'The road's a bit narrow, sir.'

They were nearing the bottom of the valley

where the road straightened out for almost a hundred yards before beginning to wind up the opposing hillside.

'Give him the bell then,' ordered Pascoe. 'It's like a bloody funeral procession!'

Obediently the driver pressed a switch. Next moment the pastoral peace was fragmented by the pulsating screech of the siren, and on the roof flashing blades of light scythed the darkling air.

The green van pulled over to the narrow verge and stopped. Pearson sent the police car accelerating by, then reached forward to switch off the lights and siren, but Pascoe stopped him.

'Leave it,' he said. 'I like a bit of *son et lumière*. It's a not unfitting way to let those gun-happy buggers up there know we're coming, wouldn't you say, Sergeant?'

But Wield did not reply. He was much more interested in looking back and wondering why the driver of the green van had changed his mind and turned round and was now heading back up the hill.

Chapter 28

'Ut puto deus fio.'

'That sounds like your lot, Dalziel,' said Sir William
Pledger. 'Didn't realize you were bringing some
friends.'

He laughed and his guests joined in, even those
who did not understand or did not appreciate the
joke. Among the latter was Major Barney Kassell,
who regarded Dalziel with grave suspicion.

The fat man shrugged and said indifferently, 'Me
neither.'

The shooting party had just returned from the
moors and, still muddy and tweedy, were taking a
hot toddy with their host in the gun-room before
retiring to hot baths and fresh linen. Kassell went
to the window which overlooked the courtyard of
the Grange where the beaters were collecting their
pay and the day's bag of pheasants, more richly
plumed than a tombful of dead pharaohs, were
awaiting their collector.

'Excuse me,' said Kassell. 'I'll just pop down and see that all's well, shall I?'

Pledger nodded and Kassell left. Dalziel looked as if he might be about to follow, but the Dutch judge who was expounding his pet theory of penal reform gripped him firmly by the elbow and the fat man, who was in an uncharacteristic state of uncertainty, let his mind be made up for him. He retrieved something of his self-esteem, however, by emptying his glass so positively that the punk-haired maid with tits like ostrich eggs, recently transferred from Paradise Hall, broke away from the French banker who seemed to think she was his personal property and came straight to him.

'Another of the same, love,' said Dalziel. The girl obliged. The judge seemed to be distracted by her imminence and lost his thread and Dalziel took the opportunity to turn away and look into the courtyard. Arnie Charlesworth was already at the window. He glanced at Dalziel and raised an interrogative eyebrow. Dalziel shook his head.

Down in the courtyard, Pascoe and Wield had got out of the police car. Kassell was talking to the Inspector, angrily at first it seemed, and then rather more calmly, while Wield stood stolidly by and regarded the colourful array of dead pheasants awaiting the arrival of the game dealer. Across by the stables, collecting their afternoon's wages, were the beaters. Two or three of them who were off-duty policemen had pulled their hats down hard over their brows at the sound of the approaching siren, and one at least, long, thin and sunken-headed, had started like a guilty thing surprised, and slipped out of sight round a corner.

A telephone rang. After a moment, a servant came into the gun-room and spoke to Pledger, who by this time was standing with all the rest peering down at the scene outside.

'Dalziel, it's for you,' said Sir William. 'You sure you don't know anything about this, old chap?'

Dalziel didn't reply but made his way to the door. He was interested to note that the sexy maid had taken the opportunity of all those turned backs to pour herself a healthy slug of the toddy. He grinned at her in passing. If abashment were felt, the indifferent mask of her face did not show it.

Outside he picked up the phone and identified himself.

He listened for a while, said, 'Jesus fucking Christ,' listened again, and said, 'Yes, why not? Not much point in doing owt else, is there?' And banged the phone down.

Back in the gun-room he said, 'Excuse me, Sir William, but mebbe you'd better come with me.'

'Come with you? Why? Is something wrong?' asked Pledger.

But Dalziel had already turned away and was marching towards the front door of the house.

There he met Pascoe, Wield and Kassell coming up the steps. The two policemen halted in surprise.

Kassell said, 'It's all right, Andy. Seems our new maid's got herself in a bit of bother.'

'Maid?' said Dalziel. 'You pair of midsummer night dreams have come here about the maid?'

His voice scoured the base of incredulity.

'She's wanted for questioning, sir,' replied Pascoe defiantly. 'Sorry to disturb you and your friends, but it's a serious matter. Suspicion of being an accessory to murder.'

'Murder?'

'Yes, sir. The Deeks case.'

'Bloody hell,' said Dalziel savagely. 'You don't half pick your moments, Inspector.'

'It's all right, Andy,' repeated Kassell. 'They'll be away in a couple of minutes. Nothing to worry about, Sir William. Just a spot of bother concerning one of the domestics.'

Pledger and most of his guests had come out of the door behind Dalziel. Pascoe let his eyes drift up to them. The only one he recognized was Arnie Charlesworth, quietly watchful, with a shotgun in the crook of his arm. Probably, thought Pascoe, he was just about the poorest in this group of rich, powerful men who got their kicks out of destroying helpless half-tame birds. Except for Dalziel, of course. Dalziel was the poorest, or ought to be. What the hell was he playing at?

'Is that right, Dalziel?' said Pledger, an edge of anger in his voice. 'Is all this noise and drama just so that they can arrest one of the maids? For God's sake, man, don't they teach you fellows anything about discretion? I'll be talking to Tommy Winter when he gets back, I assure you.'

'Your privilege, sir,' said Dalziel. 'I think you'll find the Chief Constable knows about most of it. Not the maid, no one bothered to tell even *me* about the maid.'

Pascoe found himself beyond all reason or justice being glowered at accusingly.

'What then?' demanded Pledger. 'If not the maid, what?'

Dalziel didn't respond but looked beyond the trio on the steps towards the approach road. Along it a little convoy was approaching. It consisted of two cars and a van.

'Sir William,' said Dalziel formally. 'I have reason to believe that a private aeroplane belonging to Van Bellen International has been used to smuggle quantities of heroin into the country.'

'You what?' cried Pledger, looking round at his guests. 'Do you know what you're saying?'

'Oh aye,' said Dalziel. 'Question is, do you? On the whole, I reckon not. But Major Kassell here does, isn't that right, Barney?'

'You bastard,' said Kassell softly. 'You bastard.'

He wasn't talking to Dalziel, Pascoe realized with surprise. His gaze was fixed on the indifferent features of Arnie Charlesworth.

The convoy had come to a halt and half a dozen men and a black labrador debouched. One of them, a grey-haired man with a sad face, came to the foot of the steps and looked interrogatively at Dalziel.

'Don't even ask,' said Dalziel. 'You wouldn't believe it. But now you're here, you'd better improve the shining hour. It'll be somewhere among the pheasants most likely. If Rin Tin Tin doesn't find it, you'll have to get your fingers bloody. Sir William, why don't you and your guests go back in the warm? This shouldn't take long.'

'By what authority are you doing all this?' demanded Pledger.

'Look,' said Dalziel. 'I've got a warrant here, want to look? I didn't expect to have to use it –' another baleful glance at Pascoe – 'but it entitles me to pull this bloody mansion of yours apart brick by brick if I have to. Now you can ring the DCC, or you can even ring old Tommy in Barbados, if you like, and they'll tell you the same.'

'It won't be the police I ring,' said Pledger threateningly as he retreated, followed by all the other guests except for Charlesworth.

'Sergeant Wield, think you can handle this lass single-handed? There's a Frog banker in there you're going to make very unhappy. I'd like a word with Mr Pascoe here.'

Wield glanced at Pascoe, who nodded. The Sergeant made his way into the house.

'What's going off, sir?' demanded Pascoe, looking towards the stable block where the newcomers, now wearing rubber gloves, were busy among the dead pheasants with pocket knives.

Dalziel glanced towards Kassell.

'Keep an eye on the Major, will you Arnie?'

357

Charlesworth shifted his shotgun on his arm.

'Pleasure, Andy,' he said quietly.

Dalziel took Pascoe's arm and moved him down the steps.

'I'll tell you what should've been going off,' said Dalziel. 'There should've been a man called Vernon Briggs who's a game dealer driving happily towards town with that little lot of birds in his van. I believe you passed the van on the road? Well, he was so shit scared at being overtaken by a cop car with its hooter going full blast that he turned about and set off home like a peppered rabbit. Can't blame him, can you? I mean, if you're on your way to pick up a kilo of heroin, you don't hang around when you see the filth, do you?'

'Well, I'm sorry, but how was I to know?' protested Pascoe. 'And just a kilo you say? Christ, with this performance, I would have expected at least a ton. Who are they, anyway? Customs and Excise?'

'Mainly, with some of our drugs squad lads,' said Dalziel. 'And don't be snooty about a kilo, lad, it'd set you and me up for life, I tell you. Any road, you're missing the point. There's this ring operating out of Holland. That's the biggest European market, but they're developing their UK outlets. But last winter you'll recall they lost a couple of large consignments, a couple of hundredweights or thereabouts. They've changed tactics since then, going for a lot smaller runs. This is one of them, but the drugs boys don't just want to stop this line, they wanted to follow it through to the central distribution point. The word is it's somewhere in Yorkshire; Leeds maybe, or Sheffield. Vernon Briggs was going to be the lead-in. No longer! No doubt alarm bells are ringing all along the route as he doesn't turn up.'

'I really am sorry, sir,' said Pascoe, his indignation fading.

'Don't let it worry you,' said Dalziel, belching gently. 'These fancy schemes usually turn into cock-ups. Too much pussy-footing around. Me, I was for going in feet first and kicking it out of them.'

'Them?'

'Kassell, mainly. I doubt if Sir William knows anything. But I wouldn't put my pension on it. They were buddies out in Hong Kong, so he knows Barney's not your lily-white. Still, who is these days? Except the Chief Constable! First sniff that Pledger might be involved and he was off across the Atlantic. Called it a tactical withdrawal. Didn't want to risk arousing suspicion by refusing invites to shoot. Certainly didn't want the embarrassment of being around when the balloon went up. So off he goes. Top level decision is not to tell the DCC anything. Stupid, really. He's thick but not that thick. I had to fill him in myself the other day. You should've heard him! It's all this need-to-know crap, I told him. They read too many spy stories!

'Me? Through Arnie Charlesworth. There's a big file on Kassell. Arnie was in it as an associate –

just that, no suspicion that he knew owt about the racket. And when someone spotted Arnie's lad had been shot full of junk when he crashed his car, they got the bright idea he might be willing to help if approached right. They wanted an inside man, close to Kassell, see? Then some other spark, doing a deep check on Arnie, discovered him and me went a long way back. George Asquith on the Drug Squad knew me. They contacted me to ask about Arnie first off, then gradually this other bright idea evolved, for me to get close to Kassell via Arnie who'd let on I was bendable and had done him a few favours with Customs and Excise. Anyone who's got an "in" on Customs and on police operations at the same time was like a tit in a monastery to Kassell. I thought it was a load of bollocks myself, but it went like a dream. That accident last week put the seal on it. Kassell's convinced there was a cover-up there; in fact he thinks he helped with it.'

'And there wasn't?' said Pascoe. 'You weren't driving?'

'Only as far as the road,' Dalziel said. 'Then Arnie made me change over. He's not so tired of life he wants to end up like his lad, dead in a road smash! Ironic, when you think what happened later. That Warsop woman was a bit of a bonus, really. Convinced Kassell I was bent. You can sort her and Abbiss out now, by the way.'

'Is Abbiss mixed up in this?' asked Pascoe.

'I doubt it. But he did know Kassell well enough

to appeal to him when you started leaning. And Barney asked me to lean on you. Likes doing favours, does Barney. Never know when you may need to call them in.'

'Yes. Well I'm glad you weren't driving,' said Pascoe.

'Peter!' said Dalziel in mock dismay. 'You never doubted me, did you, lad? I bet there were cocks crowing twice all over the station last weekend!'

The analogy did not have to be pursued very far to break down, thought Pascoe. It was striking him that the hunt for the hidden heroin was taking rather a long time. The searchers seemed to be going over the pheasants for a second time and the drug-sniffing dog was cocking its leg against a stone mounting-post with the indifference of one who has given up for the day.

'You're sure there was a consignment this week, sir?' he asked.

'Evidently they thought so at the continental end,' said Dalziel. 'Me, all I had to do was assure Kassell that the coast was clear, no special Customs or police activity at the airport.'

'Perhaps he was just testing you out,' suggested Pascoe brightly.

He wished he'd kept his mouth shut.

'Mebbe. If so, you're in real trouble, Peter,' said Dalziel seriously. 'It's one thing cocking this lot up if we find the stuff. But if we don't, well, questions in the House'll be the last of your worries.'

'Hold on!' protested Pascoe. 'None of this is down to me . . .'

'If you hadn't come in here on the bell with lights flashing, Vernon Briggs wouldn't have run scared, and those lads there who were set to follow him wouldn't have had to make a quick decision whether to grab him or let him go.'

'They made the wrong decision then, didn't they?'

'No. They made the only possible decision,' said Dalziel. 'Not to worry, lad. There's worse things than a career in traffic control. Leastways you only get hit by trucks there!'

The greying man with a sad face approached once more. He shook his head and said, 'Nothing there, Andy.'

'No,' said Dalziel. 'Well, I'm glad it wasn't my idea, Freddie.'

Dalziel was off-loading responsibility like a trainee stripper shedding clothes, thought Pascoe bitterly.

'What do we do now? The house?'

The two men turned to look at the building.

'Up to you,' said Dalziel. 'I'd be glad to get inside myself. It's getting a bit parky out here.'

It was true. With dusk, the wind had dropped but there was a sharp edge of frost already in the air, turning breath to visible vapour.

Kassell spoke. 'Superintendent Dalziel, don't you feel the time has come to sit down and talk this over, before you and your friends get too deep in to step back. Sir William's a reasonable man, but once roused, well, he won't hold back, believe me.'

He sounded quietly confident, but Pascoe noticed he made no attempt to move away from Charlesworth and when he looked at the gun in the bookie's hands, he saw why. The hammers were cocked! He took a deep breath and glanced at Dalziel. The thought had occurred to him that if Charlesworth were doing this for the sake of his dead son, he wasn't going to be very happy to see Kassell walk away free.

The front door swung open and Pledger appeared on the threshold, presumably having settled his guests and probably having made his phone call.

He addressed himself to Kassell.

'Barney, what's happening out here?' he asked.

'Those gentlemen down among the pheasants seem to be searching for something, Sir William,' replied Kassell. 'I don't know what it is, but I gather they can't find it. Mr Dalziel and his friend here seem to be debating about whether to extend the search into the house, I myself am limited as to movement because the Superintendent has put me under restraint of Mr Charlesworth, whose gun, you will observe, is cocked and ready for action.'

'This is outrageous!' exploded Pledger. 'I have already made representation at the highest level and I've no doubt that in a very short time, you'll be hearing from your superiors. Meanwhile I demand that Charlesworth here be made to hand over his shotgun. No one is entitled to behave in this manner in this country, not even the police, without special dispensation. So, gentlemen, let's end this farce here and now.'

There was a grimness in his voice which made him, despite his lack of size, a formidable presence.

Everyone was looking at Dalziel.

With a sudden grasp of an essential truth, Pascoe saw that all the fat man's apparent off-loading of responsibility was nothing but a show for his own peculiar entertainment. When the crisis moment came, everyone focused on Dalziel. There was no way he could escape it. Nor, in all the time Pascoe had known him, had he ever shown any sign of wanting to escape it. The grey-haired Customs man called Freddie might be technically in charge of the operation, but the decision as to whether they went into Haycroft Grange and continued the search there would be Andrew Dalziel's.

The decision was delayed by a disturbance behind Sir William. A female voice was raised in a reboant cantillation of obscene abuse, cut off abruptly as Andrea Gregory found herself thrust out into the cold air by Sergeant Wield. The girl glanced round at the curious tableau before her, decided that there was nothing in it to concern her and, focusing on Pascoe, said calmly, 'He was old, what's it matter? They should get put down anyway once they get like that, all of 'em.'

She glanced at Dalziel now, clearly including him in her euthanasia programme. The fat man said to Pascoe, 'Peter, you'd best be getting along, I think.'

'Look,' murmured Pascoe, 'isn't there any way I can help?'

'No. Just get off, that's an order. No need for you to be around when the sparks start!'

Reluctantly, Pascoe gestured at Wield and the Sergeant, who had the girl's arm in a vice-like grip, propelled her down the steps and across the courtyard towards the car.

'Super's in bother, is he?' said Wield.

'Could be,' said Pascoe.

They reached the car and Wield pushed the now quiet and blank-faced girl into the back seat and got in beside her. The driver opened the front passenger door for Pascoe but the Inspector didn't get in.

He was looking towards the stable block, beyond the dead and eviscerated pheasants, with the group of Customs officers standing by, their attention fixed on the house; beyond the more distant group of beaters, also watching the unfolding drama with keen interest; to a shadowy coign of the stable wing where the black, drug-sniffing labrador seemed to be trying to mount some struggling and reluctant partner.

Suddenly the dog let out a long and triumphant howl. Pascoe grabbed the driver's flashlight from the glove compartment and moved swiftly towards the strange couple whose relationship he had already decided was not amatory.

The Customs men too had been attracted by the dog's call, but Pascoe got there first, sending a beam of light thrusting at the dog's new-found friend.

'Hector!' he exclaimed. 'Constable Hector!'

It was indeed Hector, accoutred in an incredibly shabby gaberdine which must have been made for a creature of even greater length.

Guilt and alarm were on his face.

'It's all right, sir,' he cried, trying to push away the dog. 'Mr Dalziel knows I'm here.'

'Does he indeed? But does he know you have this strong attraction for dogs?'

He looked at the terror-stricken constable with growing speculation. Surely he looked fatter than he recalled? Less of a beanpole? Perhaps it was just the gaberdine . . .

'Hector,' he said. 'Open your coat.'

The constable sighed, like the exhalation from a reedpipe, looked almost relieved, and obeyed.

'I thought it was fair do's, sir,' he explained. 'I mean, who's to miss 'em, and we do all the work. One was for me mam, the other for me Auntie Sheila.'

Hanging in poacher's pockets, which is to say two small sacks pinned to the inside of the voluminous coat, was a pair of fat pheasants.

Pascoe removed one of them and examined it. It had been split open round about the anus. A corner of plastic protruded.

'Hector,' said Pascoe gently. 'What did you imagine this was?'

Hector looked. Then he said in a puzzled voice, 'Giblets, isn't it, sir? They always come in little plastic bags.'

Pascoe began to laugh. He was still chortling quietly as he escorted the lanky constable, danced around by the excited dog, towards the group on the steps.

'Mr Dalziel, sir,' called Pascoe. 'Constable Hector here has made a remarkable discovery.'

He slowly drew forth a long thin plastic bag from the gut of the pheasant. Through the bloodstained transparent covering it was possible to see that it was packed with white powder, perhaps a pound and a half in weight. The sad-faced man came quickly down the steps, took it from Pascoe's hand and made a small incision with his pocket knife.

First he sniffed, then he put a couple of grains on his tongue.

Turning, he nodded at Dalziel.

Hector's face during all this was showing a complex of emotions. He was not yet certain whether he had committed a very great crime or performed a very meritorious deed. But now Dalziel's voice broke out, 'Hector, lad, I don't know how you've done it, but I love you!' And the long head slowly rose from between the hunched shoulders, like a flower roused by the warmth of the sun.

'Remember, you are mortal,' murmured Pascoe as he saw the joy and relief break out on the young man's face.

Dalziel turned back to Kassell.

'Major Kassell,' he said. 'I'm arresting you on suspicion of being involved in the smuggling of illicit drugs into this country. You do not have to say anything but if you do, it'll be taken down and may be used in evidence. Sir William, shall we all go inside now? There's things to be talked about, things to be done.'

With a shattered look on his face, Pledger turned away. Dalziel urged Kassell to follow him, but the Major looked first to the man with the gun. An expression crossed Charlesworth's face which might almost have been one of disappointment, then gently he uncocked his weapon.

'Well, thank God for that at least,' said Kassell with a smile of relief. 'Dalziel, I know nothing of this business, of course, but I realize you've got to do your duty. I should like to ring my solicitor before things go any further, however. I believe that's my entitlement.'

The gun came up so quickly that there was nothing anyone could do. The twin barrels swept up between Kassell's legs and hard into his groin. He screamed, went grey with pain, doubled up.

'Arnie, for Christ's sake!' shouted Dalziel.

'I deserved one,' said Charlesworth.

'You bastard. I'll get you for this,' choked Kassell.

The bookie considered him for a moment.

'I wouldn't bet on it,' he said.

Chapter 29

'Tirez le rideau, la farce est jouée.'

It started snowing again during the course of the evening and by half past nine, when Pascoe with all loose ends carefully tied up or at least tucked out of sight was preparing to go home, it was settling in earnest.

He thought with alarm of Ellie's drive north the next day, and did not know whether he was more alarmed at the dangers of the drive or the prospect of being without her even longer if the weather was too bad for travel.

Dalziel he had not seen since leaving Haycroft Grange. Whether the fat man were in the building or not he didn't know and wasn't about to find out. There would be plenty of time to dot i's and cross t's over a reunifying pint; now all he wanted was to get back home and go to bed.

But the phone rang as he was leaving.

It was Dr Sowden.

'Just thought you might like to know Mrs Escott's fading fast,' he said rather curtly.

'Thanks,' said Pascoe.

What did it matter? There was nothing more she could tell them. It was probably better for her. What did the future hold but at best a few twilit years of being bullied by the nurses in a geriatric home? No, better by far for her to go now. And there was no point in his being there to see her go. None at all.

'You came, then,' said Sowden.

'Yes.'

'Didn't sound very interested on the phone,' said the doctor.

'I'm not . . . *interested*,' said Pascoe wearily. 'Involved, maybe. Though Christ knows why.'

Sowden grinned and said, 'I'll be off duty in twenty minutes. Let me buy you that drink we keep talking about.'

'I'm a bit knackered,' said Pascoe. 'Anyway, have you seen the weather?'

'With a bit of luck we could get snowed in some comfortable saloon bar. No crime, no one dying. Two or three days of that would probably do us both the world of good. Still, if you're too tired . . .'

He led the way into the ward. A nurse was drawing the curtains around Mrs Escott's bed.

'Isn't there, well, somewhere else,' said Pascoe, glancing uneasily at the other beds.

'A kind of dying room, you mean? Afraid not. We're pushed for space, you see. In any case, with these old folk, once you start wheeling them out to die, every time they're taken out of the ward for any reason begins to feel like a death sentence!'

Mrs Escott lay so still and with her face so composed that Pascoe thought he had come too late after all. He stood helplessly by the bedside and repeated to Sowden, 'I really don't know what I'm doing here.'

'In some of the ancient religions, last words are meant to be redolent of significance and power,' murmured Sowden.

Pascoe looked at him in surprise.

'That doesn't sound too scientific to me,' he said.

'Scientifically speaking, death is the great de-bunker,' said Sowden, feeling the woman's pulse. 'There it is. A faint flutter, like a . . . like a . . .'

Perhaps some poetic comparison had suggested itself which embarrassed him for he let the words tail off.

'Aren't there any relatives? Or friends?' asked Pascoe.

'To be here, you mean? No, no relatives that can be traced. Friends at Castleton Court, probably, but too old and not close enough to be brought out on a night like this.'

'So we're it.'

'That's right.'

Pascoe shook his head.

'Not much to show for threescore and ten, is it?' he said half to himself.

Suddenly the woman's eyes were open.

She said, 'Mr Pascoe.'

'That's right. How are you, Mrs Escott?' Pascoe heard himself saying absurdly.

'Mr Pascoe,' she repeated with an injection of urgency.

'Yes?' he said. 'What is it?'

'I saw Tap,' she said. 'He spoke to me.'

'Yes? What did he say?'

She smiled radiantly.

'Winner,' she said. 'Winner. Tap says the winner is . . .'

She stopped.

Sowden monitored her pulse once more, then shook his head.

'That's it, I'm afraid,' he said.

'Dead?'

'I'm afraid so. Nurse!'

The nurse reappeared. Sowden and Pascoe emerged from the curtains and walked together down the ward. Pascoe felt completely drained of all energy as if these old and dying people were reaching out to draw it from him.

'Last words,' said Sowden. 'Exit lines. I wonder what her friend's tip was?'

'It's not knowing that makes horse-races,' said Pascoe wearily.

As they reached the door, a patient at the far end of the ward began to make a noise. At first it was just a kind of moaning sound, but finally words came out quite clearly.

'Teeny! Teeny! Where's my tea?'

Pascoe stopped.

'Who's that?' he asked.

'That? Oh, some old boy who came in this afternoon. Had a nasty fall downstairs.'

Downstairs? Pascoe thought of Mabel Gregory's old father lying on his bed in the front parlour. Thought also of the woman's tired face and of her blank-eyed husband sitting far down the garden, smoking a cigarette and looking at nothing.

And then he thought of the news which had reached the Gregorys that evening.

'Why? You interested in him?' asked Sowden.

Pascoe shook his head. Somehow it didn't feel quite such a betrayal as a spoken *no*. Betrayal of what? Of whom? He realized he didn't want to go home to an empty house. Tomorrow with luck it would no longer be empty. Ellie would be there. And Rose. One-year-and-one-week-old Rose. Perhaps they would give him the strength to contemplate what he ought to do about the Gregorys. Perhaps.

Meanwhile.

They had reached the lifts. Pascoe stepped in. Sowden stood back and watched him.

'Goodbye then,' he said.

The doors began to close. Pascoe racked his brain for something to say. Every parting should be treated as a rehearsal for the last one; everyone should have some piece of farewell wisdom or wit at his tongue's end; but, alas, for most, even the best prepared, this was probably how it would be; the doors closing, the light fading, the lift descending, with nothing said, nothing communicated.

The doors closed. His hand shot out and his finger pressed the *open* button. The doors parted and Pascoe stepped back out into the corridor. He grinned triumphantly at Sowden who looked at him mildly surprised.

'Some rehearsal, huh?' said Pascoe. 'Now, about that drink.'